The Ghosts of Admiral

Who is watching you

Wayne Maurice Ferguson

The city was just waking up. Woodstock, Ontario, with its trees finally in full leaf, would not miss the Spenser family. As Cathy Spenser organized her youngest, the two older children pleaded with Craig to load their bicycles into the U-Haul trailer. There was excitement, tinged with sadness, as Peter and Caroline brought Gooney into the back seat of the station wagon.

"Will there be anyone in the new place to play with?" 12 year old Peter asked, as his father handed him a cardboard box. Craig Spenser smiled and ran his hand over his son's hair.

"There are still people living in the area. Mostly farmers, but they all have kids. Don't worry, Pete. You'll be busy enough investigating all the old places, I'm sure you'll make friends in no time."

Caroline stood on the doorstep, looking around the neighborhood one last time. At ten years of age, she had spent her entire life on these streets, and knew every nook and cranny where her friends could hide when they played. It was good that they were leaving so early. She didn't have to say goodbye again. It was painful, but knew that her father would not take her someplace if it wasn't safe. With all the problems in the past year, both she and her brother understood. The streets were no longer a good place to grow up. Her thoughts were interrupted by her mother's voice.

"Come on, Caroline, don't just stand there. Grab that other box and take it to the trailer. I'll take one last look around the house. Tell your brother to make sure Gooney is in the car. We don't want to have to run around town trying to catch him. He knows we're leaving and he'll disappear. Now stop dreaming and let's get out of here before it gets too hot. We have a long way to go." Cathy Spenser was still not totally convinced that moving

1

from the house was necessary, but felt that her children deserved a chance to see other parts of the world, and would be away from the evil that was spreading through the town. The near-abduction of baby Ellen from the Day Care Center, knowing only the screams of one of the older children prevented the woman from making good her escape. After that, Cathy Spenser did not take that much convincing from her husband. A chance to move back to Cathy's family farm in Saskatchewan sounded like a pipe dream at first, but the close call with her three year old clinched the deal. Taking one last look around the familiar rooms, Cathy closed the front door for the last time. Walking around the trailer and automobile, ensuring everything was battened down, Craig got into the driver's seat. Driving down Riddell St. for the last time, he thought about his future. As a Technical Writer, he could do his job anywhere. With Cathy's Great Grandfather's place sitting empty in Saskatchewan, and the opportunity to raise his children away from the increasing danger in Woodstock, this would be an experience for everyone. Turning right onto Dundas St., from this point on, the Spenser Tribe would be heading west. He would cross the border at Sarnia and then head north back to Canada. It would the first time to drive to the farm. The last time he went to Admiral, he flew to Regina, rented a car and drove to the small community. There was no way of knowing if his family could adjust to the change in lifestyle.

As long he had a reliable internet connection, he could still make a living, but taking his wife and children away from their friends of a lifetime, was a gamble.

As their home disappeared in the rear view mirror, the whole experience began to register with the family. Each one had their own memory.

As the miles rolled by, after exhausting their arguments and reminiscence, all children fell asleep, while Cathy became the navigator. Finally reaching the U.S. Border, it took a compliant Border Officer who agreed to allow a government lock to be placed on the trailer door, so that it would not have to be dismembered for inspection. It allowed Craig to pass through Michigan to the International Bridge at Sault Ste. Marie. It was a happy compromise. By evening, the Craig family were back in Canada, having cleared Customs with a grateful driver ready to find a Motel that would accommodate a family of five, with dog. Renting a cabin with a kitchen proved to be the answer. Finding a small resort alongside Batchawana Bay, Cathy agreed, it was a stroke of genius. With a place for both older children to play, it was a place to rest for the next stage of the journey. With a day to explore the shoreline along Lake Superior, both Caroline and Peter did not mention their old neighborhood, concentrating on fish and bugs found along the rocky beach, with both Craig and Cathy keeping a close eye on their offsprings.

Ellen's abduction attempt was still fresh in their minds.

The next morning, fresh from a day's rest, Craig fired up the Dodge and drove west along the

Trans Canada highway toward Thunder Bay. It was the slowest part of the trip, with truck traffic and road work, the Spenser tour arrived in Thunder Bay just in time to rent a Motel for the night. After Chinese food and a motel shower, everyone was ready to sleep. Early the next morning, breakfast at Mickey Dee's, they were ready to explore the flatlands for the first time.

Passing through Winnipeg, the next stop, as planned by the navigator, was Brandon Manitoba. Checking in late at night, the children didn't even take off their clothes before they went to sleep.

Another fast food treat in the morning, and it was on to their destination. Late in the afternoon, Craig pulled the Dodge off Highway 1 and onto a secondary road. Soon it was apparent that they were deep into farm land. Both Peter and Caroline pointed out the Buffalo and large number of cattle in the endless fields. Slowly weaving along a gravel road, the town of Admiral came into view. It was a shock. Expecting to see stores and shops, there were empty buildings and deserted houses.

Pulling up in front of the large Spenser ranch house, it took some time before anyone spoke.

"It's pretty big!" Peter said, stating the obvious. "It's pretty old!" added Caroline, also speaking the truth. Cathy looked at her ancestral domain and had a moment of panic. Was this a mistake?

There were few words spoken as the five Spensers looked at their new home. Even Gooney did not bark. After a few minutes of reflection, Craig got out, and walking around to the passenger's side, opened the door for his family to experience the fresh prairie air.

"Come on. Let's see what we've go to do to make it livable." he said, jokingly, but there were no sign of response. Following their mother up the front stairs, both Peter and Caroline looked around at the large front porch that stretched all along the front wall. Opening the door, Cathy stepped inside. The place was dusty, but was well furnished. A large bay window overlooked the Valley, where farms and grain bins dotted the landscape. Walking through to the large kitchen, Cathy Spenser, with Ellen in hand, whistled when she saw the large glass topped stove. Turning on a tap, there was no water. She looked over at Craig. He nodded his head. With both Caroline and Peter vanishing up the stairs to investigate the second floor, Graig opened the back door and crossed over to a large rear shed. Recalling the process from when he spent his summer holidays with Cathy's Grandfather, he flicked on a light. The power was on. Having previously contacted the power company, they did as promised. Studying the water system, he remembered the switch on the wall. The pump came to life. Within minutes, the water was flowing. It was a happier Cathy Spenser who greeted her husband as he reentered the house.

"Will we have hot water?" he asked as she walked with him through to the bedrooms.

"Sure. The house is heated with natural gas and so is the water. Just because the house is over 100 years old, doesn't mean we have to live in the stone age. My Grandmother made Grampa upgrade the house so she didn't have to shovel coal. It's been winterized and a new roof installed, so we shouldn't freeze in the dark. I think we should get the kids and start hauling all the stuff into the house. "Cathy suggested, seeing her husband having doubts about the move.

By the time darkness enveloped the land, the trailer had been emptied and all the boxes placed in their proper rooms. Gooney was now scoping out all the hidden holes around the building, with both Caroline and Peter checking under their beds for monsters.

After a first sleep in their new house, everyone seemed tuned to the fact that there would be no traffic noise or sirens in the middle of the night. Assembling a bit of canned food, Cathy Spenser created her first masterpiece for breakfast. It was decided that everyone would drive into the nearest town and do some grocery shopping. There was now a sense of holiday about the move to Saskatchewan. With Gooney hanging out the rear window, Craig drove into Swift Current to return the trailer and allow his family to grocery shop. It was a special time. A new town, new faces and a chance to acclimatize to a different atmosphere. Cathy Spenser could see, by the joy with which her husband and children eagerly moved around the store, the first hurdle had been successfully negotiated. Returning to the house, there was constant chatter. With sufficient food in the pantry and fridge, it was time to get acquainted with the town and its inhabitants. Walking down into what, at one time, was the center of town, it was surprising to see the buildings vacant and derelict. As they strolled along the roadway, it occurred to Craig that he had not enquired about other residents living in Admiral. It was now a deserted village. Walking up the main road, they could see the three churches were still in use. It would mean that farmers from around the area made trips into town for religious services, weddings and funerals. When he was here with Cathy before they were married, Craig never paid enough attention to anything other than trying to ride her Grandfather's horse out into the fields and along Notukue creek. Church was the furthest thing from his mind, but the farmers' daughters were always of interest. Returning to the house on the hill, it was apparent that Peter and Caroline were going to spend a great deal of time finding something to do until they could find local children to be with.

Craig could now concentrate on his work. Contacting an electronics outfit, he made arrangements to have a satellite dish mounted so he go to work. Although he had contact with an engineering firm in Regina, this new device that would allow him to work, as well as deliver satellite television for the rest of the family at the same time. Within a week, a routine was established everyone was happy with. As July progressed, Cathy could see a change in her children. Ellen would help in the garden, while Peter and Caroline were out in the fields behind the house exploring places hidden by the passing years. One day, at the evening meal, Peter revealed that he and his sister had discovered the remnants of an old church, the basement of which was still accessible. Cathy was alarmed. After all the years, anything could be hidden in the cellar of an old building. "Don't go near it, until I check it out. It may collapse on you." Craig warned, not wanting to leave the house at the moment, "I'll go with you tomorrow." he promised, passing the mashed potatoes.

The next morning, with his flashlight, Craig accompanied Caroline and Peter to a spot a short distance away from the house. Wading through tall grass, the remains of a building were hidden from sight. He was surprised that his city bred children would even attempt to walk though the jungle of weeds and overgrowth to access a broken down mass of timbers and planks. Finding the spot indicated by his excited offsprings, he could make out a door in a depression.

Working his way down to the old wooden barrier, he found a large beam had fallen down and wedged itself into the ground, blocking the entrance. With a bit of broken 2x4, he was able to pry the 6x6 out of the way. Seeing a handle affixed to the hand hewn planks, he pushed at it. It moved.

Digging away more dirt from the base of the door, he was able to pry it open. He was surprised that his heart rate had increased. He was both nervous and excited, and looking up at his son and daughter, he stepped into the dark cavern created by the church foundation. A chill ran down his spine. He could feel a presence. For the first time in years, Craig Spenser was frightened. He closed the door. He couldn't bring himself to open it again. He climbed out of the pit.

"What's in there, Dad?" both his children asked in unison.

"It's all filled with dirt." he lied, "the floor has fallen in and filled it with rotten wood, so just get away from it," Craig was anxious to get as far from this strange, evil place. "let's go home and have a cold drink. I feel like I need a Coke float." he added, trying to divert their minds away from old dilapidated structure. The offer of a treat worked. Without any more questions, three Spensers returned to the old farm house, and a welcome relief from the growing heat.

Two days later, while Craig was in the study which he converted to an electronic office, Cathy was doing dishes at the kitchen sink, watching both Caroline and Peter working on building a swing.

As she watched, a small boy dressed in a white shirt and shorts came from the surrounding tall grass. He walked up to Caroline and began to speak to her. There was something strange about the young boy. Wiping her hands on a towel, Cathy casually walked to the kitchen door. Caroline seemed to be quite animated.

Peter finally stopped what he was doing and stood with his sister. They all stuck out their arms and joined hands. It was as if they had known each other all their lives. It was an odd meeting. Gooney just laid down and watched, rather than his usual sharp barking that alerted everyone within earshot of a stranger in their midst. Cathy stepped out onto the back porch, but when she did, the little boy turned and hurried back into the tall grass. He was gone.

"Who was that?" Cathy asked, opening the screen door. Both Caroline and Peter shrugged their shoulders, "is he a neighbor?" Brother and sister looked at one another, as if unsure of the consequences for telling the truth. Puzzled, Cathy stepped from the porch and crossed over to her children. "what's the matter with you two?" Both siblings stood and looked around, looking for a place to run. Gooney came over and sat beside Caroline and Peter, as if for moral support.

"His name is Alex. He wants to be our friend," Peter replied, finally, "you said you wanted us to make friends here. Why can't he be our friend?" Peter asked, causing his mother to blush.

"I guess it's OK to play with Alex. Where does he live?" Cathy asked, wondering why she hadn't seen a house nearby, "now, clean up. It's time for lunch." she added, hoping to learn more about the strange little boy who seemed to appear from nowhere.

As time passed, the 'Alex mystery' as Cathy called it, caused Craig Spenser to spend his idle time walking the nearby trails and roads. He discovered several older houses in a cul-de-sac a short distance from the center of town. A pickup stopped him as he returned home.

"Hello there, neighbor. I see you moved into the old Romanov house. My name is George Friesen.

I have a little shop downtown. I make sweatshirts. How do like it here?" he asked, sounding like a salesman trying to make a sales pitch. Craig shook George Friesen's outstretched hand.

"Hi. My name is Craig Spenser. My wife's father, Leo Romanov, gave my wife the house when he passed away.. When her mother died, the house became vacant. I used to come here when I was dating Cathy, and remembered how much sweeter the air was than in the city. Cathy and I decided to sell the house in Ontario, and move here to give the kids an an opportunity to see what the world looks like without asphalt. How long have you lived here?"

George Friesen shut off his motor and got out of the vehicle. Standing on the side of road, the two men discussed the state of Admiral. Craig was pleased to learn there was someone else in town he could talk to. With two more children in the area, there was a chance there may be more.

"My wife will be happy to know there is another woman in town she can gossip with, even though there isn't much news to share." George commented, getting back into his truck. Craig put his hand up to stop his neighbor. "Have you ever run into a kid called Alex? He must live around here."

Craig asked, pursuing the mystery boy who seemed to have vanished. George Friesen shook his head. "No. I don't know of another kid around here that age. My kids are 8 and 13. They spend their time with me down at the shop, or hiking the fields looking for gophers, There are other kids down in the farms on the flats. They come in to town once in while to buy sweatshirts from me. Your kids will find them, I'm sure," he replied, shaking his head, "at least we don't have any bears or wolves to worry about." he laughed, as he drove away. Craig was left with the impression that his wife's concern about Alex was unwarranted.

Relaying his meeting with George Friesen to his wife, Cathy was surprised to hear of another family in the area. Apparently, there were other people as well, aside from the farm families in the Valley below.

As summer brought more heat, Cathy was becoming concerned with Craig's increased time spent in Regina, leaving her to watch over her brood. Making a sandwich for herself and Ellen, Cathy took Ellen by the hand and walked down to the village. As she walked with Ellen along the main road toward the town, it worried her that both Caroline and Peter were spending more time exploring the nearby vacant houses. Even with her husband's assurances that they were both old enough to look after one another, and Gooney would never let anything bad happen, it was still worrisome. Packing a picnic lunch in the morning, Cathy could see that Peter was very aware of his responsibility in taking care of his little sister, so with Gooney anxious to get out and explore with his two humans, she watched as they hiked down the hill to another adventure. As Cathy walked slowly along the main street, she looked in the windows of the vacant stores, with their dusty windows, and wondered what Admiral looked like all those years ago when it had a large enough population to fill 4 churches. Shading her eyes from the sun, Cathy put her face against the window of an old welding shop, and fell backwards as she saw Alex staring back at her. He was standing in the middle of the floor, still wearing the same white shirt and shorts from two weeks before. Holding Ellen tightly by the hand, Cathy crossed the street to take advantage of shade from a towering cottonwood. She sat on an old cement bench, trying to understand what she had just seen. What was Alex doing in the old vacant building. There had to be a reasonable explanation. Perhaps he entered by a back door and went in to stay out of the sun and heat. She was tempted to look again, but felt she was being childish. At 36 years of age, she couldn't be seen having a hallucination. Casually walking to the end of the street, she picked a small Crocus from a clump growing on an old building site, handing it to Ellen. The joy of her daughter's laughter drove any concern for her sanity away. She did not go back home by way of the main street, but took a back lane past other vacant houses from a bygone era. She had come to appreciate the fresh air delivered by a constant breeze that swept across the open prairie. Sitting on a discarded steamer trunk, she could look over farmland to the south, watching a tractor pull some type of large device over the ground. This was something that she had never seen on the farms near Woodstock. The land seemed endless. Growing up in Admiral, she wasn't aware of many of the things she noticed now, at 36. After her father died, her mother took her to live in Woodstock and go to school, her visits back to see her grandparents were made less often. When her grandmother died, she returned for the funeral, but after that, she never thought of it until she visited grandpa Arvid, with Craig as her boyfriend. She wondered if Craig would ever see the beauty that she finally understood. From this particular location, Cathy could make out the curve of the earth. It was a revelation. Looking over to her right, behind her, she could make out the remains of another house. On a whim, she took Ellen by the hand and made her way along a deer trail to the site. The house was still intact. Stepping carefully onto the porch, she entered by way of the partially open front door.

Although weather had attacked the interior, there was a room where glass in the windows prevented the bed and dresser from being damaged. Cathy tried to imagine the family who once called this place home. Opening a dresser drawer, she found old socks and underwear.

They were still in surprisingly good condition, without mice destroying the fabric. Moving the underclothes aside, Cathy was surprised to find a Bible. Lifting it, she discovered a thick envelope. Sitting on the bed, she carefully opened the flap. Inside were a number of photos and letters. Feeling like a voyeur, there was moment when she thought about putting it back, but started to read.

With Ellen leaning against her mother's arm, she took great interest in the photos. Giggling at the sight of people in old clothes and funny shaped automobiles, she asked her mother about the large animal attached to a wagon.

"Is this Santa Claus?" Ellen asked, running her finger over the shiny surface. Cathy laughed.

"No, sweetheart. That's a horse, not a reindeer. This is how people got around in the old days before cars and trucks." Ellen nodded her head, as if in understanding. "it's hard to believe this house could be that old." Cathy added, thumbing through the small stack of neatly inscribed envelopes. Pulling one from its hiding place, she carefully opened it. Holding it up to the light, she began to read…

"Bruno is not able to work again this week. Gunther took his place on the plow. We hope to have twenty acres in seed by the end of the week. We lost another calf when the dugout dried up and the mother couldn't feed her. We may have to butcher another cow while there is still enough meat on her to make it worthwhile. It will keep us in meat until it goes bad. Maybe two weeks. Maria is leaving for the city. She hopes to get a job and feels guilty about leaving us alone to run the farm.

I told her that she has to decide for herself. She knows there will be one less mouth to feed if she leaves. I don't want her to go, but things are not getting any better. With Bruno laid up, it will take longer for the crop to be planted. The damn wind will probably blow away what little seed there is anyway. Hope things get better soon.

Love and kisses. Greta…

Cathy was now depressed. Seeing someone giving up on life was unsettling. She had to remind herself that the person who wrote this was probably dead and buried. Assembling all the photos and letters, she placed them in her bag, along with the sandwiches she and Ellen were supposed to eat on their journey. With a shrug, she took Ellen's hand, and together they left the old house, still thinking about the former residents and their hard life.

A short distance along the trail, she was alarmed by the sound of someone running through the tall grass, but was relieved when the faces of her other children appeared on the path ahead. There was surprise on everyone's part. Cathy could see both Peter and Caroline had been exploring in earnest. Both their shiny faces were covered in dirt, but still beautiful to an appreciative mother.

"Are you two finished for the day, or are you going to have a night shift?" Cathy asked, following along, assuming they would know the way home. Upon reaching the back yard, Cathy could hear loud voices at the front of the house. Walking around to the sound, she discovered a very large, bearded man standing over Craig, shouting in his face. Turning to her children, Cathy handed off Ellen. "Take your little sister in the house, while I find out what the problem is." she said, with the 'don't argue with me' tone that all three children knew well. Taking their little sister into the front porch, Gooney was free to assault the stranger. Growling and snapping, he was eager and ready to tear the leg from this stranger. The man kicked at the offending attacker, until Cathy screamed at the intruder. Gooney stopped attacking, and the big man stopped kicking.

"Who do you think you are?" Cathy asked, standing right up in the man's face. He backed up a step. He looked at Craig, then at Cathy, contemplating his next move.

"We want you out of here. You have no place in Admiral. There is no place on earth fit for a Romanov. Your family is poison. Your father was no better than his father. The whole Romanov clan is diseased. You reek of evil. The Romanovs have been the Devil's partner since time began.

We want you out, and will not stop until you and your corrupt family have gone back to Hell, where you belong." He paused for a moment, then turned and left, walking back to his pickup truck, where several members of his family were waiting. Cathy stood and watched as the man got into his truck and drove away. She turned to Craig, who, with fists clenched, was ready to explode.

"Who in Hell does that guy think he is? Do you know who it is?" he asked, not looking at his wife.

"I think he's a preacher for the Immaculate Church of God. I've never seen him before, but my Grampa used to tell me to stay away from their Church. They are an orthodox sect who believe that anyone other than their religious group are Satanists. My Grandfather owned most of Admiral. He even owned the land their Church was built on. I think, if I wanted to, I could go to Court and have them thrown off the property. They probably know that. That's why they're nervous about me coming back to the homestead." Cathy replied, taking Craig's arm, leading him back to the house. As they entered the porch, all three children rushed to their side.

"Who was that, Mommy?" Caroline asked, "is he going to kill Daddy?" The question was written on the faces on her sibling's faces. Cathy opened the door, herding everyone inside.

"Come into the kitchen. I'll make lunch and try to explain your ancestry." Cathy said, taking Ellen by the hand. With everyone seated around the large kitchen table, Cathy Spenser set about explaining her upbringing to a captive audience, while assembling sandwiches and soup for her crew. As she worked, Craig placed glasses and cups on the table. It was the least he could do for the woman whose past had always been a mystery. While assembling the food, she spoke.

"My Great great grandfather, Peter Romanov, arrived in Canada from Russia back in the late 1800's. He landed in Montreal and was told about the free land here in the west of this new Country. As a machinist, he got a job helping to build the railway across the prairies. When the CPR cleared the line through Shaunavon, he spent his last pay cheque on land here in Admiral. Little by little, he increased the size of his farm, to include where Admiral is now. He didn't name the town." Cathy laughed, as she could see her audience was paying attention, "His son took over the farm and started building grain elevators all along the rail line. As more farmers began to ship grain by rail, they made a great deal of money. The Romanov name became connected to anything that made money. With two grain elevators in this area, a town was built around them. My great grandfather built this house. It was the biggest and nicest in town, so people became jealous. I was in University in Toronto when I met your Dad. He was interested in where I was born, so we came back here to visit my family. For some reason, my grandmother liked your Dad." Cathy reached over and took Craig's hand, "and my grandfather put him to work fixing up the pump house. It was decided, then and there, that your Dad would be better on a computer than a pipe wrench. We were in Woodstock when my mother died, and I came back here for the funeral. We closed up the house, and went back to Ontario. That was many years ago. I know you all have friends back in our old place, but we'll see how things work out here. Your Dad tells me there is another family over in the little subdivision by the school. The man that was here today acting like an idiot, belongs to a group of farmers that have always been a little bit different, so don't worry about him. You have every right to be here. Now, where did you two go today? Did you find any new places?" Cathy asked, sipping on a coffee placed before her by an appreciative husband.

"Alex took us to an old building and showed us a dead body." Peter said, as he bit into an egg salad sandwich. Cathy looked over at Craig and could see he was ready to jump on his son.

"You saw Alex today?" Cathy asked, not acknowledging the dead body remark. Craig looked over at his wife. The dead body remark left him pondering his son's sense of humor.

"Yeah. We were with him all the time. He knows a lot of places. He said he might take us to a special place next time." Peter commented, taking a drink of milk.

"And he doesn't wear shoes. Mommy!" Caroline added, feeding a small piece of bread to her little sister. "he must have tough feet," she added, laughing as she looked over at Peter.

"I don't want you to spend so much time with Alex," Cathy said, trying to understand how Alex could have been in two places at once. 'we don't know anything about him. Where does he live?"

Peter shrugged. "I think he lives beneath old church behind us. I asked him if he would show us, but he got mad and said he wasn't allowed to show anyone." Craig thought about the door beneath the old destroyed church, and the cold fright he felt when he stepped into the darkness. He could not picture anyone living in the damp, blackened ruins.

The next morning, Craig called the RCMP Detachment and spoke to the Police about the confrontation. "Oh, you must mean Siegfried. He's the leader of a religious group living in the area. There are quite a few of them around. He's all bark and no bite." the Constable said, "we've spoken to him a few times about problems, and he usually cooperates. I wouldn't lose too much sleep over his threats. Lots of smoke, but no fire, if you know what I mean." he added, trying to make it sound like the visit was a normal occurrence. Craig left the conversation feeling like the religious groups had a hold over the RCMP.

He would have to find out more about the Immaculate Church of God. Concerned that his work was suffering with the interruptions that the move to Admiral had caused, Craig decided to overlook the Preacher's tirade and concentrate on his job. Cathy could see that her husband had withdrawn into his office and worried that the Preacher's threats would change the atmosphere in the house, especially when Craig refused to stop work to have dinner with her and the children. This was concerning. Peter and Caroline could see their mother was not happy as they sat and ate in silence, their father's chair empty.

"Is Daddy mad at us?" Caroline asked, not quite understanding her father's new attitude.

Cathy shook her head. "No, sweetheart. He's not mad at us, but he has a couple of jobs that have to be finished. He promised some people that he could still work from home. Do you remember how he went to work every morning? Now his office is downstairs, and sometimes he has to go to Regina. Just give him some time to catch up on his work, and he'll be eating with us again." Cathy explained, not really feeling she spoke the truth. It was possible that the Preacher frightened her husband. He was not accustomed to being talked to by people like the Preacher. Saskatchewan had many different religious sects that were imported from Europe during Canada's early days. They had strident views and strict beliefs. The Romanovs were chosen as targets because they refused to join any particular sect.

Cathy thought about those early days, while she was growing up, and the discussions she heard in these very rooms. Her Grandfather, Arvid, was the last of the Romanovs who had control of Admiral and the surrounding farms. Many farmers were still paying rent into the Romanov bank account for their acreage, as well as government had to bow to the Courts when it came to taking over Romanov property in the former town of Admiral. Although it was no longer regarded as an official 'Town', Cathy, as the sole survivor of the Romanov family, was now the only person standing in the way of all the property reverting to the Province. When Craig told her of the conversation with the RCMP, and Police hesitance to interfere with the Preacher and the Church, it was proof that the pressure was on her to relinquish Romanov ownership of all the lands. That evening, while Craig was busy in the basement, Cathy sat down with the bag of photos and letters. She was pleased when her three children joined her on the bed, sorting through the old, smelly paper and shiny images.

The first letter chosen by Caroline was dated September 12, 1929.

My Dearest Sylvia
Sven is out in the south section, The crop is good this year and the price is the best in years.

We are thinking of buying a larger harvester. The new ones have gas engines, and Brother John is happy that he doesn't have to feed and look after all the horses or fiddle with that miserable steam machine. I can't wait to see how it works. How is Lucien? I hear that they are moving to Vancouver I hope he and Marie find a small farm. At least the weather will be better, but I will miss Marie at our get-togethers.

Martin's son is working for the Romanovs at their elevator. He says it's hard work, but the pay is good. He very seldom sees old man Romanov. The CP elevator is bigger, but doesn't pay as well. I'm going into Swift Current next week to see a Doctor for my back. John said I should take the train rather than travel by car. The new Ford rides so nice, and I don't have to wait around in the city for the trip home. Teddy said he can take a few days off to drive me. I think he just wants to get away from the fields, but John figures he and Tim can handle the harvesting while Teddy drives me to the Doctor. I think it will be nice break for both of us.

Will write you when I return..

Love.. Melanie Popov. xoxoxox

It took a minute for Cathy to realize that to realize that this letter was never mailed. There was no envelope. What happened to prevent Melanie Popov from mailing it?

Cathy thought about the house she visited where she found these letters and photos. The people had normal lives and wondered whatever happened to the town and the residents. When she was born, it was still a Town. The Hotel had burned down, but the Bank and Grocery store were still operating. She attended the school, which was now closed, but there were other kids to play with.

This eighty year old letter was a connection to the past that showed the Admiral was a busy, lively place. She looked over at Caroline and Peter, who were giggling at funny looking people in the old photos. Ellen was asleep at the foot of the bed. Searching through the stack of musty papers, she discovered an envelope with a letter still inside.

Opening it, she took out the film-like paper and carefully unfolded it.

It was dated November 10, 1929

Dear Melanie.

How are you making out with the downturn. Harold is out of work at the machine shop. No one is buying the equipment, so there's no service work. I hope you got your crop sold before the bottom dropped out of the market. The farmers in the area are stocking up as much as they can, because there is no way of knowing how long this downturn will last. I guess all we can do is hope that the government can make a deal with the Americans for a better price for our grain. With no money coming in, it won't take long before we will have to start selling our bodies. (that's a joke). I don't think your family would appreciate men knocking on your door, even if they had money in their hands. I hope the post office doesn't close down.. Take it easy, kiddo…

Love you lots… Johanna

Peter and Caroline picked through the pile of photos. "Who's this?" they kept asking, and Cathy had to explain that the pictures were from a time long before she was born. She recalled a couple of the family names, but the town was deteriorating even when she was born.

Picking up another Letter, the envelope had the name of a Lawyer that Cathy recalled, but the faded post mark was August 20, 1931.

Haroldson / Gordon Law Group
Saskatoon, Saskatchewan

Dear Mr. Martin Popov

After considerable discussion, we have no choice but to foreclose on your account. Having had no payment since July, 1930, we have been advised that the Bank can no longer carry the Popov overdraft. We have made arrangements with the Bank to leave the sum of $500. in your account to assist you in your transition. We understand the reason for your lack of payment, but our business also relies on punctual remittance. This Depression has taxed the financial system to the brink and beyond. Whenever this world wide disaster ends, we will be happy to accommodate your business once again.

Yours truly
Jeremy Haroldson, QC.

Cathy read the words and felt the pain that the original recipient must have experienced upon opening this letter. Having your credit cut off, and your Bank account seized, without any recourse while trying to operate a farm, would mean no more fuel, seed, or machinery parts. Without a large pot of money salted away, there would be very few farms that survived. They would have a few cows, pigs or chickens to provide meals in the summer, but winters would be brutal without being able to stock up on firewood or coal. Cathy thought back to her life as she was growing up. As a Romanov, she never experienced any hardship. Her Grandparents and Mother always had food, milk, and fuel for the large furnace in the basement. She barely remembered her father, Leo. He was killed when she was three. Her mother never explained how he died, and her Grandmother never talked about him. She had seen photos him and thought he was quite handsome. The kids in school always treated her with deference, but she never completely understood why. It wasn't until she was older that came to realize that most of the kids she went to school with owed their livelihood and success to being supported and financed by a Romanov. When she left for school, her grandfather, along with a housekeeper waved goodbye.

Years later, she returned with Craig in tow. She smiled when she recalled how bad Craig was at doing anything that required mechanical ability. The fact that he could make a living describing how things work to the purchaser of anything from an electric razor or power saw, yet have no idea how use them himself, had always impressed her over the years. Her attention was brought back to the present when Caroline tugged at Cathy's sleeve.

"Here's a picture of Alex!" her daughter said, with Peter crawling over the bed to verify the photo.

"Yeah. It is Alex. How did the picture get in with all these old pictures?" he asked, taking the photo from his sister's hand and holding it up to the light.

"That can't be," Cathy said, not really paying attention to her son's question, but took the photo from Peter, casting a glance at the image in passing, then stopped. Bringing it to her face, she studied the old tintype and shook her head, "It certainly looks like Alex, but these photos are over eighty years old, so it must be a relative." she added, trying to understand how the boy in the picture was identical to the little boy she saw in the window, in fact, wearing exactly the same clothes. Deciding to put away the bag of letters and photos away, she took Peter and Caroline to the bathroom to do their pre-bedtime routine. After putting them to bed, Cathy returned to place Ellen in her bed in Caroline's room. All the time she performed these nighttime duties, she couldn't shake the image of Alex. As Craig came upstairs from his office, he could see his wife was pre-occupied.

"What's new?" he asked, as he made a cup of warm milk, studying Cathy's face for some clue.

"Nothing. I've just been looking at some of the old photos and letters I found in the house down the lane. They are from the late 20s and early 30's. They had a hard time here during the Depression.

My Grandparents were not well liked, even then." she said, sitting down to join her husband in a nighttime snack. It was the only time in the past two weeks that they could spend together, with Craig totally involved with a large contract that would pay for the whole year. She understood the need for him to work away home in Regina, and would have to grin and bear it. It was a surprise when Craig dropped the bombshell.

"I'll have to fly to Japan in two days. The client wants me there for some hands-on technical instruction. They want me to go to the factories that make their products to get a first hand look at the process. I'll take the truck so you can have the car to pack the kids around." Craig said, as if asking for his wife to pass the sugar. Cathy stared at her husband in disbelief.

"How long do you think you'll be gone?" she asked, not looking at Craig. It would mean that she would be alone if Siegfried returned with his gang of crazies. Craig could feel a sudden chill in the room.

"Probably at least a week. Maybe two. You'll be alright here with the kids. This is your home. I'm feeling like just a visitor. The Company is paying the fare and their Company President wants to meet me in person. It's a chance to really get involved with their marketing and sales. There could be big money in it for us." Craig reasoned,," and we may make enough money so we can move to a farm somewhere down south. Maybe South Dakota. Wouldn't that be cool?" Craig stopped talking and took a drink of warm milk. Cathy couldn't believe what she was hearing. Her husband of fifteen years wanted to move out of Canada and go to the States. It was a shock to learn he wasn't happy being in her hometown. She thought back to the visit by the Preacher and how frightened Craig appeared to be of the bearded man. The fact that the RCMP wouldn't investigate was another trigger. She stared at Craig. What happened to the man she married?

There had to be more to his sudden desire to leave Admiral. Cathy Spenser got up and crossed to the sink. She couldn't bring herself to look at her husband, so she walked out of the kitchen.

"You can sleep on the couch, tonight." was all she could think of saying. She didn't look back at her husband. Craig sat and watched his wife leave. He knew he had made a mistake, but with a chance to make some real money and move away from this deserted town, he was going to take the trip to Japan, certain that Cathy would come around as soon as the big money started rolling in.

The next morning, Craig was packed and ready to leave. Peter and Caroline were puzzled why their mother and father didn't speak to one another, but as Craig got into the pickup, he knelt down and hugged his two older children, not even approaching Cathy holding Ellen, who was waving to her departing father. Gooney sensed there was an unhappiness in the family and never went to be scratched behind the ears by the man of the house. Moments later, the pickup truck rattled down the driveway and onto the main road. Within minutes, he was out of sight, leaving his family wondering if they would ever see him again. Cathy led her children back into the house.

"Where is Daddy going?" Peter asked, as he settled down to his Rice Crispies. Caroline was also waiting for an answer. Cathy took a moment to concoct a reasonable lie.

"Daddy's going away to see a man about another job. He'll be back in a couple of weeks."

It was all she could think of to make it appear that she and their father were still happy together.

"Caroline and me are going on a treasure hunt. Alex showed us another house where he said the School Teacher lived." Peter said, eager to get out into the deserted town. Cathy watched as Ellen finished her egg, knowing it was going to be a long two weeks without her husband.

Three days later, Cathy was gathering clothes for laundry, when the phone rang. It had been silent for weeks. The voice on the other end was not familiar.

"Hello. Is this Mrs. Spenser. My name is Staff Sergeant O'Neill. Your husband called the Detachment the other day. Have you had any more problems with Siegfried? I've spoken to him about the incident the other day. He seems to think that you will stir up trouble, being a Romanov, I mean. I understand from him that he doesn't believe you should be in Admiral." It was a statement that caused Cathy to wonder if she was in Canada or some banana republic. The Sergeant made it sound like she was responsible for any problems that occurred in the past hundred years of Admiral's existence. There was a temptation to get angry, but keeping her temper under control, she replied, "My family has been in this area for one hundred and thirty years. The Romanovs have built the area with grain elevators and farms, bringing in people from every Country to work and build a community. I am the last of the Romanovs. I will not be frightened off my land by some heretic who believes they have more rights to this land than I do. In fact, I own the very land Mr. Siegfried's church is built on. In fact, it was my grandfather who built the damned church. If he thinks he can frighten me and my children from this place, he will find that a Romanov does not take being threatened lightly. Tell your friend that if he comes onto my land again, he will discover a totally different response than he received from my husband. He and his kind can go to Hell!"

Cathy hung up the phone. A switch inside had been turned on. Her family had survived for over a one hundred years in the area. They provided jobs, built stores, houses and multitude of grain elevators. She was not about to allow some bearded religious freak to chase her out of her home. Taking Ellen downstairs, Cathy was a woman on a mission. Looking through the old filing cabinet in Craig's office, she found the dossier that her mother kept, and had offered to her daughter before she died. Cathy was now interested in its contents.

Leafing through the most recent additions, she came upon the name of the Law firm that handled the executor duties. The McCleod / Gordon Law Group was located in Saskatoon. The name was somewhat familiar. Dragging Ellen away from Craig's computer, Cathy went upstairs and phoned.

After a short discussion with a suspicious Secretary, Cathy was finally connected to a young male voice.

"Good day. Mrs. Spenser? I'm not sure if I can help you. What is it you would like?"

"Good morning. My name before I was married was Romanov. Your firm was executor of my mother's will. I would like you to send me an itemized copy of my account." There was a momentary silence, and Cathy could hear the Lawyer mumbling instructions to the Secretary.

Moments later, he returned with a more contrite attitude.

"Yes, Mrs. Spenser, I have your file here. But the way, my name is Barry Gordon." He was about to continue when Cathy interrupted him. "Did you once have a partner named Haroldson?"

"Yes. That was my father's partner. He passed away many years ago. I took over from my father and teamed up with a fellow law student, Ben McCleod. It appears the Romanovs have been clients of our firm for many, many years. What can I do for you. It says here your name is, was, Catherine Romanov. Your mother was Ruth Romanov. When she passed, she left all the Romanov titles to you." there was a long delay as Barry Gordon shuttled through papers, "we have been looking after all the paperwork and documents since then. In fact, Haroldson / Gordon have been connected to your family since the early 30's. According to this, we have been collecting fees for providing this service for over 80 years. I don't know if you would like this discussed over the phone, but you have substantial holdings in both Alberta and

Saskatchewan. Do you want me to send you an accounting by email?" Cathy could hear him breathing heavily.

"Yes. That would be a good idea. I would like to know where I stand as far as to what I own." Cathy replied, hoping that the belief in her Romanov name was not just wishful thinking.

"Fine. I'll have my Secretary assemble all the data and send it to you. Just send me the eMail address and we'll get that off to you. Thank you for calling. It's good to see the Romanov name hasn't disappeared completely." Hanging up, Cathy sat back and wondered what was left in the pot.

Within the hour, sitting at the computer, Cathy was surprised at the number of documents appearing on the screen. Printing them as quickly as possible, she was astonished at the results. Assembling the many spread sheets and bank statements, she looked over at her youngest child. "At least we won't starve to death, sweetheart."

As sole beneficiary, Cathy Spenser had 4.1 million dollars in the bank, 31 million dollars in real estate and 1.1 million in annual revenue from oil leases and royalties. Looking over the stack of receipts and lists of properties, it took her breath away. The Romanovs, over the years, had invested in everything from oil to land. Looking through the real estate holdings, she found what she was after. A map of the Admiral area and the property owned by the Romanov family. Her family. The Immaculate Church of God, held services in a church built on property whose taxes were paid by the law firm every year. With that information, Cathy Spenser had the ammunition she needed for the next time the Preacher came around to harass her and her family.

Sorting out the different maps and diagrams, one fell to the floor. Ellen immediately latched onto the rebel piece of paper. Sitting her daughter on her lap, Cathy separated the bits and pieces into their respective piles. Taking the paper from Ellen, Cathy studied it for a moment and was about to place it in the appropriate section, when a small drawing caught her eye. Holding it so the light made it more legible, it was the outline of a building. Sorting through the various piles, she found a corresponding photo. Placing the two images side by side, it became apparent that it was of a Church. Having been born in Admiral, she thought she knew every building in town, but she had never seen this particular hermitage. She set it aside, intrigued with its design and puzzled about its location. By noon, with Ellen's questionable help, all the new documents were placed in their appropriate drawers. It was time for her other offsprings to return from their foraging sorties, hungry and eager to tell her of the new adventure.

Although half an hour late, Cathy was grateful to hear them arrive on the back porch. Arguing about the size of a deer, they bounced into the kitchen, and went immediately to the kitchen sink to wash off the prairie dust that seems to be ingrained in their skin. She smiled as she recalled doing exactly the same thing as she grew up in this house, but with an old fashioned enamel sink that seemed to be from the stone age. The Contractors did a good job of modernizing the house, with new faucets, showers and toilets.

"What did you two do, today?" she asked as they sat down to their soup and grilled cheese sandwiches. Casting glances at one another, Caroline answered.

"Alex showed us another old house. It had a basement with an old bicycle. Peter tried to take it up the stairs, but he's just too weak." That comment drew a kick in the shins by her brother.

"Well, I didn't see you trying to help!" Peter shouted, embarrassed at being portrayed as less than superhuman, "it was as if it wouldn't let me take it out of the basement. It kept getting heavier."

Caroline laughed at the suggestion, which made her brother stick out his tongue. A retort that was ignored by his younger sibling. Quiet settled over the table as both Peter and Caroline thought about the experience.

"Why didn't you get Alex to help you?" Cathy asked, replenishing their orange juice.

"He disappeared someplace." Peter explained, "one minutes he was talking to us from the stairs, then he went up into the house and we never saw him again. Maybe he had to go home. Anyway, I never got the bike. I wanted to fix it up and ride it. Why did we have to leave our bikes back home? Why couldn't we bring them?" It was a question Cathy asked herself. Craig said he forgot to place them in trailer, but, when she suggested he return and pick them up, he got angry. Seeing that he was upset at leaving the city, she accepted his anger and did not press the matter.

"Maybe we'll go into Swift Current and buy new bikes. I think I'll get one too. Maybe I'll get one for Ellen. We can ride downtown and wherever there is still pavement." Cathy suggested, knowing that bikes would be useless on the rough gravel roads surrounding Admiral.

"That's OK., mom. We like hiking in the fields around here. We always run into Antelope or Deer. The other day, we saw a Coyote with pups." Caroline said, finishing the last of her orange juice.

"You kids have been all over this place in the last month. Come downstairs, I want to show you something." Cathy said, as she cleaned away the dishes. There was sense of excitement as Cathy and her brood went down into the basement. Pulling out the photo and drawing of the Church, she spread them out on the ping pong table. It took a moment for both Caroline and Peter to study the images, but finally Peter picked up the photo and nodded his head.

"It could be the church up behind the house. The one on top of the hill," he said handing the photo to his sister, "Dad went into it and ran back out. I think he found something that scared him." her son commented, puzzling Cathy.

"He never said anything about a church up behind the house. I was born here and I don't remember seeing a church up there." Cathy admitted, feeling stupid for not being aware of her surroundings, "tomorrow, you can take me up there to see it. If It's there, it belongs to me." she said, finally. Peter and Caroline looked at each other. They could hear a tone in their mother's voice they had never heard before. Taking Ellen by the hand, the four Spensers went back upstairs to watch television. Tomorrow would be another day of adventure.

Peter was up at daybreak. The thought of taking his mother to a new site was exciting. He thought back to the day he saw his father disappear into the basement of the old church on the hill. He also remembered the look of fear on his face, and the hurry to get away from the destroyed building.

Maybe, today, with his mother along, he will get a chance to enter the basement and see what frightened his father.

"How far away is this church?" Cathy asked, joining her son as he dropped a piece of bread into the toaster, "it must be pretty old if I never saw it before, although my mother and Grampa told me not to go past the fence at the end of the north field." she added, warned that there were wells in the field that she could fall into. Believing it was for her own good, Cathy Romanov listened to her Grandfather and mother and didn't venture up the the hill through the old cemetery. Feeling adventurous with her children's exuberant goading, she packed a lunch, and together, they left the yard. Closing the gate behind her, for the first time in 36 years, she would head into the field west of her house. Walking through the uncut grass, she could make out the valley in the distance, and familiar landmarks from her youth. Following the trail that Peter, Caroline and Alex had been using to access the top of the hill, she had the unsettling feeling of dread. Tripping suddenly, she prevented herself from tumbling on top of her three year old, and barely missed a small cross planted in the tall grass. Kneeling, Cathy was surprised to see a metal plate affixed to the base of a crucifix.

In memory of Alexander Popov 1834-1920

She wiped the dirt from the plaque and thought about the house where she found the photos.

She used to play with a Jenny Popov. Her father was a mechanic for the car dealership in Shaunavon. It was just as Admiral was beginning to fail.

"Are you OK, mommy?" Caroline asked, holding Ellen's hand. Cathy looked up at her daughter and smiled. At least she found the cemetery.

"I'm fine, honey. I guess I have to watch where I'm walking." she replied, getting up and rejoining her crew. A short time later, they arrived at the remains of a building.

"Is this it?" Cathy asked, as the explorers looked at the ruins. Peter walked through the overgrown weeds to a clearing. There, among the broken boards and rubble, was the entrance to the basement. That feeling of dread returned. Cathy looked around at her children. They were expecting her to enter the dark hole in the ground. Carrying the basket over to a fallen timber, she sat down and opened it, withdrawing the sandwiches and juice boxes. It was an attempt to change the focus from the church to food. It worked. Suddenly, her brood gathered around, finding a place to sit down and enjoy a picnic. Although there was laughing and joking, in the pit of her stomach, Cathy knew she would have to enter the doorway. It was just a portal to the basement. She thought back to the photo and hand drawn image from the day before. It was obvious that this building was in the same condition when she was younger. It would account for her not seeing it from the house.

As the drinks and sandwiches were consumed, the time to show her children that their mother was brave, arrived. Peter got up and walked down the rotted stairs to the mysterious doorway. He looked up at his mother. She could no longer delay. Cathy Spenser was going to have to enter the unknown. She felt silly being frightened of a doorway. It was just an entrance to an old building.

As Peter, Caroline and Ellen waited, Cathy carefully made her way down the steps, and stood in front of the old wooden door. Partially open, it would take a slight push to clear the cobwebs and bits of wood blocking the way. Taking a deep breath, she stepped inside.

****

The air was hot and filled with dust. She looked around and found herself in a house filled with people. She recognized her Grandfather, but he was only in his thirties. Her grandmother carried a plate of chicken breasts to the dining room table.

"Cathy, hurry up and bring the gravy. It's on the stove." Her grandmother was pretty, and young.

Immediately, Cathy went to the kitchen, retrieving the small bowl of hot sauce. It smelled so good.

Carrying it back to the dining room, she placed it on the table in front of two young girls and an older boy.

"Sit down, Cathy. Your father wants to get supper out of the way so he can get back out with the workers and bring in the rest of the crop. We've only got another two weeks before the weather changes."and handing her husband the plate of carrots, asked. "Petrov, do you want more carrots, or have you had enough?" Cathy sat down and handed mashed potatoes to her brother sitting beside her.

"You're lucky you don't have to go out in the field today, Cathy," he said, passing the potatoes along the table to his other sister. "Papa, how are we going to get the tractor started with no belt?"

Arvid asked, spilling the gravy on the tablecloth. Cathy's father looked along the table at his eldest son. Petrov Romanov did not trouble himself with minor problems.

"I told Tommy Popov to run into town and get a new one. Now, when you finish supper, go out and give Jeremy a hand. He's not that good with horses. By 1930, I want to be able to get another

31

tractor, then we won't have to worry about horses. We can put them out to pasture. It will be good to have two machines to run the harvester. I spoke to a fellow named Curtis who said he can have a new harvester here by November. It's too late for this year, but we'll have it ready for next year's crop. With another section in wheat, we're going to need the machinery to do the work. With the price of wheat this year, we should have no trouble paying for another machine." There was general agreement around the table that 1929 had been a good year. With threshing just about complete, the Romanovs looked forward to having more machinery to speed up harvesting.

After supper, Cathy went up to her room and looked out over the fields to the south. She could see her brother and field hands bringing the horses into place to start threshing. Off to the north, the town of Admiral looked busy. The Hotel was booked up with CPR workers. Her father built the rooming house, complete with a Bar, to support the rail company in exchange for constructing a siding for the Romanov grain elevator. CPR even agreed to build a railway station to accommodate visitors to the town, even though Shaunavon was larger. To the west, Cathy could make out the new Fordson tractor pulling three hay wagons at once. She marveled at how much more the machinery could do than the teams of horses. Now that the Romanovs controlled six sections in the vicinity of Admiral, it was up to her brother to find enough water for all the fields. Her concentration was interrupted by a voice in the doorway.

"What are you doing up here?" It was Abigail. Two years younger but devoted to the farm.

"Just watching the boys. I see Tony Mercedes is out helping his father. What's he like?" Cathy asked, sitting down at the dressing table. She began to brush her hair while her sister took up perusing the local young males as they worked the fields. With threshing and baling under way, it was all hands on deck, except for the girls of Petrov Romanov's family. Daughters of other farm families in the area were part of the work crew. In the dust and heat of a Saskatchewan autumn, they worked alongside their fathers and brothers, but Petrov could afford to hire replacements for his three young girls. It was embarrassing at times, when they all met in town. Dressed in the fine clothes brought in from New York and San Francisco, Cathy, Abigail and Dorothy stood out when they rode into Admiral in their new Model A Ford, while their neighbors arrived in wagons and buckboards. No one was starving, but the Romanovs had accumulated the land and business contacts, allowing Petrov to pick and choose where his wheat and barley was sold, receiving the best price. With four grain elevators along the CPR line, the Romanov name was emblazoned on the side of all but one, for everyone to see.

Abigail sat next to her sister, and began to whisper. "I went out on Blaze the other day and met Tony down by the creek. He said his father was thinking of buying a quarter section next to our land. He asked me to not mention it to Papa, but if the Mercedes' bought that piece, they could cut off the water to our south east section. I don't know what to do. Should I tell Papa, or just keep my mouth shut? I feel like a traitor. I like Tony, but I'm a Romanov. What do you think I should do, Kate?" Abigail took the brush from Cathy and began combing her sister's hair. Cathy could see the dilemma. If she didn't tell Papa, and he found about Abbigail's prior knowledge, he would be furious. If she told Papa, he would buy up the land before the Mercedes and Tony would never speak to her again.

"If Tony told you about the land deal, he must know you would tell Papa. He may be hoping you do. If Papa buys the land, he'll need to keep the Mercedes on to work it. I think it was a trick to keep a job. I would tell Papa that you heard in town that the quarter section was up for sale and let him figure it out. If he sees that he could lose access to the creek, he'll be at the land registry in the morning. At least it will guarantee you get to see Tony again." Cathy said, watching her sister's reaction in the mirror. Abigail stopped combing and smiled. Handing the comb to her sister, she turned and hurried downstairs to relay an overheard rumor to Petrov. Cathy knew what her father's reaction would be. The Mercedes would be assured of a plot of land, a house and job for years to come, and Abigail would still be able to see her beau. As September turned to October on the Canadian Prairie, the weather became cooler. It was time to prepare for winter.

Petrov was happy to be able to give the teamsters a bonus for their work with the horses, knowing that their job was becoming tenuous with the purchase of more tractors. A shipment of coal, parked on the Romanov siding, was quickly unloaded and sold to anyone with a freight wagon and money. Along with a small amount of wood, the coal kept the house and workshop warm during the long, cold prairie winters. Cathy was just entering the front door of the main house, when she heard her father curse. It was not an unusual event, but this was a more guttural expression than an offhand remark of displeasure. Crossing into the living room, she could see he was standing at the fireplace warming his hands. Her mother offered her husband a cup of coffee, but he waved it off.

"I tell you, Tzeitel, those idiots in Washington will destroy Canada. The stock exchange in New York has just dropped 12 percent. We have not received payment for this year's crop yet, and now they say that we may have to wait to get our money. We've got thousands of dollars tied up in machinery and equipment, and it has to be paid for by the sale of our wheat and cattle. If the Stock Exchange crashes, and there are no more investments, there will be no money for anything. We can get through this winter, but unless we see some money in the spring, we'll have to sell off our land and elevators." Cathy could see her father was more concerned than she had ever seen him before. This was serious. Going to her mother's side, Cathy could see that her normally unflustered parent was ready to cry.

"What can we do?" Cathy asked. Petrov turned and placed a hand on Cathy's shoulder.

"Don't worry, Kate. I have friends in the government who know what's going on. I'll contact them to see how bad it is. I'm sure it will blow over quickly, but in the meantime, we will live our lives as usual. We have an auction coming up to get rid of a few head of choice feeders, so we should get a good price. That will tide us over until seeding next spring. Until then, I'll keep an eye on the market and try to keep the lights on. Now, let's forget about the stock market and have lunch. Tomorrow is Tuesday, maybe we'll get better news. That night, Petrov was busy on the phone, speaking to friends and businessmen about the state of the Country's finances. Tuesday October 29, 1929, the bottom fell out of the stock exchange. By Wednesday night, Petrov was in mourning. The company he had been dealing with, had invested heavily into the Stock Exchange, and had lost every nickel. It meant that the wheat in the Romanov grain elevators would not be paid for. After the last few years of increased prices for the product from his fields, the same bin full of grain was worthless. It was like being put up against a firing squad. The oil company wanted payment before any more fuel would be delivered to Romanov farms. Creditors demanded immediate transfer of funds, but the American bank failures caused Canadian Banks to tighten lending policies, a fact that drove Petrov Romanov to threaten to start a farmer's credit union.

The bad news of October 1929, was followed by a winter in which there were very few happy moments. With the coal bin filled and wood in the shed, days were spent inside the Romanov house making quilts and staying away from the neighbors. Those around the Admiral area were jealous of the family living on the hill. Looking out the window, Cathy could see the brutal wind pushing snowdrifts against windbreaks, with starving cattle huddling for warmth while waiting for feed that never arrived. As winter progressed, the lack of money in the system took its toll on businesses. Although some CPR section crews stayed in the Romanov Hotel, the company was slow to cover their costs. To the south, in the United States, life was shutting down without any kind of disposable income. In the Romanov house, there was still food on the table, and milk in a bottle, but the root cellar was being emptied at an alarming rate. Tzeitel Romanov, although a magician able to feed her brood with meager food supplies, knew that this frugal lifestyle was going get even more sparse as winter snows deepened. With a constant wind chilling bodies to the bone, preparing a hot meal was the only way she could remain sane and not let her family see the bleak future. Walking down into the town, the three Romanov sisters could feel the eyes of their fellow citizens burning through their warm winter clothes.

The few stores were closing without customers having money to spend. Everyone was pulling back, trying to save whatever funds they had left for a long winter. As the cold dragged on through to 1930, news from the United States was grim. The Depression had wiped out so many investors and small companies, that soup kitchens were becoming the norm. Farmers in the American mid west were finding no sympathy. The realization that this downturn in the economy was not just a blip, but could last into the summer, forced many farmers to wait for the warm weather, long after normal seeding time. Whatever seed they had in bins would have to be kept until there was money available to buy the grain produced. It was a gamble. The farmers who planted seed would either live or die with their farm. As spring arrived in Saskatchewan, so did the army worms. Even in the Romanov house on the hill, there was no respite. Tzeitel went from room to room, sealing off the doors and windows, trying to prevent the crawling worms from entering and dropping onto plates of food and into coffee cups. It was another indication that 1930 was going to be year of misery. As Spring progressed into summer, Petrov decided to seed only one quarter section, giving employment to a large crew who were without any means of support. The Popovs, Mercedes and the teamsters were happy to have something to fill their days and put food on the table. With the shortage of fuel, tractors were used sparingly, while horses were eyed as food, they would be kept safe until there was no other choice. Rumors that the Romanovs had a cache of food caused problems for the girls as they made their way to the fields with lunch baskets. Vagrants tried to drag them off into the bush, threatening them, stealing their baskets. Only the intervention by Arvid and his steel fist prevented anything more serious from happening. There was no mention of what happened to the thieves, but when word was passed around that stealing from a Romanov was a death sentence, the girls were given free passage. As summer dragged on, there was hope that the crop planted would have buyer, a sense of hope arose in the community. There was a feeling that things were about to improve.

Heat, dust, worms and grasshoppers soon dashed any thought of relief. As Cathy sat at the bedroom window and looked out over the dried fields, she had the feeling of despair. She felt dirty. With creeks drying up, and the well next to the house taking longer to refill, it seemed the world was deserting the Romanovs. She ran the hairbrush through matted blond locks that appeared to be turning to straw.

"What are you doing?" Dorothy asked, as she came in and sat on the bed. Cathy's youngest sibling was Petrov's favorite. She was small and dainty, unlike Abigail and herself. Cathy looked over at Dorothy and smiled. Just turned 13, she was last in the line of Romanovs and Cathy wondered what kind of life she would lead. It probably wouldn't be farming.

"I'm just trying to figure out how to wash my dirty hair without water." Cathy replied, running her fingers through the mop-like string attached to her skull. Dorothy laughed.

"Your hair? I have been wearing this dress for three days now, and I can hardly move in it. Arvid checked the well and it's barely coming in at all now. We'll have to wait the whole day before we have enough to cook with. Arvid went down to Notukue creek to fill up the barrels so we can at least wash the dishes. I wonder what's going to happen this year? I wonder if Papa has enough money to keep the farm working?" Dorothy rolled over on her stomach and stared at her older sister, "did you see Abigail visiting Tony the other day? I saw her take Blaze out of the barn and disappear down through the field. Do think they'll get married?" she asked, studying her hands. Cathy laughed at her romantically inclined sister. "I don't know Dotty. It's kind of a tough time to think about getting married, especially if they plan to have kids." Cathy thought about her own life. At seventeen, she was ready to find a boyfriend, but had delayed any search until she left for school in Swift Current. There were probably older boys in the city who weren't afraid of her father or the family name. She handed the brush to Dorothy with the unspoken plea for a hair brushing.

Kneeling on the bed, Dorothy began an ancient ritual of women the world over. As she passed the bristles through her sister flowing curls, she began to hum. It was a quiet moment in a confusing time. With the dust, heat, worms, grasshoppers and no money coming in, there was no way of knowing how much longer the Romanovs could afford to live in the big house on the hill. With passing of summer, it was time to take what few crops they could from the field. A threshing team assembled horses and wagons. The new harvester, which hadn't been paid for, was towed out into the quarter section that had some moisture. The wheat was stunted, but the grain seemed firm and full. Within three days, the gang of workers had taken off the crop and found that result reasonable for such a dry season. It was time to find buyer for the year's labor.

Several calls to friends in the government brought no relief. Although the price had not bottomed out, any revenue would barely cover the cost of growing the wheat and oats. Petrov Romanov felt the market was going to recover, and spent the last of his savings on new seed and paying off the crew who had not seen a pay cheque for months. It was a grateful group of men and women who felt money in their hands. It meant they could buy food and medicine for those who suffered most from the constant dust and heat. The summer and fall of 1930 brought a realization that staying in the Admiral area would be test of their faith in the Romanov magic touch. As September arrived, Cathy could see that her father was being worn down by the constant need to explain to creditors and workers that they would have to wait, have patience and believe that the Canadian government would come to the rescue. A year after the Wall Street disaster, news that there would be very little help from the people in Ottawa, who were not suffering the same fate as those who lived on the prairies. With coal becoming a scarce commodity, and wood almost non-existent, there was sense of panic, driving people to their churches for solace. The four chapels in the area had full attendance, especially when a soup kitchen was established in the basement. Abigail was becoming more distant at family dinners. When asked by her father the reason for her silence, she just shrugged. Having just turned 15, Abigail was suffering from being love-struck. She was now fixated on Tommy Popov, and even quiet talks by Cathy did nothing to quell the fire that was burning within her younger sister. Although the Romanovs were not a church going family, Petrov did what he could to help with funds to purchase food for the kitchens. November and December of 1930 came with brutal winds and the drying up water holes and wells. People gathered in the churches to keep warm, knowing there was no heat at home. Cathy and her sister, Abigail, who was growing taller by the month, helped in the Church of Lost Souls located a short distance away from the house. Operated by a man of the cloth by the name of Brother Daniel, he was no fan of Petrov Romanov. The mistrust was mutual. Petrov viewed the leader of the Church as a charlatan and fake. With long, unkempt beard and black eyes, he gave off a sinister aura that was hidden within. Petrov tried to convince his daughter to stay away from the evil presence, but such advice was met with protests. Even with Cathy's warning, Abigail believed that Brother Daniel was sent by God to save her from the torments of farm life, and only he had the answer to her salvation. There were many other farm families who had fallen under Brother Daniel's spell. Petrov did his best to stay away from any conversation regarding the Church of Lost Souls. Having learned from his father the foibles of becoming involved with religious zealots, Petrov was well aware of the Romanov name being linked to the assassination in 1918 of the Tsar and his family in Russia. It was a constant reminder that there were people who associated the name with death.

A small supply of coal was delivered to the Romanov siding, so that Churches could be provided with some relief, being able to keep their parishioners warm, if not fed. Christmas was not a time of joy in Admiral. A snow storm, combined with brutal cold and unforgiving wind, kept everyone indoors. Cattle and horse were sacrificed for the common good. At minus 35 degrees, it was an act of mercy to butcher the animals, who, with no hay to eat, would stand in one place and die. Petrov did his best to save Blaze from the slaughter, knowing that his daughters loved the animal, and couldn't bring themselves to talk about their beloved horse being used as stew. Three large Clydesdales, owned by a government official, were stolen from the man's corral and within the hour, were cut into steaks and distributed to the starving citizens of Admiral and Scotsguard.

The thought of tearing down one of the town's grain elevators had become the main topic of conversation during the cold winter night. There would be enough wood to keep everyone's stove filled for the remainder of the winter. It was generally agreed that the Romanov building was safe, as it was built with more concrete than the smaller CPR facility. Word came from the CPR that anyone causing damage to their structure would be prosecuted to the full extent of the law.

There was general agreement that being thrown in jail would guarantee a warm place to sleep and a full belly. It seemed to be a perfect solution. One way or the other, they would have a warm place to live.

Just after Christmas, the destruction commenced. With wagons drawn by human power, little by little, the large building was dismantled. Within a week, it was just rubble. Every piece of combustible material was gone. With a few government dollars allotted through the Post Office, the remaining citizens of Admiral survived until the Spring.

With a warmer breeze and melting snow, a feeling of optimism could be felt throughout the prairies.

Petrov discussed relief with government officials, hoping that grain prices would rise, allowing any crop planted in the spring, would have a reasonable value. With no guarantee of success, it was a difficult decision by Petrov, who was the only person in the area who had enough seed to make planting worthwhile. With a work crew who were eager to get back to work, Petrov held a meeting of those farmers and families in the town square in front of the Post Office. Although there was still no rain to fill the dugouts and guzzles, from the winter snow, there would be just enough moisture to have the seed germinate. It was more of a gamble than usual, but there was no choice. With seed supplied by the University, the crew could plant Crested Wheat grass as a by-crop. If the normal crops suffered, the wheat grass would at least provide feed for the remaining cattle.

"Are the Romanovs getting paid for us breakin' our backs?" A voice from the rear of crowd caused a flurry of sniping by farmers who had lost everything and were just hanging on, with no place to go. "Brother Daniel said that you were hoarding all the money and food the government sent. You drive around in your new car and your useless daughters flaunt their expensive clothes in our face." It was a verbal attack that was not surprising, but the underlying hate with which it was delivered, was concerning.

Petrov expected a few unhappy neighbors to be suspicious, but he was in too deep to not try anything to survive. The government had supplied enough fuel to run the tractors, so that he didn't have to fire up the old steam driven machinery. Petrov Romanov would have to stem the vitriol if there was any chance of getting cooperation from his neighbors.

"I have been assured by our Member of Parliament that everyone would get paid if they helped with planting." With a promise of actual money, the grumbling subsided. Once the plan was decided on by farmers in the surrounding countryside, there was an excitement that hadn't be felt since the Depression first reached the prairies. As soon as the field could be accessed, the men and women set about preparing the earth for the seed drill. With the wind constantly blowing dried out topsoil across the fields, the task was even more miserable. Cathy and Abigail were busy filling the drill with seed, riding on the back of the wagon, choking in the swirling clouds of fine sand particles that engulfed them, even though they wore wet cloths over their faces. The heat, dust, wind and thirst took their toll on everyone out on the flatland. Cathy looked longingly at the dried up creek along the edge of field, and remembered when she and her sisters would walk barefoot in the cool water, looking for frogs which had already been wiped out by hungry neighbors. It seemed like a lifetime ago. Within three days, the quarter section was planted. With the help of two students from the University, they also planted Crested Wheatgrass as an experimental crop. There was definite release of energy as Petrov assembled everyone at the edge of the roadway and handed out 50 dollars to everyone who participated. The money was part of a grant delivered by the Member of Parliament, and was given full credit for the government's largesse. It was a much happier crew who visited the grocery store, even though the selection was meager. The money would go a long way to salving the suspicions of the religious groups, especially those who hung on Brother Daniel's every word, who believed that, because the elder Romanovs did not attend any of the four churches in the community, that they were in league with Satan. Tommy Popov, who was closing in romantically on Abigail Romanov, was a member of the Church of Lost Souls and did his best to convince Abigail to attend. When Petrov was made aware of the young man's intentions, he was adamant. There would be no daughter of his ever again setting foot in the Church that he felt was a cult rather than a legitimate religious entity. Abigail was in tears when she met Cathy in the hallway.

"What's the matter, Abby?" her older sister asked, as they sat on the bed. Sobbing into a handkerchief, Abigail Romanov seemed inconsolable.

"Papa won't let me see Tommy any more. He says that he just wants to convert me to some kind of zombie. He thinks that the people who attend that church behind us are not really interested in praying, but just want to bring young girls into the flock for unnatural reasons. What am I going to do? Tommy thinks I should go with him to a meeting tonight, just to see what the Church is all about. He wants me to meet him at the Church. What will Papa do if he finds out I disobeyed him. I'm afraid he'll kill Tommy." Abigail looked to her big sister for support.

Cathy was now faced with a dilemma not of her making. She was also beginning to have doubts about the small Church on the hill behind the Romanov property. Although Abby was now 16 years old, she was still too young to marry Tommy Popov, especially in these times where there was no money or work. The problem was postponed by the arrival of Dorothy, who was in a state of panic.

"Cate, Abby, come quick. The place has gone crazy!" The discussion around Tommy and his desire to wrap Abigail in a cocoon of faith was immediately forgotten as the three sisters ran downstairs and out onto the front lawn. It was like scene out of a bad nightmare. Wave after wave of grasshoppers flew and hopped across the lawn. In minutes, the insects had devoured anything edible as they moved across the lawn. From their vantage point, the three Romanov girls could see the fresh green shoots of the recently planted crop being leveled by the millions of grasshoppers. As they stood and gathered their skirts tightly around heir legs, they watched the destruction, and joined by their father and mother. The sound was deafening. With millions of wings snapping in their haste to find food, and the click of their mouths, it was an invasion unlike they had ever witnessed. It was the description of Armageddon from the Bible. Retreating into the house, door and windows which were opened to refresh the closed up house, were once again sealed against a new threat. Army worms were disgusting, but the oppressive sound outside reached a new level of alarm. Nothing was safe.

Anything edible would be consumed. Even Rabble, the dog that seemed older than the house, found a safe place upstairs under Cathy's bed. There was no going outside. The family would be trapped indoors until the swarm moved on. There was no mention of Tommy Popov. Arvid volunteered to go to the pump house to check on the water level. Although Notukue Creek had dried up, the Romanov well was deep enough to still have water seeping in. Preparing to kill any intruders when the door was opened, everyone watched as Arvid made his way through the wall of wings to the door of the pump house, finally disappearing inside.

Turning on the tap, they waited. It was becoming a hardship. Washing clothes or dishes had to be planned days ahead, but they had water, unlike a lot of their neighbors. Filling kettle and jugs, there would be enough for two days, at which time they would have to pump it up by hand once again.

The pantry had been empty for some time, and only Petrov's connection with the Railway Company allowed deliveries of food sent by Christian churches back east. Word that the prairies were suffering more than the manufacturing regions of Canada prompted several church groups to package foodstuffs and send them by train to be distributed along the line. It was a welcome treat to have condensed milk for coffee.

June 2, 1931 was turning point for the people of Admiral. With the realization there would no crop to sell, no water in the dugouts or groceries on the store shelf, the fact that there was not even any gasoline for their cars so they couldn't leave, was the final blow. There was a feeling that the Romanovs were hoarding all that they needed, so a group of farmers and townspeople assembled to march onto Petrov's house and take anything of value.

In the Romanov dining room, Petrov passed the wheat cakes over to Tzeitel, apologizing to his beleaguered wife for not having enough butter to share with his family.

"I'm expecting a shipment from Winnipeg this afternoon, so we might have a bit more cream to make some home made butter. That should be fun" then looking around the table asked, "where is Abby?" Cathy and Dorothy both looked over at Arvid. As the eldest sibling, they felt that he was responsible for his sister's whereabouts. Arvid suddenly had a look of concern that was unusual for the 19 year old. It took a moment for him to answer.

"I checked her room this morning, because I heard her talking to someone last night. I thought it was with Cathy. Now, that I think about it, it could have been Tommy." he replied, looking quite sheepish. Petrov looked at his son and was silent for a long moment.

"Kate. Go check and see where your sister is. Your brother seems to, suddenly, have a poor memory." It was a request that was immediately obeyed. Cathy ran upstairs to the bathroom and bedrooms, and was surprised to see some of her recently cleaned clothes were missing. Checking under the bed, the blood drained from her face. The suitcase was missing. Cathy sat on the bed and thought about the ramifications of her 16 year old sister running off with Tommy Popov. Steeling herself for the reaction, Cathy returned to the dining table with her news.

"I think Abby has gone with Tommy." Cathy said, as she sat back down to her wheat cakes.

She looked over at Dorothy, then at her mother, then, finally, at her father. It took a moment for the information to sink in, but Petrov closed his eyes. Finally he stood, and taking a last drink of coffee, turned and walked out the back door. Arvid got up and followed him, as did Tzeitel and her daughters.

"Where are you going?" Tzeitel shouted, as her husband closed the gate behind him. Arvid stood for a minute and watched his father walk down the trail to the Popov house, but joined Petrov in his quest to find Abigail. Within minutes, they arrived on the Popov front porch. Petrov pounded on the door. Moments later, Gladys Popov appeared, wiping her hands on a dish towel. She seemed confused. "What is it, Petrov? What do you want? Martin isn't here right now. He's in town at a meeting." There was a definite fear appearing as she saw Arvid step onto the porch joining his father. Petrov was vibrating with anger.

"Where is my daughter?" Petrov asked, fists clenched, "and where is Tommy?" The question seemed to confuse Gladys. She looked through the screen at the two Romanov's and sensed that this was serious. "I don't know where your daughter is. Which daughter?" she asked, still confused as to why the two neighbors were at her door.

"Abigail is missing. We think she has gone with Tommy. Could you please ask your son where my daughter is." Petrov asked, trying to keep his anger under control. Gladys could see that the elder Romanov was concerned about his daughter. She nodded understanding.

"Just a moment, Petrov. I'll go and get Tommy for you. You can ask him if he knows where Abby is." Petrov could see that his neighbor had no idea where his second oldest daughter was. Moments later, Gladys Popov returned to the door. "He's not here.

I don't where he is. I thought he was upstairs, but he's gone. You think he's gone with Abby?" she asked, genuinely concerned.

Petrov Romanov realized that his neighbor was telling the truth.

"Do you think that Tommy and Abby are together?" Gladys asked, seemingly not aware of her son's attraction to Romanov's young daughter.

"Have you ever seen them together, Mrs. Popov?" Arvid asked, now concerned that perhaps his sister had left home by herself. It was a frightening thought. The woman hesitated for a moment, trying to decide if her son was in trouble.

"I've seen her riding your horse into the fields where the boys were working, but I don't know who she was going to see. Tommy doesn't tell me much. Maybe, when Martin returns, I can ask him." Gladys offered, hoping to put an end to this inquisition. Petrov could see there would be no answer forthcoming from his neighbor.

"Thank you Gladys. I'm sorry to have troubled you." With that feeble apology, Petrov turned and left the woman, who seemed as concerned as he was. Walking back up the trail, there was no conversation. Arvid could see his father was more concerned now that there was no sign of Tommy. With the problems in farming, having Abigail vanish without notice was serious enough, but if she was with Tommy, it would mean that she would be running away to get married.

"Maybe Mom has heard from her?" Arvid said, trying to think positive. As Petrov and Arvid reached the gate, Dorothy ran out to meet them. Grabbing their hands, she was crying.

"They took all our food, Papa. They just came in and took everything." Petrov could see his daughter was angry as well as frightened. Entering the house, Tzeitel came to Petrov. She had been crying as well. "I can't believe our neighbors would so cruel!" she said, as she opened the cupboard, "they took all the food. Bread, flour, milk, they even took my canning kettle.

What is wrong with these people. Luckily, they didn't discover the entrance to the root cellar, or they would have found all our vegetables." she added as she sat at the kitchen table.

"Who were they? What are their names?" Petrov asked, running his hand over the empty pantry shelves. This was an affront to him and his family. It would have to be rectified. Dorothy was eager to supply the details.

"The Petersons, Mercedes, Popovs, Gundersons, and even the Carsons," Dorothy took Arvid's hand, "come. I'll show you what they did to the front door. They broke it when Mom tried to keep them out." Arvid followed his little sister to the living room. The glass paneled door was hanging by one hinge. Petrov followed them into the room. His focus was not on the door, which could be fixed, but on something more important. Kneeling he took Dorothy by the shoulders.

"You said the Popovs were here. Both Tommy and his father?" The answer came from Catherine, who was carrying a broken dish from the dining room. "Yes. Tommy was here. I tried to talk to him, but he was like a wild animal. They reminded me of the grasshoppers. They came in, and in minutes, had taken whatever they wanted, and left. I've known these people all my life, and it was like I was dropped into a prison riot." Tzeitel entered the room and put her arm around Cathy.

"You say Tommy Popov was here? Who did Abby run away with?" Petrov asked, not expecting an answer.

"Well, we can only hope that she is with someone who will treat her well." Tzeitel offered, knowing that having her daughter missing was foremost in her husband's mind, "meanwhile, we have to clean this place up. They tracked in dirt with their filthy boots." Cleaning house was not on Petrov's mind, at least not at the moment. He would deal with the thieves in due course, but at the moment, he wanted to find his missing 16 year old daughter.

"Arvid can stay here and help. There's something I have to do." Petrov said, as he left by the open front entrance. Tzeitel could see there would be no changing her husband's mind, so she accepted the fact that he was on the trail and put her effort into cleaning up her home.

Petrov walked up the trail to the Church on the hill. Passing by gravesites, he remembered when he helped his father build the Church. He was only young, but could see that, as the first Church in the community, it would bring farmers together. The first Preacher was a farmer who held services only on Saturday. He lasted two years. The next, was a Catholic Priest who held services on Sunday, but insisted everyone had to convert to Catholicism. He lasted three years. There was a time when one of the wives became the Minister. She lasted ten years before she died. The Church sat empty for many years until the present Preacher, Brother Daniel arrived. He was a dark, strange man with eyes that penetrated the soul of his audience. Petrov did not like him at all, but although Romanov's owned the land, did not want to antagonize his fellow farmers. Now that his friends had turned against the Romanovs, there would be no love lost if he shut down the Church.

Arriving at the front steps, he opened the double doors and stepped inside. It was as if Brother Daniel knew he was coming. Standing at the pulpit, he spread his arms as if gathering in the sheep.

"Welcome to the flock, Brother Petrov. I was wondering how long you could stay away from my little bit of heaven. Would you like to confess your sins? I am ready to listen to your innermost wants and needs." he said, in a tone that sounded like it came from God himself.

"I'm not here to listen your crap, Daniel. I'm here to find my daughter. Have you seen her?"

Brother Daniel descended from his elevated position to face the visitor. Petrov was surprised at the man's size. He seemed to have grown in stature, as well as ego. Trying to avoid the Preacher's mesmerizing gaze, he looked around at the dark interior of the old wooden structure.

"Which daughter would that be?" Daniel asked, " you have three beautiful young ladies, especially the oldest one, who would make someone a lovely wife. If I wasn't a man of the cloth, I might be interested. Who are you looking for?" Daniel walked past and caused Petrov's skin to chill.

"Abigail. She is only 16 years old. I can't find her. Have you seen her? Did she show up here?" Petrov asked, hoping the answer was 'no'." Daniel continued to walk away from his guest.

"Ah, yes. The lovely Abigail. Perhaps she has seen the future and decided to look elsewhere for solace and comfort. She was quite sweet on a young man, and the young man in question was eager to take advantage of the opportunity. Because of my vow of silence, I can't divulge the name of the suitor, suffice to say, he would make a formidable father for their children."

The thought of Brother Daniel having knowledge about Abbigail's whereabouts, caused Petrov to test God's judgement and strangle this pompous fool.

"If you know anything about my daughter, I would advise you to tell me. You are on Romanov property. I can wipe this Church off the face of the earth, and you will be allowed to watch me do it." Petrov was ready to tear the building apart with his bare hands, if only to wipe the smug look from Brother Daniel's face. The Brother's response was surprising.

"I guess you haven't been paying attention to your government correspondence. I applied to the government to have this Church and graveyard removed from the tax rolls. So, Mr. Romanov, if you attempt to destroy this place, you will be committing a crime, for which you can be arrested and thrown in jail. This is Holy Ground now, and I have the blessing of both God and government to that effect. As far as Abigail is concerned, I wouldn't worry about her. I'm sure she is in a good place, away from your paternal grasp, and in the arms of someone who really loves her. Now, Petrov. Go back to your family, and take care of the ones you have left. I would certainly keep an eye on Cathy. A beautiful girl like that in these trying times is vulnerable." With those words, Brother Daniel disappeared into a side door leading to the Manse, leaving Petrov with clenched fists and an even greater determination to destroy this evil place. Walking back down to the house, he was no longer concerned with his missing daughter. His job now, was to discover what had to be replaced in the house and plan retribution for those responsible.

After all the work he had lined up for the surrounding farmers, who did not have his connection to government funds, they turned on him and his family. There would be a penalty for that mistake.

Back in the house, he was surprised a how normal the place felt. Arvid had repaired the front door, and his girls had retrieved food from the root cellar, so that the pantry looked replenished. He would have to take a trip with the CPR road crew to Swift Current and arrange for a shipment of milk and perishables. It would give him chance to touch base with his government contacts. The visit with Brother Daniel had shaken him. If the government had changed Romanov's property configuration without notice, someone would be losing their job.

With September 1931 coming to a close, the Romanov family prepared for winter. With no longer any concern about his neighbors, Petrov didn't even ask if they needed help. Their traitorous pillaging had broken the ties with the people in the area. If they wanted his help, they would have to ask. He could no longer even become fixated on Abigail's absence. Brother Daniel obviously knew where she was and hinted that, wherever she was, or whoever she was with, she was alive and well. Disturbing news throughout the winter caused some handwringing, when two more children went missing. The RCMP sent out a squad to help with the search for the children, but they were never found. There was some interaction between Petrov, Arvid and the neighbors who took part in the search. A couple of the transgressors came and apologized for their actions, but the rest were still staying away from admitting guilt. By the spring of 1932, the Depression had winnowed the local population considerably. Petrov's connection to Ottawa proved to be the only reason several farmers held on. Forming a cooperative with the surviving group of hard nosed land owners, Petrov was able to pry more money, seed and fuel from the government agent, allowing the assembled farmers to plant the Crested Wheat and drilling a deeper well. With oil being found in neighboring Alberta, there was a hope that the same good fortune would occur in Saskatchewan.

There was great jubilation when the drill struck water. With a guaranteed supply of water, and a means of pumping it, it would be possible to raise small fields of vegetables, rather than rely on wheat and oats to pay the bills. With no easy access to fuel, the farmers once again turned to horses for transportation. As if nature had deserted them, the farmers hung on with nothing more than faith to cling to. The Church of Lost Souls was filled to overflowing with people who had nothing more than Bother Daniel to give them hope. Brother Daniel was supportive to the families whose children had, apparently, wandered off. Another search was conducted. Petrov Romanov's house was used to hold an investigation held by the RCMP. The latest two children, Jeremy Klassen and Jacob McLaren vanished within days of each other, and it was suggested that wolves in the area were targeting the boys and girls, who spent a good portion of their time playing in the fields, out of sight of their parents. It was troubling. A couple of the men were equipped with rifles and ammunition, and with guarantee of food, became wolf hunters, in search of the elusive animals. They stopped when the first snows revealed no prints, other than deer, moose, pronghorn and rabbits.

The Spring of 1933 was brutal with a deadly cold wave and wind. Dust storms persisted throughout the year, and Cathy had finally left for school in Swift Current. Dorothy was now the last of the Romanov girls. With no word on Abigail's whereabouts, Petrov became a recluse. It was up to Arvid to look after Romanov business and he was surprised to find the extent of his family's reach. His grandfather, who built the house, had been busy purchasing plots of land in the area, as well, his father continued the aggressive strategy by erecting grain terminals, all but one of them were still standing. With the Hotel having been closed for two years, he felt it would be in CPR's best interests to reopen the rooming house for their work crews. Petrov could see that Arvid was even more business oriented than himself. With rent from various properties resuming, Arvid purchased oil leases in Alberta. It was a calculated risk, but within a year, money from oil discoveries brought relief from the past few years of abject poverty.

By 1934, Dorothy Romanov was becoming a beautiful young lady. Petrov smiled as his favorite daughter tried on new dresses ordered from Sears. Farmers in the surrounding area were beginning to see a modest return on the fields they planted. For those who were left, all the bad will from the raid on the Romanov's house was forgotten, almost. Arvid was affable and with a good business sense, was able to corral a number of farmers to use the Cooperative to deal with creditors and the federal government. With a relief system to cover some farming costs, Arvid was able to expand his holdings in Alberta. It was an important meeting between Arvid and

Petrov that changed the Romanov future.

Sitting on the front porch, overlooking the valley, Petrov was in a good mood. Arvid was happy to see his father coming out of the morose frame of mind. Sipping on a bottle of home made beer that was produced in one of Romanov's own breweries, Arvid was startled when his father mentioned Abigail.

"My life has not been the same since Abby left." he said, without any prompting, "I should have made Brother Daniel tell me what he knew, but I thought she would return, or at least contact your mother or me, but he sounded like he knew where she was, and he seemed confident she was going to be alright. It's been four years. She should have told us where she was, or sent a Post Card." Petrov took a sip of beer, but had the look of a man marooned on an island. Arvid felt sorry for his father. Losing Abigail was a turning point in his life. He seemed to lose the desire to be the best farmer and business man in the area. In the years since Abby left, his father had aged considerably. Arvid knew exactly what his father meant. Having dealt with Daniel sparingly, he could manipulate people into doing his bidding. It was all in his eyes and voice.

"I'll go tomorrow and speak to him again. Maybe I can jog his memory." Arvid said. Petrov looked over at his son, and knew that Arvid was capable of doing severe damage to any Individual who got in his way. After finishing one more beer, it was decided that Arvid would take over all responsibility for the Romanov fortunes. At 24 years of age, it would be a big job. With properties and leases in both Saskatchewan and Alberta, oil becoming a large part of the portfolio. It was possible the Romanovs could regain, and even surpass the riches his grandfather and father had accumulated. The following day, Arvid walked up the hill to the Church of Lost Souls. Reaching the front door, he could hear voices being raised in the Manse. Crossing through the nave, he reached the door to the Church living quarters and stepped inside. He couldn't believe his eyes. Brother Daniel had Dorothy partially disrobed. As she tried to escape, Daniel ripped her dress off and screamed at her to stop resisting. He did not see her brother until Arvid reached reached an arm around the Preacher's neck, dragging him away from a struggling Dorothy. "Get out of here, Dotty, I'll look after Daniel!" he screamed, as his sister gathered her dress and ran for the door. There would be no quarter given this day.

"I can explain," Daniel pleaded, as Arvid wrapped a hand around the neck of the false prophet. Driving a fist into Daniel's face again and again, Arvid did not stop until all resistance ceased.

Picking up the limp body, he carried Daniel out into the cemetery. Seeing pieces of Dorothy's clothing stuck to bush alongside the trail down to the house, Arvid went directly to the barn. Within minutes, he had the tractor forks against the wall of the Church of Lost Souls. There was a great feeling of release as the walls came crashing down, like Jericho. An hour later, the place was just a rubble pile and the body of Brother Daniel was buried beside his Grandfather's old dog, Rufus.

It would remain unmarked.

There was no need for either Tzeitel or Petrov to ask as to the fate of Brother Daniel. It took six months for people to stop visiting the remains of the Church. There was a rumor that God had demolished the Church, even though tracks from the tractor's steel wheels led directly down to Romanov's barn. Everyone agreed that God works in mysterious ways, and it was best not to question His methods. Without the presence of the Preacher, there was movement to one of the other Churches for salvation. The great dust storm of April 1935, was not felt as far north as Admiral, but it was a turning point in the fortunes of many farmers on the flatlands. Wheat was being purchased once again, if only by the government as a means of doling out relief.

Petrov still had the ear of many politicians in Ottawa, but with a change in Parties, those who held power before the election, were now on the outride looking in.

With oil creating a bulk of Romanov's income, Arvid was able to take time to do what was becoming a chant by his mother.

"You should take a trip into Regina or Medicine Hat and find yourself a nice girl. Although it's probably a good idea to stay away from Regina with all the strikes and problems they're having."

Arvid smiled at his mother. He had been thinking the same thing. The girls around Admiral were either too old or young, so, with an approved haircut, and driving the family Model A, which was filled with gas, Arvid tempted the vagaries of the open road, and left for Medicine Hat. Two days and two flats later, Arvid Romanov pulled into a parking space vacated by a large delivery truck.

Looking up and down the street, he was searching for a hotel for the night.

Along 2nd street, he entered Jim's Café, and was immediately struck by the look of the place. Nothing in Saskatchewan prepared him for the modern architecture and activity.

Medicine Hat was a busy place. Sitting in a booth, he perused the menu. Moments later, a young girl came over clutching a note pad.

"What can I get for you, sir?" she asked. Arvid didn't look up immediately, but finally he raised his head to look into the eyes of a vision. He was awe struck. He had been in town for only ten minutes, and felt his luck was changing for the better. Forgetting how to speak, he stammered.

"I'll have the ham and eggs, a coffee and piece of, it says here, home made apple pie. Is that true?" The girl was equally struck dumb.

"Uh, yes. It is. My Uncle makes it every day. As you can see, it seems to be a popular choice." she said, looking around at the other patrons who were devouring their baked wedges of heaven.

"OK, you've convinced me. By the way, is there a Hotel in the area? Something not too fancy."

Arvid asked, still staring at the Waitress, "I'll only be here for a few days." he added, not knowing why. The girl smiled and nodded. "Yes. There is one over on 5th street. The Hotel Corona is not fancy, but I know the owner. They keep it clean, and they serve beer downstairs, if you get thirsty." she offered, smiling at her new customer. "tell the desk clerk that Margaret sent you. They might give you a discount." she added, stifling a laugh.

"How do you do, Margaret, My name is Arvid." The young Romanov felt that his search for companionship was going to be successful.

Taking his time with the second piece of pie, Arvid Romanov couldn't keep his eyes off the Waitress. It seemed to be mutual. Crossing to the counter to pay for his excellent meal, a large man came from the kitchen, and wiping his hands on a dirty apron, looked his customer up and down.

"That'll be $2.50. cash. You new in town?" he asked, taking the money from the visitor

"Yes. I'm here to look for a business opportunity. I hear Medicine Hat is a growing town." Arvid, said, looking through to the kitchen. Margaret was watching him. Taking out a hand full of bills, he made a flourish of paying for the meal. He nodded to her and smiled. The man studied Arvid for a moment, then handed him his change. "We open at 6. " he said, " in case you want breakfast." Turning his head, he looked back at his Waitress, "but Margaret doesn't start until noon." he added, smiling. Arvid nodded understanding, then turned and left Jim's Restaurant.

Following Margaret's advice, Arvid drove down the block.

As he drove through town, he could see a large group of men carrying signs. It was an assembly of men assembling to catch the train to Regina. It was part of the march on Ottawa. He heard from a gas station owner that unemployed workers were gathering to ride the rails in an effort to put pressure on the government for employment relief. The CPR had set aside box cars especially for the purpose, feeling it was safer than having people jump on and off the moving freight trains, risking death or injury. Avoiding the throng, Arvid found the Corona. He noticed that most of the buildings in town were built from brick. Having helped his father build in the Admiral area, where the most common material was wood, here in Medicine Hat, brick seemed much more sensible, and durable. Parking on the street in front of the Hotel, Arvid could see that he was in a busy part of the town. He smelled the aroma of beer as he passed the open bar room door, but, not being a great beer drinker, was not enticed to enter the dark interior.

The Desk Clerk was happy to see someone with money enter, and was even more cheerful when Arvid said he wanted the room for a whole week, at 3.50 a night, with bath, paid up front. Walking up to the second floor, he was impressed that there was no smell of alcohol in his room, which faced the street. Placing his bag on the bed, he looked out and could see his Ford parked at the curb, along with a dozen older Model T's. Sorting out his clothes, he was surprised to find that there was hot water in the sink and the toilet actually flushed. It was something that the Romanov boarding house, with attached Bar in Admiral could not emulate. Feeling excited about being in the busy town of Medicine Hat, he checked his finances. He had enough cash for two days, then would have to locate a Bank of Montreal to access his account. After a stroll along 5th street, he found a restaurant in the Cecil Hotel that served steaks. It had been quite a while since he was served food by someone other than his mother, and in the quiet of the dining room, he thought about his reason for being in Medicine Hat, and smiled. How would he go about finding a girl?

The Waitress who served him was pleasant and quite pretty, but in her forties.

"You new here in town?" she asked, as she placed a slice of lemon meringue pie in front of him.

"Yes. I come from Saskatchewan. It's first time time I've been here. It's pretty busy." Arvid commented, as he tasted the slice of heaven, " looks like a bunch of guys riding the train. That happen often?"

"They must be headin' to Regina for the March on Ottawa. I hope they keep goin'. It makes me nervous to have a whole gang of men with no jobs or home prowling the streets. I hope the Cops are on them. Things are getting better around here, but the train keeps bringin' more trash to the city. " the woman said, her bitterness toward the vagrants obvious. Then, aware that she was sounding excessively bitter, suddenly smiled, and added, "I hope you find what you're looking for." then placed a hand on Arvid's shoulder. It was a comforting gesture that made him leave a one dollar tip. As evening finally drew to a close, Arvid prepared for bed. Unaccustomed to street noise at night, it wasn't until midnight that he fell asleep. His awakening was hastened by being pulled from the mattress and punched in the face by a man who appeared drunk. Arvid was quick to respond with a clenched fist to the attacker's nose. He could feel bone break. In the dimly lit room, he could see another man rummaging through his pants and shirt, coming up with his wallet and a roll of bills.

"Got it! Finish him off and let's get out of here!" By this time, Arvid's attacker was busy striking him with a baseball bat, although blood was pouring from his nose. Between swings, Arvid was able to deliver three more blows to the man's face. He finally gave up, and cursing, joined his partner exiting the room. Arvid was left standing in the middle of the room, naked and badly bruised.

Turning on the light, he looked in the mirror and could see he was going to be black and blue by sunrise. Avoiding the blood on the floor, he got dressed. Finding his wallet under the bed, he was surprised to find his personal identification intact. The money was gone, but he could get more from the Bank. Going down to the Front Desk, he found the Clerk asleep in his chair. Waking him, he described the assault, but could see that there would be little sympathy from management.

After an intense discussion, he was finally coerced into calling the city Police.

The arrival of the City Police was more like a comedy routine than a serious investigation. It was even more incredible when Arvid discovered his Model A had been stolen, using his key. He could only hope the engine backfired and broke the thief's arm. Now, with no car, he was stranded in Medicine Hat.

"You say you come from Saskatchewan. Who knew you had money and a car?" Sergeant Polaski asked, "did you talk to anyone when you came into town.? You got friends here?"

Arvid thought back to his activities. "I had lunch at Jims Café, then came right over here to the Corona." Arvid replied, not understanding the connection.

"You talk to Margaret?" the Sergeant asked, writing in his notebook, then glanced over at his partner. They cast a knowing look. " this isn't the first time we've heard this story. She guides you over to this hotel, and probably figured you had a few bucks. The goons who clobbered you and stole your car will probably slip her a couple of bucks once they sell it. How much did they get?"

Arvid began to feel like a fool. He was a rube in the big city. "I had about 22 dollars in cash, but they left me with my I.D., so it's not that important." Arvid realized instantly that 22 dollars to an underpaid Policeman would mean a great deal. Feeling the investigation was over, the Sergeant had his partner take a photo of Arvid's injuries, and left super rich Mr. Romanov to lick his wounds. Finally, the first night in Medicine Hat came to an end. As Arvid waited for the Banks to open, he sat at the window looking at the spot his car once occupied. There was a gentle knock on the door. Opening it, he found a young girl who was obviously nervous about disturbing the occupant.

"Excuse me sir, but I hear you had a problem last night. I clean the rooms, and was told to look after you." she blushed when she realized how that sounded, " I mean, I'm supposed to see if you need anything." Arvid was instantly mesmerized by her innocence. He nodded his head.

"Yes. Thank you. The fellow bled a little on the carpet. I don't know what you can do about it." he said as he stepped aside, allowing the housekeeper to enter. She walked over to the window and drew the curtains back to allow more light into the room. She stood and looked at the carpet, then up at Arvid. She smiled. "My name is Patricia. I hear you come from Saskatchewan. I guess you don't have a very good opinion of the city now, " she laughed as she rolled up the stained throw rug. Arvid knelt down to lift the bed and helped move the carpet. As they struggled to pull it free. their eyes met. There was no need for words. It was too late to retreat. Arvid carried the unruly bundle out, placing it on the housekeeping wagon. There seemed to be an aura surrounding them.

"I'll find another rug for you." Are you going to be here for a while… uh.." There was a pause.

"Arvid. My name is Arvid Romanov. Yes, I'll stick around until you return, then I have to find a Bank of Montreal" He felt stupid explaining his activity, but wanted to extend the time he had with Patricia.

"If you need a guide around the city, I really don't start work until 11 am. That's check out time, so after that, I'm working the rest of the day. Homer asked me to see to your room, because he was embarrassed that he missed the guys who attacked you. How do you feel? You look pretty bad." Patricia asked, as she ran her hand over Arvid's swollen cheek. He reached up and held her hand.

"I'm OK. I've been hurt worse getting bucked off a horse." he admitted, lying just a little. Patricia smiled, but did not pull her hand from his, "I would appreciate your help."

Returning to the cart, she pushed it down the hall, then turned, and asked, " do want to come with me to help me with the new carpet?" The housekeeper did not have to ask twice. Walking with her to a small broom closet at the end of the hall, he waited until she unlocked the door, and then placed the old carpet into a bin. As they stood in close quarters, there was a heat generated more by emotion than the summer weather in Medicine Hat, Alberta. Selecting a new carpet, together they returned to the room and rolled it out into its proper place.

Waiting outside the hotel entrance, Arvid was surprised when Patricia came out and joined him She had changed from her housekeeping uniform and into a flowery dress that was perfect for the occasion. Arvid did not feel the pain from his beating, he felt only the joy of being with Patricia, a person he had known for only an hour. It was as if it was destiny. The Romanovs, being a non religious family, were not accustomed to the feeling of being controlled by a deity regulating emotions. He knew what love was. He felt it from his mother and father as well as his sisters, but this was different. This affection he felt for this human by his side was unique. There was no way to describe the emotion. Patricia turned on an emotional switch that he didn't know existed.

Reaching 2nd Street, Patricia went with Arvid as he spoke to the manager. Entering the office, the Manager stuck out his hand. "Welcome Mr. Romanov,. My name is Roger Cullen," then saw Patricia standing at the counter, "Patricia, come on in," and moments later, she standing beside Arvid as the Manager sat on the edge his desk. " how's your father?" he asked. Arvid was about to answer, when Patricia spoke up.

"He's opening up another shift. There is a company in Vancouver who want large pots for planters on city streets. It should employ another thirty people." she said, as if reporting to a shareholder. The Bank Manager smiled, then turned to Arvid. "You've got a smart girl here, Mr Romanov. The Dixon family operates the largest brick and pottery in the west. Now, what can I do for you?" Arvid was still gobsmacked with the news that this little girl who worked as a housekeeper for the Corona Hotel, was connected to a local pottery business that he noticed coming into town.

"I was attacked last night in the hotel, and some money stolen. I have an account with this Bank. I would like withdraw one hundred dollars, as well, I have to buy a new car to replace the one they stole." he added, as further evidence of his loss. With the mention of a new car purchase, Mr. Cullen drew more attentive. "Very well, Mr. Romanov, give me your particulars, and we'll get you on your way." There seemed to be no problem with having Patricia present while Arvid relayed his intimate details to the Bank Manager. Within ten minutes, a teletype returned with the OK from Montreal. Arvid was given permission to spend whatever he wanted for a vehicle. With the news that he had two very important people in his office, Mr. Cullen suggested that he take them to lunch. It was just good business. As the meal progressed, the Manager could see that Arvid Romanov was not just a young man passing through town. There was money buried in the Saskatchewan farmer's past.

"Did you ever think of investing in land or business, Arvid?" Cullen asked, as Patricia became more attentive. She was also interested in her new boyfriend's intentions. Arvid nodded.

"My Grandfather, Peter, came from Russia in 1889 with his wife when he was 21 years old. He worked for the CPR, but kept his eyes open for any opportunity to improve his life. With any spare money, he purchased abandoned farms and plots of land. He was fortunate to buy a large portion of a town that was being built along a new rail line. As the population and farming grew, he built a grain elevator. By the time my father was ten, my grandfather owned a good portion of the acreage surrounding the little community. He built three more elevators, and the CPR built a siding for him. When my father was 21, I was born, but my Grandfather died from pneumonia. My father expanded the farming business when steam engines were running the farm equipment. Lately, with the discovery of oil in the Turner Valley, he's also picked up a few oil leases on property around Lethbridge. The Depression has slowed down the farming end of the business, but there is more money coming in now from oil than wheat. I'm not going to turn down an opportunity to help the family if a good deal comes along." Arvid stopped and look over a Patricia, "besides, I may need extra income if I find someone to share my life with." Patricia visibly blushed.

Roger Cullen nodded agreement. "I'm glad to hear that, Arvid. Since my business is money, I get to hear about deals all the time. Up north here in Alberta, there is a new area opening up. It's around a place called Fort McMurray. They found oil leaking out on the ground. It's mixed with sand, but there seems to be no end of it. I don't know how they would ever separate the sand from the oil, but that's not my area of expertise. They're selling deeds on the land up there for $10 dollars an acre. If you're interested, I can facilitate a deal for as many acres as you like. Will you have speak to your father first?" Cullen asked, sipping on the last of his coffee. Arvid shrugged.

"No, I can make the decision. Get me fifty acres. I expect you will have a charge for doing this, so just tack that on. While you're organizing that, Patricia will have to go back to work and I have to shop for a new car." Arvid reached across the table and shook Mr. Cullen's hand. The deal was done. Patricia reached over and took Arvid's hand. "I don't have to go back just yet. The Corona Hotel is owned by my Uncle. I work there just get out out of my Stepmother's way."

Mr. Cullen laughed at the revelation. " You should listen to this young lady, Arvid. I know her stepmother, and I guarantee, that it is a matter of self-preservation." With an elevated feeling of good humor, the three left the Dining Room, the Banker to complete a deal for land, and the other two in search of transportation. Within the hour, Arvid was seated in a brand 1935 Chevrolet Master Deluxe, with Patricia directing him to the Dixon Pottery Factories.

"I want you to meet my Dad." she said, sitting beside Arvid, as he tested the power of his new six cylinder automobile. With electric start and soft springs, he was actually happy the thugs stole the old Model A. Stopping at the security gate, the guard waved to Patricia, and Arvid was allowed through and into the massive yard filled with all types of tile and pipes, pots and tubs.

Walking into a large building, past rows of castings and unfinished molds, Arvid could see that the Dixon Pottery business was labor intensive. Reaching the end of the building, they climbed stairs to the office. A Secretary jumped up to hug Patricia, and Arvid could see that he wasn't the only person who could see inner beauty that matched the visible, lovable bits.

"Is Dad here?" Patricia asked, " I want him to meet Arvid." she said, taking Arvid's hand.

"He just went down to the pump house." the Secretary replied, just as a large, mustached man entered the office. Patricia ran to him and hugged the surprised parent.. Taking him by the hand, she led him to meet 'her young man'. Arvid could see Mr. Dixon sizing him up, but he finally stuck out his hand. "How do you do, sir. My name is Arvid Romanov. Your daughter has been kind enough to show me around Medicine Hat. This is quite an operation you have here."

Mr. Dixon nodded and held Arvid's hand for a moment, then nodded agreement. "Hi. I'm David. Yes, it gets a little hectic around here. How did you meet Patricia? Is that your new Chevy downstairs? How do you like it?" David asked, leading both he and Patricia into the office, "do you want some coffee?", then turning to his Secretary, " Gloria, get some of those fresh baked cookies from the lunch room." and finally settling in behind his desk, he added, " God, I love those cookies. OK, sweetheart. Where did you meet this big galoot?" He sat back in his swivel chairs and studied Arvid.

"He's staying at the Hotel, but a couple guys beat him up and stole his car. He comes from Saskatchewan." Patricia continued the story of their meeting, and Arvid could see her father was absorbing every word. With the arrival of cookies and coffee, the conversation took on a more personal tone.

"How long are you going to be in town, Arvid?" Dixon asked, as he munched on the home grown cookies, "Patricia knows everything about this town. I think she would enjoy showing you around."

"I wouldn't think of spending my time with anyone else." Arvid replied, looking over at Patricia who was sitting beside him. She took his hand and held it for the next twenty minutes and four more cookies. Having survived scrutiny by her father, Arvid bid goodbye to Gloria, who offered to place cookies in his pocket, and with Patricia by his side, left the grounds of the Dixon pottery complex.

As the afternoon progressed, it was time to return to the Corona Hotel.

"Are you working today?" Arvid asked, as they pulled into the Hotel parking lot. Patricia was running her hand over the new upholstery, and smiling. "I'm not going to work until tomorrow." she replied," my Uncle has an Indian girl who fills in from time to time. I didn't show up for my 11 o'clock shift, so he probably got her to clean the rooms. No that busy anyway. I'll be in my room if you want to talk." she commented, as she got out of the car. Arvid watched as Patricia entered the rear door of the hotel. One thing that had been stuck in his mind for the past day, was that he didn't want to leave Medicine Hat without Patricia. There was something about this little girl that connected with him.

Was he just being stupid? Did the beating from the night before loosen some brain cells? Locking his new car, a definite improvement over the open Model A, Arvid entered the back door and climbed the stairs to his room. He could hear loud voices from the rear hallway. It sounded like Patricia.

Moving quickly along the hall, he reached an open door. Looking in, he saw Patricia trying to push away a drunken man who was attempting to put his arms around her. The man, with his back to the doorway, failed to see Arvid standing behind him. Arvid tapped the drunk on the shoulder.

"Fuck off, Ricky. Find your own woman!" he screamed, as he tried to corral Patricia's arms. When he turned his head to face his partner, he was surprised to see was it not Ricky. Arvid smiled when he saw the man had a large patch over his nose. The man's eyes opened wide when he realized Arvid was the person he had beaten with a baseball bat. Leaving Patricia, he turned to face Arvid.

"Want another beating, asshole?" Arvid grabbed the man by the shirt and drove him in the face with a determination bordering on cruelty. "this one is for stealing my car, " then struck again, 'this one is for hitting me with a baseball bat," and another blow crunching more bone. "this one is for Patricia, " and another blow landed on the face of the luckless thief, " and this one is for me."

Blood sprayed everywhere as the man tried to defend himself from the series of bone destroying blows. Putting his hands to his face, he staggered back against the wall. He was trying to maintain his balance while adjusting to life without breathing. Grabbing him by the collar, Arvid rushed him to the open window, and threw him out. Despite a feeble attempt to prevent his flight, the attacker flew well, but landed poorly. Landing with a crash on a shed behind the hotel, he lay there for a minute, then, with blood trickling down the metal roof, he slid to the ground and staggered away.

Arvid turned to Patricia who ran over and hugged him, trembling with the thought of how close she had come to harm.

"Do you have to stay here in the hotel?" Arvid asked, "can't you live with your Dad?" Patricia did not answer immediately, but walked back over to the open window. There was more to the story of the Dixon family.

"My stepmother hates me. My mother died four years ago, and Cynthia stepped in. She had money from her first marriage, and convinced my Dad that the only way to save the business was if they got married. Dad was so concerned about having to lay off seventy-four workers, that he agreed to the arrangement. I know she's only in it for the money, and I think she became the major shareholder, which means that she can take over the business and sell it. That's her plan. I heard her discussing it with her lawyer. My Dad built that business up from one kiln and four helpers. It breaks my heart that he doesn't see what Cynthia is doing. You see how nice he is. He knows the brick and tile business, but is terrible when it comes to dealing with women. I don't know how much longer Gloria is going to stick around. She loves my Dad, but Cynthia treats her like dirt. I'll be OK here. That guy you threw out the window, has a buddy. His buddy is a thief. He steals and sells his loot to another guy down by the railway yards. I think you taught him a lesson." she said, as she closed the window.

"I was going to stay here for another couple of days, but I can rent another room for you, if you want?" Arvid said, as he tried to sort out his feelings for Patrica Dixon. She sat on the bed and looked at Arvid. There was a moment when a decision was made that would have lasting consequences. "Can I go home with you?" Patricia asked, tears welling up in her eyes. Arvid's heart almost stopped. It was the same question he was going to ask. He sat beside Patricia and held her hand. There was quiet acceptance that this would be a permanent arrangement. They kissed for the first time.

"If we're going to be together, we've got something to do. We've got to tell your father and get his blessing. If you're coming back to my place, you have to be prepared for a lot less excitement.

Admiral is a small farming community, and not a busy place like Medicine Hat." Arvid held Patricia close, and wondered what his mother and father would think of his miraculous find.

"As long as we're together, I would live in a sod hut. I love you, Arvid. I can't think of being with anyone else." Patricia whispered, as she placed her head on his shoulder.

"OK. Let's go talk to your Dad." Arvid said, lifting Patricia to her feet. After a kiss, they left to start a new life together.

****

In a downtown Montreal office, two men sat and huddled over an inter-office memo. The larger of the two, younger, bearded and aggressive, handed the smaller man a folded piece of paper.

"This note we received from one our friends in Medicine Hat mentioned a request for funds by a fellow called Arvid Romanov. He's got the money alright, but, as our friend pointed out, his grandfather's name was Peter Romanov. He apparently arrived in Canada in 1889.

I checked with out friends in Moscow, and they did a check on this Peter character. You might be surprised at what they found. After a discussion with the records bureau they discovered this Peter Romanov was born on May 6, 1868. " The small man behind the desk shrugged his shoulders.

"So, what's so important?" he asked, adjusting his glasses, reading over the memo.

"What's important?" his partner replied, "it is the same date that Nicholas was born. Either someone made an error in recording the date, or this Peter Romanov was the Tzar's brother.

According to our informant in Medicine Hat, the fellow that withdrew funds for a land deal up in the north of Alberta, and a new car, is Peter's grandson. That means that when we got rid of the Tsar, we left a Romanov alive. We have to complete our task. We have to ensure there are no more Romanovs alive on the face of the earth. What do you think?" The small man sat back in the large leather chair and looked at the ceiling. It was a serious situation. As a true Marxist, there could no way to leave a remnant of the Russian monarchy alive. Killing off the Tsar and his entire family in 1918 was the only way to eliminate any link to the royal past of Russia. If the public were to discover that the Tsar had a brother who lived and thrived in Canada, questions would be asked about the strength of the Communist Party. The Bolshevik revolution was supposed to eradicate the bourgeoises, so their job was not complete. I thought we killed them all, so to leave the family alive would be a mistake. All remaining members of the Romanovs in Canada would have to be eliminated. Send out some of our men to finish the job. It's been only 18 years since we got rid of the Tsar, but if word spreads that there are still some of his family members alive, it will be a circus. I'm surprised that they haven't been noticed before. Do whatever it takes to finish the job," Taking off his glasses, he cleaned them with a small cloth set aside for the purpose, " as well, transfer any funds they've accumulated over the years to the Party in Moscow. It shouldn't be too hard to convince our friends in Ottawa that it's in the best interests of the Country to get rid of these remnants of the Russian monarchy."

With the decision made, the bearded man left the office to set the purge in motion.

****

In the Office of the Prime Minister, there was a silence as the P.M. looked over the RCMP's list of subversives. He shook his head, throwing the paper on the desk in disgust.

"We've got to get rid of these traitors. I don't care what you have to do, I want these damned Communists and Bolsheviks rooted out and sent back to Russia. Our Ambassador in England tells me that Mr. Hitler is flexing his muscles, and we don't need a bunch of traitors on Canadian soil if we are dragged into a damned war. Get rid of them. The reason I called you in here, Commissioner, was to make certain it was kept confidential. We don't need the Press warning all these spies in advance. With an election coming up, I want to make a statement that my government will not tolerate another Country operating on our soil. Hand pick your crew and sweep these left wing traitors out of Canada. I know it's serious, because I have a friend in Saskatchewan who deals with farmers and trades people constantly. He tells me that the Communists have been mobilizing the workers out west, urging them to have a general strike. In the midst this depression, we don't need a bunch of rabble rousers stirring the pot. Do what you have to to put an end to this nonsense. Now, go do your job. I'm placing my faith in you and the RCMP to rid Canada of this scourge of Communism." The Prime Minister sat down and turning in his chair, looked out over the Ottawa river, hoping that this show of force will endear him to the Canadian voter.

The Commissioner left the P.M.'s office, feeling that he was chosen to clean house of all the rabble that were causing trouble in the West. Within the hour, he had his team chosen, and contacting the CPR, was assured of transportation for his Officers and undercover Police. They would make their move before July 1st. With boxcars filled with strikers and unemployed on their way to Winnipeg from Vancouver, he would have to ensure the leaders were picked up before they reached their destination.

****

In Medicine Hat, after a surprisingly short conversation with Patrica's father, Arvid was simply asked to treat Patricia with respect and not hurt her. It was also the first time that Arvid had ever seen a woman in six inch stiletto heels.

Cynthia arrived at the office in time to organize everyone's life. It was apparent that the Stepmother was in total control of David Dixon. Leaving the Dixon Pottery Works, Patricia held onto Arvid like a drowning sailor grips a lifebuoy.

"Well, I guess that pretty well means we are going back to Saskatchewan." Arvid said, laughing at the vision of Cynthia and her 300. dollar shoes. Stopping by the Bank, Arvid went to the Manager's office.

"Mr. Cullen. We're leaving now. If you could send all those papers to my home in Admiral. I'll see that they get signed and sent right back." he said, as he stood in the doorway. A look of panic came over the Manager's face.

"NO...no.. uh, just a minute Arvid." Cullen got up from behind the desk and went over to his visitor, "the papers will be arriving first thing in the morning. It would save a lot of trouble if you could be here and sign them right away, that way we save a lot of time and fooling around with the crappy mail system." He seemed quite agitated. Arvid was puzzled. It seemed odd, but could see Cullen's point. "That would mean we have to get place for the night." Arvid said, aloud.

"That's OK. I'll pay for the room. In fact, they have a Honeymoon Suite over at the Cecil. I'll arrange for you and

Patricia to stay there for the night. It would be perfect. When the papers get here in the morning, you can sign them and be on your way. It will be my way of giving you two a chance to get some proper rest." He winked as he spoke. Arvid smiled at the thought. It was true that he and Patricia had not yet spent a night in the same room.

"OK, Mr. Cullen. I'll take you up on it. Give the Cecil a call, and we'll stay until the morning." And so it was done. As the Manager watched Arvid Romanov walk out of the Bank's front door, he looked over at his desk where all the deeds were laying. He had just bought more precious time.

The Honeymoon Suite was not quite as imagined. The difference between it and the usual room, was a mirror on the ceiling and a fancier bathroom. There was some awkwardness as the Bellhop opened the door, since the young man went to school with Patricia, and was somewhat upset that someone else had managed to steal the woman of his dreams, especially a tall, good looking farmer with money. Once in the room, the awkwardness persisted. Both Arvid Romanov and Patricia Dixon were not accustomed to sleeping with the opposite sex. It would be a learning experience for both of them, but there was no doubt about the attraction. They were meant for one another. Bathing together, with the newest modern convenience, showering, was more about exploration and fascination than insemination. Falling asleep in each other's arms was the culmination of their lives to that point.

The next morning, refreshed and ready to face the world together, Arvid and Patricia left the Cecil Hotel, convinced that there was nothing they couldn't accomplish. Driving over to meet Mr. Cullen, Arvid was planning his return to Admiral with his new love. The house was big enough to accommodate his mother, father, sisters and Patricia and he was certain they would love Patricia as much as he did.

Entering the Bank, Cullen was waiting for Arvid.

"Did you enjoy your stay at the Cecil?" Cullen asked, walking with Arvid into the office. The deeds were all in order and ready for the new owner's signature. Arvid could see that this was a very legal procedure and was impressed with Cullen's attention to detail. Within minutes, the documents were signed, witnessed, and with a firm handshake, Arvid said goodbye to the Bank Manager, eager to rejoin his companion and continue his life.

Unaccustomed to the new style door on the Chevrolet, he felt quite awkward getting into the car. The 'suicide doors' were a new wrinkle in the car's design, and felt it would not last long. Driving out onto 5th Street, he looked over at Patricia. She had that look of someone who was still in the Cecil Hotel. Driving east out of Medicine Hat, he could see that there were many men still walking the streets, with no job or place to go. The trains were loaded with men on their way to Ottawa. It made him feel somewhat guilty that he could afford a new car and return to a house with food and future.

As they reached the farmland on the outskirts of town, the green of the surrounding land was startling in comparison to the brown, dry land around Admiral. The Palliser Triangle was living up to its reputation as being the driest portion of Saskatchewan. Approaching the Alberta border, a new Ford car came up from behind, and as Arvid pulled over to allow the vehicle to pass, the passenger pointed a revolver at him and fired. The bullet came within inches of Arvid's face, taking out the passenger's window. Patricia tried to make herself as small as possible, looking over at Arvid for some kind of explanation. The Ford began to crowd Arvid off the dirt road, trying to force the Chevrolet into the field where it would have no chance of escape. The shooter took aim again, but Arvid stepped on the brake and hit the rear bumper of the Ford. Veering wildly across the road, the driver tried to regain control, but was now sideways on the gravel surface. Seeing an opportunity to ram the car, Arvid also saw the gunman take careful aim at the Chevy windshield. It would be a close encounter. Before the shooter had a chance to pull the trigger, Arvid rammed the side of the Ford. It flipped immediately, with pieces and parts flying off the car like confetti. The shooter flew out of his door, and Arvid could feel the man's body as the Chevy ran over it, almost dislodging Patricia in the process. She hung on, literally, for dear life. When the Ford stopped rolling, Arvid jumped out of the destroyed Chevrolet and ran to the driver, who was pinned beneath the wreckage. The entire weight of the Ford was resting on the man's chest. He was having great difficulty breathing.

"Why are you trying to kill us?" Arvid asked, kneeling over the dying attacker.

"I was told to get rid of you. You're a Romanov. Ask your father." he whispered with his last breath.

Arvid looked at him and tried to understand the cryptic message. The man was dressed in a clean shirt and pants. He was not an unemployed laborer. He was a hired killer. Walking around the wreck to the body lying on the road, Patricia got out to join Arvid. It was a gruesome sight. The man's head was nearly completely severed. Kneeling down, Arvid felt in the man's pockets, finding a wallet. Opening it, he found the phone number for the Bank, and Roger Cullen's name written on it. Arvid's blood ran cold. He had been set up by the Bank Manager. As they stood next to the destroyed vehicles, an Army truck arrived from the east. A soldier got out and surveyed the wreckage.

"What happened?" he asked, as he motioned others to hook up the cars to the truck.

"This guy cut right in front of me but rolled his car. I ran into it. I guess that new Ford V8 is just too much gun for some people." Arvid said, taking the two bits of luggage from the scrapped Chevrolet with only 80 miles on it.

"You folks want a lift back into town?" the Sergeant asked, as the wrecks were pushed off to the side of the road, "we were sent here to keep an eye on the guys coming from Vancouver on the trains. I'll tell the Police what we found. It's up to them if they want to do anything about it. They can figure out next of kin and whatnot." Within minutes, the road was cleared off, the bodies dragged to a ditch with small tarp placed over them. Jumping into the rear of the covered truck, Arvid and Patricia rode back into the city like farm workers going to a job.

Arriving in Medicine Hat, they were dropped off directly in front of the Bank. Both entered and went directly to the Manager's office. The look on Roger Cullen's face needed no explanation. He knew that his role in the attempted murder had been uncovered.

Arvid held up the business card. "The next time you send someone to kill me, make sure you find somebody who can drive. Your hit men are Coyote feed now. So, here is what's going to happen. You are going to buy me a new car. A Ford, this time. Fully equipped, and if I have any more trouble, I will mention your name to my father. You know he has contacts in Ottawa and Montreal."

Roger Cullen was about to cry. He had failed to complete his mission. He had no choice but to do as Arvid asked. Picking up the phone, he called the dealership, and within minutes, a new car was ready to pick up. "OK, Arvid. I'm sorry about this serious lapse in judgement. I hope we can still do business in the future." he said, walking with his unsmiling customers to the front door.

As Arvid and Patricia placed their bits of luggage in the new Ford, there was a feeling of invincibility when it came to their union. Once again they drove east out of Medicine Hat, knowing that someone was watching them. Passing the accident scene, the coyotes and crows had already discovered the dead bodies. "Serves them right!" Patricia commented, as the scene disappeared in the rear view mirror. Arvid was impressed with the new car, and doors that opened the right way around. Within hours he could see familiar landmarks he had grown up with. Pulling into the driveway, Dorothy was the first one out to greet him. Arvid walked around to the passenger's door, and opened it, helping Patricia out onto Romanov land. Dorothy stopped for a moment and studied Patricia, then hugged her.

"You're pretty!" she said, holding Patricia's hand. Moments later, Tzeitel and Petrov came out to see who was driving the new Ford. There was a feeling of family that Patricia had forgotten existed. Dorothy hung onto Patricia's arm as they all went into the house. Petrov winked at Arvid and nodded his head. "Nice car." he said, as everyone settled around the dining room table.

Within days of arriving home, it was as if Patricia Dixon was born into the Romanov family.

She enjoyed cooking and working around the house, and Dorothy had another girl to talk to.

****

In Regina, the March to Ottawa stalled, and with instructions from headquarters, the RCMP, along with the City Police did as they were told. Surreptitiously, they rounded up the ringleaders, communists and agitators, placing them in sealed boxcars, transporting them to Montreal to be placed on ships in chains. Over one hundred union leaders, bolsheviks and communists were removed from Canadian soil. The Prime Minister would take the heat for the confrontation in Regina, but was happy to be rid of a good number of troublemakers.

****

With Arvid back home, it was time to ask his father about the comment by the dying gunman.

Sitting in the workshop, Arvid brought up the subject, without having to explain where he got the information. If there was a movement to kill the Romanovs, then they would have to be more careful. Petrov recounted the day back in 1918 when his father heard about the Tsar and his family being murdered by the

Bolsheviks. Petrov was very upset, but had no reason to think that anyone in Canada would want to kill him or his family. Was that the reason Abigail was taken? Was she taken as a warning? It was a troubling thought. Arvid suggested that it was because the Romanov's were making money while others were out of work, As oil revenues increased, the Romanovs would become the target of those who wanted a piece of the action, but Petrov believed it went much deeper.

As 1935 passed into history, and the new government in Ottawa began to spend more money, there was a sense of optimism around Admiral. The Depression was being written into history books. The marriage of Patricia and Arvid was attended by farmers from around the area. It was also time to celebrate a better harvest and rising grain prices.

In the spring of 1937, Patricia gave birth to Leo. Arvid wasn't crazy about the name, but had to admit, he was a good looking boy. News from Europe was grim. Germany was ramping up their army, but sales of grain were brisk. The Romanov elevators were being cleaned, ready for the first crop in seven long years. Some moisture had returned to the Palliser triangle, and with the new varieties of wheat, improved tractors and harvesters, farming was becoming profitable again. Watching Leo grow made the hard work tolerable. With Cathy back at home from University, she became Patricia's new sister. Along with Dorothy and Tzeitel, the four Romanov women were a force to be reckoned with in the reviving Saskatchewan town of Admiral.

In 1939, as September began, word that Germany invaded Poland shook the financial community loose. Suddenly, the world wanted Canadian wheat and oil. Petrov Romanov was concerned when the Prime Minister arrived in the driveway with his entourage. Arvid was surprised when the P.M. stuck out his hand while his Security detail kept an eye out for any crazy who might take exception to the Prime Minister's visit.

"How do you do Arvid. I expect you're wondering why I'm here. I want to talk to you and your Dad about enlisting your help to get our agriculture organized." he said, as Petrov exited the house.

With a large smile, the P.M. he greeted the elder Romanov with hug. Arvid was surprised to see such an amicable greeting. The Security team looked at one another and shrugged. As the P.M., Petrov and Arvid entered the house, the armed escorts relaxed and lit up cigarettes. This was going to be an easy surveillance job.

Introducing Tzeitel and the girls to the P.M. prompted the women to surround the men with coffee and baked goods. Knowing that the war was foremost on the mind the Prime Minister, Tzeitel guided her daughters upstairs to the sewing room to attend to more important duties.

Settling into one of the large leather chairs, talks began in earnest.

"Petrov. I have been in discussions with Prime Minister Neville Chamberlain. I fear for our safety. He believes that Hitler will not attack England, and wants to sign a peace treaty with the Germans.

I think he's wrong. We've got people living in Germany, and they say that Poland will be just the start of Hitler's campaign. Canada has to be ready in case we end up in another Great War. You have the ear of all the farming community. They listen to you. If the shooting starts in earnest, we are going to need food, and lots of it. This damned Depression has crippled our output of grains. Because we are part of the Commonwealth, we are going to have to help Britain when the bullets start to fly. We have to get our farmers back to work. I'm prepared to release funds to you to prime the pump, as it were. I've always been impressed at how you survive the problems out here in Saskatchewan, so I know the you can drum up the business and get production moving again. With an election coming up in March next year, I have to ensure we get back in to fight a damned war. We have the winter months to get organized, and one of the things is getting the Army, Navy and Air Force up to speed. I'm going to declare war when I get back to Ottawa, but the conscription thing is going to be a problem. When you came to Ottawa last year, I followed your advice and made certain that the Minister of Agriculture actually knows something about farming practices." The P.M. took a breath and tested one of the many cookies laid before them.

"What are you going to do about Quebec?" Arvid asked, "they seem dead set against the war."

The P.M. sat back and closed his eyes. "Yes. The French don't want to fight for Britain. It's the same old thing as during World War 1. They run and hide in the woods, but if things spread, and get out of hand, I think they'll change their minds. I'll worry about that when we get to it. In the meantime, Arvid, can I count on you to help me organize the shipment of agricultural supplies.

With your father organizing the farmers, I need someone with a mind like yours, and that eidetic memory to make sure the supplies get to where they're supposed to. I can see a chance for a black-market in produce. I'm banking on the Canadian people voting for the Liberals next March. I have no idea how big this thing is going to get, but it won't matter if I don't get re-elected, we could be in for a confusing time. Can I count on the Romanovs to make it work?" The question was unnecessary. Both Arvid and Petrov shook the hand of the P.M., making the pact complete.

"Do you want to stay for lunch?" Petrov asked, as the three men stood and looked out over the last of the harvesting crews out on the southern quarter sections. The P.M. shook his head.

"No. I've got to get back to Gull Lake. The CPR has a train waiting on the siding. The gang out there who are supposed to be protecting me get a little antsy if they don't eat on time. I don't want to be murdered by my own security team. It would be embarrassing." As the trio walked to the limousine, voices could be heard. from the second floor window. Looking up, Petrov could see the women waving to their guest. The P.M. stopped and walked back to a point beneath the window.

"You ladies are going to be a major part of the preparations and delivery of services in the upcoming months. We will need your commitment and dedication to accomplish all that we need to do. Because of you, we made it through the bad times before, and I know you will come through once more. Thank you Tzeitel. I hear that Catherine is now a Registered Nurse. Excellent. With Dorothy and Patricia at your side, we will overcome any problems that arise. Thank you again. Stay safe. We need you." Waving to the suddenly silent women, the P.M. got into the car and closed the door. Arvid was impressed with the fact that the P.M. did his homework and learned the names of his family. It showed that there was considerable importance to his visit. He would await his instructions and security clearance.

As winter closed in on Saskatchewan, overseas, Hitler was proving to be a threat to all of Europe.

The P.M. was true to his word. Arvid and Petrov received credentials that would allow them to access any facility in Canada. With a winter storm blowing snow up against the windbreak, even the cattle seemed know their fate. As Canada and rest of the Commonwealth prepared to go to the defense of the Island situated only 20 miles from France, Petrov set about contacting famers and ranchers, while Arvid set up distribution points for all the goods sent to Montreal and Halifax. Working with other departments, Arvid was now required to leave the Romanov farm and travel across the Country to meet with shippers and suppliers. In March 1940, William Lion MacKenzie King was reelected, ensuring both Arvid and Petrov would keep their jobs.

As Arvid prepared his overnight bag, Patricia sat on the bed with Leo, who at three years of age, was becoming a handful. Arvid could see David Dixon in his son's frame. Rather than long and lean, Leo was large boned and solid, like his grandfather. He would be a Romanov, but with a fist the size of dinner plate.

"How long do you think you'll be gone?" Patricia asked, holding Leo on her knee. Arvid sat beside his young wife, knowing that there was no way she could know what the future would bring. With fighting in Europe growing more ferocious, Canadians would be called upon to give more to the cause. This was a new experience for both of them. Arvid was called by his Country to provide a service, and he had no choice. Picking up Leo, he kissed him on the forehead. Handing his son back to Patricia said, "I don't know where I'm going to end up, but a lot of people are going to lose their lives unless the Germans can be stopped. They want more land, and they don't mind killing people to do get it.

I've been asked by the Prime Minister to do a job, and I'm going to do it. You'll be alright here with Mom and Dorothy. I know Cathy will have to leave, because she's a Nurse and she'll be needed in the hospitals back east. I don't know what I'll be able to tell you when I call or send a letter. They have a security check on anything we say or write. Just look after yourself and each other. The sooner we get rid of Hitler, the sooner I'll be back home here with you." Arvid said, kissing Patricia one last time, then grabbing his duffle bag, he went downstairs and out to a waiting car driven by a uniformed soldier. Patricia waved from the window, but Arvid was already gone. As they watched, Dorothy came up behind her.

"Both he and Papa will be back before you know it." she said, taking Leo from Patricia, "now, come on downstairs and help Mama bake more cookies for the bake sale downtown." Together, the sister and wife of Arvid Romanov knew that it was brave talk, but it was all they could do in the face of a growing war across the ocean.

Arvid was delivered to a waiting train car in Gull Lake, where a Sergeant saluted. It was apparent that his job was going to entail dealing with all ranks of the military. Two days later, he was in Trenton, Ontario. Once there, he was fitted with a uniform, and ribbons signifying his rank as Commander in the Canadian

Navy. He was also considered a Colonel in the Army, but as most supplies would be shipped by water out of Montreal or Halifax, it was decided by the Prime Minister's staff that Arvid would be more effective with an elevated rank in the Navy. Having been briefed by the Department of Defense, he hit the ground running. Setting up a chain of command, everything edible that was to be shipped overseas would pass by Commander Arvid Romanov. By the autumn of 1940, the war in Europe had spread throughout the various Countries, creating more refugees and death.

With a good harvest in Canada, Petrov, in charge of the agriculture end of the system, contracted with farmers and cattle ranchers in Alberta, Saskatchewan and Manitoba to process meat through slaughter houses and packing plants, establishing a base price that would allow a small profit, but still have the products inspected. The last thing he wanted was having someone die eating the food sent overseas. Being shot at was dangerous enough. As the war entered its second full year, 'U' boats were causing more havoc in the North Atlantic, so shipping goods was a crap shoot. Merchant Mariners risked their lives to deliver the precious food and munitions to England. Top military commanders were at loss to put an end to marauding submarines entering the Gulf of St. Lawrence. Ships leaving the St. Lawrence river were easy prey as the slow moving vessels made their way out of the river into the wide open Gulf. Without aircraft surveillance, the ships were vulnerable. Hundreds of men and a million tons of supplies sank to the bottom. By 1941, Arvid was asked to go to England and sort out the receiving end of the supply line.

April 1941, Arvid Romanov was aboard the Calliegh Maiden when it left the port of Montreal, bound for Liverpool. Rather than take the train and board a ship in Halifax, Arvid decided to sail directly from Montreal. Boarding the ship as a Commander was confusing for the sailors on board. Arvid was a civilian Commander, but was to be treated exactly the same as the Merchant Captain. He was hitchhiking to England, but his role aboard ship was that of an Adviser. Sailors snapped a salute whenever they were in his presence. It took a while for Arvid to become accustomed to returning the required gesture. Three days after leaving the Canadian Port, and squeezing through the Strait of Belle Isle, the old vessel making ten knots, poked its bow into the North Atlantic. With a cold wind blowing in through a broken window in the cabin, loaded with coal, fuel and dried food, it was not going to be a quick passage. As night fell, the ship's Captain tripled the watch.

Not only was there fear of submarine attack, but icebergs drifting down from Greenland could sink the old ship just as easily. The plan was to join a 100 ship convoy one hundred miles east of Newfoundland. There were three more ships following the Calliegh Maiden, but there was no sign of them to the stern.

At 2 bells, the shift was changing. Not being able to sleep, Arvid joined a seaman on deck. It was cold and misty, with only the trail of glowing plankton showing where the ship had been.

"How did you end up on the Calliegh, Commander?" Seaman first class John Quigley asked, as he and Arvid walked toward the bow on the port side. It was almost pitch black. On a ship this old, having been pressed into service from the Gulf, it was not equipped with the latest in radar or sonar. It was strictly compass and courage that steered the ship toward its destination. John turned to light a cigarette, but Arvid stopped him. "Don't light that out here. Go inside to light the match." he said, making it sound like an order from God. John was about to open a hatch, when there was a blinding flash that temporarily left them both stunned. Hanging on while the Calliegh seemed to lift completely out of the water, finally it was silent, then the roar of an explosive deafened them. Hanging on to a deck rail, Arvid, said. "let's get to a lifeboat. This ship is going down." Already the Calliegh was listing at ten degrees. Making their way the short distance to the nearest stanchion, they were joined by two more sailors. With light from by an increasingly large fire, the four managed to release the boat from its cradle.

"Where is Captain Munroe?" Arvid asked, as they lowered the double ender into the rising sea. The water was only ten feet from the gunwale. There would be no second chance to get this boat free of the sinking ship. Working together, it was finally floating free in the cold Atlantic.

"He's gone. The torpedo hit directly underneath the bridge. I saw a couple more swabs jump off the stern. Maybe we can pick them up." the sailor shouted, as the explosion increased with each passing minute. Arvid's greatest fear was that the whole ship was going to blow up, taking everyone with it. Unfastening the oars from their nesting place, where they had rested since the ship was built 30 years before, the seaman put their backs to the job, placing as much distance as possible between them and the flaming hulk that now had its deck flooded. By the flickering light, they could make out several people still on board, awaiting their cold, wet demise. Arvid looked at the humans who knew that their death was immanent, and wondered what was passing through their minds. Was it someone back home, or was it knowing they would never fulfill their childhood dreams. It didn't matter, seconds later, they were gone. After the wash from the sinking vessel churned the water around them, the sea became quiet once again.

Ten minutes after the disappearance of the Calliegh Maiden, with everyone laying down in the boat, keeping the cold wind from causing hypothermia, there was a strange sound. It was a hum. John Quigley sat up.

"I think it's another ship. We're going to be rescued." he said, with the excitement of a child at Christmas. The others all sat up, searching the horizon for any sign of lights from an approaching vessel. Unbelievably, a large metal shape rose beside them. It was the sail of a submarine. John was about to shout, hoping someone inside would hear, when Arvid grabbed him, pulling the surprised tar back down into the bottom, holding a firm hand over his mouth. The sub continued to rise out of the depths, until moments later, several men came out to view the damage they had caused. With the lifeboat being so close to the sail, the men shone their flashlight some distance away. From Arvid's vantage point, he could make out that two of the submariners were carrying machine guns. They were going to make certain there were no survivors. Laughing, satisfied that their mission was successful, they reentered the sub, and as the boat moved forward, the row boat was spun around with the vortex it created. Shortly after the encounter, the sub sank out of sight. Arvid let John go. Although upset at being manhandled, his shipmates told him that Arvid saved their lives. There was no question. The Germans were going leave no witnesses.

As night passed into morning, cold began to seep into everyone's bones, making the tossing of a building sea more difficult to stomach. Lethargy took the place of observance. One of the seamen found the emergency kit up underneath the bow cover. It contained dry food and cans of water. Checking the date, it was decided that they would draw lots to see who would take the first sip. It fell to Arvid to decide the fate of his fellow survivors. Breaking the seal, he put the can to his lips while his three companions watched to see the Commander's reaction. It was cold and sweet.

He wanted to gulp the whole thing at once, but realized that, with four cans, if they used it sparingly, they could all last two more days. Moments later, the others drained the liquid over their dry lips.

With a chocolate bar sized bit of dried meat, and the water, they were ready to face another night. The second night at sea was more like a dream. Arvid could feel himself hallucinating. John woke up in the middle of the night, and tried to jump overboard, but his two friends held him against the gunwale. " We're all going to die.!" he screamed, trying to break free, but was pinned to the floor.

Salt spray had soaked through their clothes, chilling flesh to the bone. Arvid had to speak up.

"Yes. That's right. We're all going to die, but not tonight. As long as you're all with me, you will not die."

The words caught the imagination of his fellow shipwrecked sailors. The tone Arvid used to ease an implausible situation made it seem possible. A calm settled over the four men as they unfolded the rotted blanket from the kit. Another night passed, but as the sun came up. it was apparent that the ocean was completely still. Dead calm. As the sun rose in the east, the sound of a motor droned through the mist. Moments later, a large flying boat flew only 1000 feet above the waves. The men all stood and began to wave their arms. It veered in their direction and flew directly over them. The RCAF roundel emblazoned on the side meant that they would soon be aboard. Ten minutes later, the large hull skimmed over the ocean and pulled up alongside the stranded seamen. It was a delirious quartet who accepted the hot coffee freshly made in the galley of the large aircraft.

"What are you fellas doing out here? You fishing?" The airman laughed, as he handed each grateful sailor a chocolate bar. It was like a T-bone steak, "are you Commander Romanov?" he asked, seeing the soggy insignia and Commander's bars on the sleeves and epaulettes.

"Yes. I was on my way to Liverpool. How did you happen to find us? Were you looking?"

"There were two ships behind you. The one directly behind was torpedoed and sank. The third one picked up the survivors. They reached the point where the Calliegh Maiden should have been, but found just debris and oil slick. We know the drift rate of material, so we just flew the route until we found you. I'm glad we got to you when we did, otherwise we would have to go back for fuel.

"Well, we're glad you went the extra mile." Arvid commented, as he sat back and enjoyed the fresh biscuits.

"We'll be heading back to Gander to refuel. You can find out from your boss where you are supposed to go." The airman commented, as he laid out clean coveralls for the drenched passengers. It didn't take a second suggestion to change from the wet clothes to something dry and warm. The droning engines, and a soft pile of extra tarps made falling asleep non-negotiable.

Within an hour, the large water bird landed on the pavement in Gander. Taxiing to the fuel tanks, within moments, the four rescued shipmates were being driven to the command center for debriefing. It was hub of activity. Maps and charts spread across walls and tables showed every possible point where there had been a submarine attack. Colonel Wilkins, C.O. of the center, singled out Arvid, taking him into his office away from the madness in the main room.

"Well, Commander, you are one lucky son of a bitch. My crew tells me that they were turning to come back when they saw you in the water. We'll fix you up with a proper uniform. I've been told to get you to England as quickly as possible. We can either put you on another freighter, or get you into a Lancaster that we're ferrying across the pond. Your choice." Wilkins said, as he sorted through a stack of papers on his desk. Arvid looked out the window at a very busy airstrip, and could see reconnaissance aircraft being fueled up. Thinking back to the time spent soaking in a small boat in the middle of the Atlantic, the choice was simple.

"Do you have an extra parachute?" Arvid asked, as the Colonel stood beside him.

"Don't blame you." Wilkins laughed, as he went to the door, shouting orders to his Adjutant. Within minutes, a new officer's uniform was delivered, along with a packet of papers to be read and destroyed en route. Handing the new clothes to Arvid, Wilkins left to allow some privacy. "You can use my razor, Commander. The bathroom is just through that door." he added, as he left the room.

2500 miles away, in Admiral Saskatchewan, Catherine Romanov was packing her night bag, assisted by Dorothy, Tzeitel and Patricia, who were unhappy to see Cathy leave, but understood, as a Registered Nurse, she was needed for the Canadian war effort. Hearing only news that was censored by the Canadian government, it was difficult to know the truth.

"Where do you think they'll send you, Kate?" Dorothy asked, hugging her older sister. Cathy shrugged. With just a phone call, she was told to meet the Commanding Officer at the Regina armory. From there she would be transported to where she would be of most value. At 27 years of age and unmarried, she was ideally suited to be sent overseas. It was a thought that permeated their conversations since Cathy was notified of her induction into military service.

With a final hug and tear, mother, sister and Patricia watched as she got into an Army Jeep that would take her away. As it disappeared down the driveway, Tzeitel could only wonder what her family would look like whenever this terrible war was over. With Petrov, Arvid and Cathy off to somewhere in the world, she held both her daughter and Patricia close. They would concentrate on raising Leo so that he would be the remaining Romanov at the end of this madness.

Cathy looked over at her driver. He was quite handsome in his uniform, but as the little vehicle bounced over the gravel road, she couldn't think about romance. She had no idea where she would spend her time during the duration of the war. Four hours later, they pulled up in front of the Regina Armory. The driver helped Cathy out and guided her through the massive building to C.O.'s office a the rear. There were several soldiers standing around talking as Cathy entered the room. With just a nod of the C.O's head, everyone cleared out, but not before checking out the young woman dressed in civvies. Closing the door for privacy, he motioned for his guest to sit.

"Hello, Miss Romanov. I'm glad you could make it on such short noice. My name is Major Thompson. I'm the Commanding Officer here in Regina. Things are heating up overseas, and we're putting together a squad to help. We have three other Nurses, such as yourself, so that the four of you will be air lifted to England. We'll be leaving in two days for Trenton. We have made arrangements for you and the other girls, excuse me, Nurses, to bivouac in one of the new trailers behind the armory. It will give you a chance to get to know your fellow Nurses before we leave. If you have any questions, let me know, and my Adjutant will see that you are looked after.

You are now in an area where we have to maintain complete secrecy, so I'm afraid you won't be able to tell your relatives where you are going. I realize that it is draconian, but it applies to me, as well. My wife thinks I'm shuffling papers in an Office in Vancouver. So, go meet your fellow nightingales, and be ready at 0600 on Wednesday. We've all got a big job to do, and there is no time to waste. Any questions Lieutenant?

"Lieutenant?" Cathy stopped and turned to face her new Commanding Officer..

"Yes. As a R.N in the Service, you automatically become a Lieutenant. Don't let any of the enlisted men push you around. You have the authority to issue an order and have it obeyed. So go help us win this damned war. Any more questions?"

Cathy was impressed at the Major's attitude. "No. I guess we'll all have to play it by ear until we get to where we're needed." Cathy said, as she picked up her bag and followed the Major through the back door out to a cluster of house trailers.

Thanking her immediate superior, she opened the door to the newly painted trailer and stepped inside. It was like old home week. Two of the nurses were from the same class in the hospital where she did her internship. The other was Chinese, and it was immediately apparent that she felt like an outcast. Cathy went directly to her and introduced herself. Within the hour, the

89

four women were exchanging hospital stories. Cathy felt good knowing she would be with friends when they eventually arrived in the war zone.

O600 came early Wednesday, 2nd of April, 1941. Cathy and her nursing sister were loaded into a Van and taken to the Regina Airport. A large, twin engined plane was warming up on the tarmac. Along with her three compatriots, fifteen soldiers, complete with duffle bags, were seated in the noisy fuselage, and moments later, were airborne. It was her first time in an aircraft, and watched apprehensively as solid ground disappeared beneath the wings. There were smart remarks from a few of the young soldiers about the Nurses, but a sharp word from the Sergeant quieted all the scuttlebutt. He reminded the mouthy ones that they were in the Army, and not at the soda shop or local ice cream parlor. Refueling at Sanderson field allowed the passengers to stretch their legs, but a half hour later, the Lockheed Hudson lifted back into the sky, aiming for Trenton Ontario.

Three hours later, the plane landed at the military airport. Cathy could feel excitement in the air. There were planes constantly landing and taking off, and the fifteen soldiers who kept up constant chatter during the flight, were now suddenly quiet, faced with the reality of going to war. With a new Commandant, an older lady in a military uniform, the four Nurses were led to a small school bus, and transported to a house on the outskirts of the Air Base. It was a chance to have a bath, and a with the added new convenience, a shower. It was a relaxing evening as Cathy got to know her fellow conscripts better. Jane, Shirley and Mia became close during the evening, with the sound of aircraft buzzing overhead. It was a bonding time. There was no way of knowing if they would be serving together, or spread around to various hospitals. After a good sleep, they spent the day being fitted with flight suits and shown how to use the parachute strapped on their back, with the assurance that one of the crew would be there to assist them, in case of emergency. That evening, under the glaring lights of a huge hangar, the Pilot spoke to them as they assembled at the rear of the four engined Lancaster, prepared to say good bye to Canada. Cathy guessed that he was probably younger than she was, and said a silent prayer that he was as confident as he appeared. Cathy was impressed with the way all six crew members were silent and listening to their young Captain. This would be a different ride than from Regina.

"Hi. My name is Henry Collingworth. This is kind of a special trip for all of us, Lieutenant. We have been chosen to take this new Lancaster to England. We know it flies well, but this will the first one that we take across the ocean. My crew and I have been flying her for the past week, and she's a beauty. Because things are heating up across the pond, we have been chosen to take you ladies with us. There is not much room in the Lanc., so quarters may be a bit snug. We'll be flying at around 10 to 12,000 feet, so there should be no need for oxygen, but just in case, Johnathon, our Navigator, will show you how to wear the masks, and what to look for if we have to climb above the weather. We'll be landing first in Gander to refuel, so take advantage of the washrooms, because, after that, it's a long haul to Greenland. Now, let's get on board and get settled. We've got a war to win." With that, the crew helped the Nurses through the side hatch. There was general agreement that being inside the shiny new monster was preferable to standing on the tarmac in an April wind.

The Nurses were placed in the small area that contained a bunk and seat and given sleeping bags to ward off the cold. The crew all introduced themselves, as they moved to their respective positions. With a stern word from the Pilot that everyone was on a war footing, and there would be no hanky panky on his aircraft. Cathy and the other Nurses were happy to hear that they weren't going to have to fight off the horny crew members as they flew through the night to Gander. Although it was awkward, the girls managed to get to the washroom before the long flight to Greenland. Colonel Wilkins was surprised to see the four young

91

women crammed into the tight quarters of a Lancaster Bomber. It certainly wasn't the normal compliment in the big aircraft. At 0400, the engines started and the plane took off for Greenland. Cathy pulled the soft bag around her and went to sleep with the mesmerizing drum of the 4 Merlin engines propelling them closer to the war.

Six hours later, including an hour of waiting for the runway to be plowed, it was a grateful crew and passengers who were treated to the hospitality of Greenlanders. After a three hour layover, the Lancaster once again took flight. The next stop was either Iceland or Norway. En route, the Navigator was told that Norway was no longer available. If the Pilot wanted to refuel, he would have to stop in Meeks field, Iceland. There was a discussion between the Pilot, Navigator and Radio Operator over whether or not to just bypass Iceland completely and fly directly to the Faroe Islands, but in the end, the Navigator won out, and the Lancaster landed at 1200 hours. By that time, it was a group of very hungry aviators who invaded the lunch room set up for ferry crews as they made their way from America to England. With a chance to use the bathroom and have a wash, Cathy and her companions, with an opportunity to free themselves of the flight suit for even twenty minutes was like being reborn. After all the hours of being in cramped quarters, listening to the constant drone of the engines, and at times having to rely on air bottles when the pilot rose above the 12,000 foot altitude, it was a happier group who assembled to climb into the fuselage of the waiting Lancaster.

Within minutes, they were airborne, flying southeast to Ireland and the next stage of their deployment. Since the Nurses were not fitted with radio, they had no way of communicating during flight, making the trip feel even more isolating. Two hours after lifting off from Meeks Field, the plane suddenly made a violent maneuver that shook everyone awake. Cathy looked up to see the mid gunner swinging around in his turret and heard the rattle of the Browning 50 caliber gun. Holes appeared in the skin of the fuselage only inches away from where she was laying. Struggling to free herself in the close quarters, she worked her way up to the gunner's turret. He was bleeding, but still swinging around and firing. Sitting in a canvas saddle, he appeared to have a gun shot wound in his right leg. Looking down, he screamed at Cathy.

"Go help Jimmy in the back. I think he needs your help." then spun around and fired the gun once again. Dropping down to the tunnel that extended to the tail of the plane, Cathy found Jane and Mia already out of their sleeping bags and at the tail gunner's turret.

"It sounds like we're being attacked." Jane shouted, as she reached the rear of the Lancaster.

Hanging on as the aircraft dove and twisting to shake the pursuer, they arrived in time to see Mia trying to pull the tail gunner from his seat. He appeared to be dead. With the three women taking a grip of the man's flight suit, they pulled him free from the cramped seat. Mia immediately climbed in and with the skill of a trained sniper, pulled the slide handle, readying the Browning to fire its 50 caliber bullets at whoever was trying to knock the Lancaster out of the sky. Both Cathy and Jane could see a plane diving at them to finish the job, but Mia swung the turret to meet the challenge with a volley of shots that ripped through one wing of the passing German aircraft. Bits of fabric and metal flew from the plane, and rather than turn and climb, it began to spiral away at an angle toward the ocean. Johnathon, the Navigator, came back to join the women.

"What the hell happened?" he asked, as he saw Jimmy Mitchell lying off to the side, " is he dead?"

"I don't know. I can't tell." Jane said, trying to find a pulse. Johnathon looked up and saw Mia at the turret in control of the Browning and understood why the German attacker disappeared into the ocean. Helping Cathy place Jimmy in a more accessible spot, Johnathon nodded his head. "I've got to go back to help us make the Irish coast, and it looks like you girls have everything under control. Unless we get another visitor, we should be landing in an hour. Good work." he added. "Shirley is with Tony." as he left to join the crew in the cockpit. Jane opened Jimmy's zipper and put her face against his chest. She closed her eyes, then shook her head. "He's gone. It looks like he took a round through the heart," she said, checking him further. With the sudden violence waking up the remaining crew, it was good to know Mia was a sharp shooter.

Cathy moved forward to see if Shirley needed any help with the mid gunner Tony. As he remained seated in the turret. Shirley had cut away his pant leg and was treating the wound so that he didn't leave his post. Being close to Norway, it was possible another plane would find the Lancaster and attempt to knock it out of the sky. Watching her fellow Nurse, Cathy realized that it would be the first patient they had in the war. Seeing that Tony was content to have a pretty girl working on his leg, Cathy made her way to the cockpit. She was able to see exactly what the Pilot and Navigator had to put up with in order to fly the bomber. Climbing over the bulkhead, there was very little room to move. Sitting beside Arnie, the Radio Operator, Cathy waited until he removed his earphones.

"How's Jimmy?" he shouted., keeping one speaker pressed against an ear. Cathy shook her head.

"He didn't make it. How much farther until we land?" she asked, knowing that Tony may have a more serious wound than just a through and through. Arnie turned his head and nodded toward Johnathon. "talk to Johnny. He's the map guy. Too bad about Jimmy." he added, then turned back to his radio controls. Moving to Johnathon, Cathy could see he was too concerned with his calculations to speak to her. Carl, the Flight Engineer leaned back and pulled Cathy closer so he could speak without shouting.

"Go see Henry. He wants you to take the Aussie back to be the tail gunner. Our radios stopped working." Cathy nodded understanding and crept beside Henry, the pilot as he worked on controlling the Lancaster. He pointed to the ladder leading to the Bomb Aimer's compartment. "Tell Jordon to go back and take over from Jimmy. I think he's hurt." Cathy shook her head, and turned her thumb down. There was a look of shock on Henry's face, but he shrugged and motioned for her to continue down the ladder into the bomb aimer's comportment. Jordan was surprised to see Cathy in his cramped quarters.

"What's happening up there, Lieutenant?" he asked, " my two-way stopped working. Are we going to crash?"

Cathy had to pause for a moment to understand the Australian accent, but shook her head.

"Henry wants you to go back and take over from Jimmy. He's dead and Tony is injured." Cathy said, leaning into Jordan's ear. There was a look of confusion on the Australian's face, but, finally he squeezed by Cathy and crawled up into the cockpit. She could hear Henry shouting orders to his bomb aimer, and realized that this simple ferry flight to England had turned into a fight for survival. Laying on the pad used by Jordan to see bombing targets, she could see why he was so isolated from everyone else. This job took total concentration. Although there were two guns mounted above the bombardier's location, it would be difficult for the crew member to reach the guns in the event of an attack. As she lay in the prone position, she could see the ocean pass beneath the plane. Without warning, the Lancaster began a sharp bank to the left. He heard Henry scream to his crew. "Hang on everyone. We've got another one. Seconds later, a smaller plane appeared beneath the bomber. Without thinking, Cathy crawled up to position herself in the gunner's seat, and recalled seeing Mia pull back the slide handle, Cathy did the same.

With heart pounding out of her chest, she strapped herself in and hung on while Henry tried to keep the Lancaster from becoming flotsam in the north Atlantic. As the bomber twisted and turned to shake the persistent German fighter plane, Cathy gripped the gun like it was part of her body.

As the little plane turned to attack directly from beneath, Lieutenant Cathy Romanov, Registered Nurse, although taking the Nightingale oath, became a warrior, pressed the trigger with her thumbs. The Browning 50 caliber guns came to life and spit lead out at the moving target. The vibration shook Cathy to her core, but the feeling of power was intoxicating. She could see the pilot of the plane as it climbed to make strafing run, but turned when his propellor shattered, with bits ripping into his left wing. There was no way to avoid the hundreds of pieces of lead spewing from the barrel of the Browning, and as it passed in front of the Lancaster, the underside of the fighter plane disintegrated, showering the Lancaster with debris, causing one of the Merlin engines to catch fire. Trembling with emotion, Cathy felt the Lancaster level out and, on three engines, resume its course southward. Cathy detached herself from the nose gun and climbed the ladder to the cockpit. Henry looked down at her as she emerged from the 'hole' and offered a 'thumbs up'.

"I'm sorry!" she shouted, as she stood beside the Pilot. "are we going to make it?" she asked, looking through the side window at the smoking engine. Henry smiled.

"We can fly on two engines, so with three, we're good. Nice shooting, killer," he said, laughing. "we're almost over the Faroe Islands, so we'll try to land and see what more damage we have. Just stay here. Pull down the dickie seat and hang on. I hear from Arnie that they're just finishing the runway, so it might get a bit bumpy. " Cathy looked over at Johnathon who, after extinguishing the fire and feathering the propeller, reached back and pulled down a small folding chair attached to the fuselage. Seating herself, and following good advice, watched as Henry Collingworth controlled the Lancaster, slowing for the approach to the new runway. It was as if the bomber was landing on the ocean. One moment, they were over water, moments later, she felt the rumble as rubber tires rolled over the new gravel airstrip. As the aircraft rolled to a stop, several jeeps pulled up to greet the newcomers. As the first Lancaster to arrive from Canada, it was regarded as a novelty. Several mechanics poured over number two engine, inspecting the damage caused by the debris strike. It was determined that the damage was minor, contained to the one motor. The plane could be flown on to Prestwick on three engines. The crew, which included the four Nurses, was treated to celebratory coffee and sandwiches. Within the hour, they were back in the air, aiming for the mainland and Scotland.

With the arrival of the Lancaster in Scotland, Cathy, Jane, Shirley and Mia were received by a Hospital unit, completed with surgeon and ambulance. Their help would be desperately required by Doctors in the middle of the blitzkrieg. With German bombs falling constantly since September of 1940, the need for medical help was extreme. Cathy was assigned to a Hospital in Barrow

Her Canadian companions were sent to other Hospitals throughout Scotland and England. This was Catherine Romanov's first experience with massive casualties caused by the bombing of Barrow by the Luftwaffe. It was heart stropping. The sound of the air raid siren, and the controlled panic of people as they tried to squeeze into make-shift bomb shelters, drove home the need for an end to this madness. It took only three days to understand and appreciate the resolve of her co-workers to survive and win this battle with Mr. Hitler.

Over in Gander Newfoundland, at the ungodly hour of 0400, Arvid Romanov watched out a trailer window as a Lancaster Bomber took off for Greenland. Colonel Wilkins stood beside him as the huge aircraft lifted from the runway.

"Too bad you couldn't take that one, Commander, but they've got four Nurses on board. Those planes aren't designed for passenger comfort. I have no idea where Collingworh, the

Skipper, is going to put everyone, but there is another Lancaster due to land in the morning. There will be room for you on that one." Wilkins commented, adding, " the layover will give you time to see how the aircraft ferry system works." Arvid was impressed at how cooperation between the Canadian and British government allowed aircraft to be built and flown to England. The war had not yet stirred the Americans to action, but with ships being sunk daily by German submarines and seeing firsthand the ferocity of the German Navy, he felt it would not be long before an American freighter would be targeted.

Later in the morning, a low hanging mist greeted Arvid as he stepped out of the trailer and walked toward the Lancaster that was being refueled for trip to Greenland.

Equipped with flight suit and parachute, he felt adventurous. Approaching the rear of the plane, a group of airmen greeted the passenger with a modicum of respect.

"Good morning, Commander. My name is Captain Derrick O'Reilly. Are you ready to fly? I hear you had a bit of trouble the last time you traveled by water." he laughed, as he and his crew entered the rear hatch, "I hope we don't get our feet wet on this trip. This is the second Lanc. to make the trip across the pond, so we know they will fly that far. Let's go." Arvid was happy to be surrounded by a crew of fellow Canadians who were eager to be airborne and get the job done.

The rumble of the tires and roar of the Merlin engines signified the Lancaster was on its way across the Atlantic, albeit by a circular route. Seated on a cot in the center of the plane, Arvid could not imagine how four Nurses could have possibly have fit into the same space. Listening to chatter by the crew, Arvid began to appreciate the work that went on to make this all possible.

Arriving in Prestwick without incident, just past midnight, Commander Arvid Romanov thanked all the members of the crew for a safe flight. He was not told of the harrowing experience by the crew of the Lancaster that was parked in a hangar nearby. Within the hour, he was picked up by an Officer Cadet in a Land Rover and transported to Command Headquarters in Glasgow.

Major Lithgow greeted him with a salute, which felt odd to a Canadian without military training. As a civilian with a military title, it was an unusual situation.

"We're glad you made it in one piece, Commander. With all the Luftwaffe activity, we never know when the next assault will happen. Lieutenant Cosgrove will show you to your quarters, and after you get settled, you and I are going to take a trip. We have supplies that have to get to our people in Antwerp. My boss, Field Marshal Alexander, thinks that you can do this job without drawing attention to the military. We need to have someone who can work behind the scenes and not be connected directly to the British High Command. I can tell you, that if you succeed in this secret mission, we will be that much closer to pushing Hitler back to Berlin, where we can crush him." Lithgow said, making a fist to express the emotion. Arvid was beginning to understand his purpose. Following the Adjutant, Arvid was taken to a makeshift barracks set up with sandbags and netting. Soldiers in full battle dress were assembling to be taken to areas outside the city that had been hit by the Luftwaffe several times trying to destroy the shipbuilding capabilities. With anti aircraft guns set up to defend against the constant overflights by German bombers, there was no question that he was in the middle of a war zone. With shipbuilding and a long runway as targets, everyone was aware that any night could be their last. After three hours sleep, the Lieutenant was at Arvid's side, shaking him awake.

"Major Lithgow wants you to see what your assignment is. We're expecting another wave of Heinkels tonight, so the sooner we get you on to your way, the better." Arvid visited the latrine, had a sandwich and within twenty minutes, was in a Land Rover with Major Lithgow and Lieutenant Cosgrove heading for Edinburgh. Everywhere along the road from Glasgow, there were signs of damage caused by errant bombs. It appeared that Scotland was not waiting for the Germans to invade their Country, and were ready to protect their land. It would be a fight to the death with the fierce Scots.

"The Field Marshal was made aware of the plan, and believes that you can pull it off. He has been assured by Churchill that, whatever happens, the Canadians will stand by us." the General looked over at Arvid and smiled. As they reached the outskirts of Edinburgh, Arvid could see the Castle sitting atop the bluff, and wondered why the Germans hadn't destroyed it first. Turning off the highway, the Land Rover drove down to a wharf located on the Firth of Forth. There was no sign of any military presence in the area. Quickly entering a small building adjacent to the wharf, Arvid was surprised to find a command center operated by a number of women. From the outside, this was just a work shack, but it had been converted to a communications hub, receiving information from throughout Scotland. Walking down a flight of stairs, they came to a steel door, guarded by two very large and intimidating Scotsmen. Saluting, they opened the door for the Major and Arvid.

Once inside the concrete bunker, it became apparent that this place was off limits to anyone without security clearance. Maps on the wall showed various troop concentration of both British and German troops. A second room concentrated on the air war. Arvid felt concerned that he was now vulnerable if he should ever be captured. Major Lithgow opened a door to a smaller room with desks and teletypes constantly clicking away. Men and women in civilian clothes worked in cubicles, apparently keeping track of all the information being collected in the adjacent rooms.

Finally, opening a nondescript little hatch, they stepped out into a tunnel leading to the river.

A pair of speed boats were tied up along the dock. They were still being loaded with weapons. The soldiers loading them stood at attention when they realized the Major was present on the wharf. With a quick wave of his hand, the men resumed their work. "You can study the plans tonight." then leaning closer to Arvid, whispered, "tomorrow, you and your crew will leave for your destination." It was apparent by the Major's actions, that this was indeed, a secret mission, but had nothing to do with supplies to Antwerp. The Antwerp mission was obviously a cover story. Returning though the complex, the Major stopped at a young woman's desk.

"Charlotte, will you please show Commander Romanov to the apartment. Make certain he has the May file to study." The woman stood and opened a small safe beside her, withdrawing a file, handing it to Arvid. She smiled, and he could see that, despite the war going on outside the doors of this underground command center, life and love goes on.

Walking to a wall, she pulled open a drawer on a filing cabinet, and like magic, the whole cabinet swung away, revealing a hallway to a series of doors. Apparently, this was where all the workers stayed so that they did not have to leave the building. Following Charlotte, Arvid was surprised when she stopped at a door, handing him a small metal card.

"This is for your apartment, Commander. Just insert it into the slot." Arvid did as instructed. The door clicked and opened. Thanking Charlotte, he stepped inside. The room was small but well appointed, with a bathroom off to one side and bedroom on the other. A menu on the coffee table had a list of food that was available from the kitchen. It was obvious this complex was built and designed long before the war. Sitting in the easy chair, he opened the 'eyes only' file.

He now understood why there was so much secrecy involved with his arrival in Scotland. He was a Canadian and not involved with the British government. If he were to be captured, he was expendable. The British could deny responsibility. Reading over the details, he accepted that the results would be worth the risk.

He would have seven other men with him to take the boats out into the bay to the Isle of May. One of them would be a scientist who knew how to operate 'a device'.

Arvid stared at the words. 'A device' So this was the reason for all the secrecy. With an eidetic memory, he perused the documents, locking in the pertinent details that would require precise timing.

Feeling he understood the plan and its need for his participation, Arvid closed the file and ordered a steak and potatoes from the menu. He would see if a T bone in England was acceptable compare to grass fed beef from Saskatchewan. A half hour later, a knock on the door, and two young ladies entered, with utensils, condiments, plates of vegetables and a sizzling T bone steak. One of the women laughed when she set the plate on the table in front of the Canadian.

"The Major warned us that you might want to test us, so we went to our Scottish Chef, and he had a few of these sent down from his cousin in the Highlands. During the rationing, I hope you appreciate what it takes to smuggle this kind of food past thousands of hungry soldiers." After they placed the food, they sat on either side of the visiting Commander, as if waiting for the big reveal. Arvid smiled at his companions and picked up the tools. Knowing that the British held their forks differently than Canadians, he purposely remained Canadian, and sliced off a piece of the succulent meat.

Placing it in his mouth, his audience awaited the decision. Arvid was shocked, It was perfectly done, and tender as veal. He smiled, and the girls leaned over and kissed his cheeks.

"I guess that means we can tell the Chef it was a success. Hazel said you wouldn't like it, but I guess she was wrong." the younger girl said, with the air of a winner. Arvid cut another piece and offered it to Hazel. She hesitated for a moment, then gladly accepted the tidbit. As she chewed the morsel, she closed her eyes, and finally swallowing it, she smiled,

"Aye, that is good. Thank you Commander. I'm happy to be wrong. We'll leave you now to enjoy your meal. Please call us if you want anything else." There was a hint of romance in her voice.

Arvid smiled and nodded. "Too bad I can't tell my friends about the great food and service in this hotel. Thank you." He noticed they curtsied as they closed the door. Finishing his excellent meal, Commander Arvid Romanov was ready for sleep and eager to see what the next day would bring.

300 miles to the south, in London, Catherine Romanov, Registered Nurse, was pulling a small child from beneath a collapsed portion of roof. Since leaving Barrow, the bombing had been incessant, and hundreds of buildings in London had left burning and in ruin. There seemed to be no end to Hitler's desire to break the English spirit. With hospitals suffering direct hits, it was becoming difficult to find a safe place to treat patients. There was no shortage of hands to help move bricks and broken bits of lumber to access those who were strong enough to call for help. Cathy's initiation into the horrors of war was sudden and brutal. The trip down though the countryside by truck, past check points and crashed aircraft still did not prepare her for the disaster that was London. She could see the smoke from miles away, but to actually be in the midst of the conflagration was a whole new experience. Thrust into the belly of the beast, she was dropped off at a tent that had been erected to treat the walking wounded. With streets blocked by debris, there were no short cuts, so bodies and those still alive were brought to the tent. As part of the triage unit, Cathy had to decide who could be saved and those who were beyond human help. Serving with a Dr. Goldsmith, who was inducted from the Polish Army, together they were overwhelmed by requests to save relatives that were already dead. It was heartbreaking, but as the days past, catching sleep when and where she could, it became a race to the bottom. It seemed the more people she treated, the more death and destruction occurred.

The nights were filled with sirens, explosions and cries for help, but after a time, huddling with others in bomb shelters, Cathy Romanov accepted the common belief that it was just a matter time before another one of the Heinkels dropped an egg that would find them, as it did on the 12th of April. St. Thomas Hospital had been bombed before, but still managed to operate and remained open despite being across from the parliament buildings and on the Thames river. Cathy was finally happy to be able to have equipment and supplies to work with, rather than having to tear bandages in half to patch up a bleeding wound in the back of a lorry. Each night, the sirens would wail, and people would run to an undergone shelter. Having helped dig survivors out from beneath a buried Anderson shelter, the concrete bunkers and old unused tram tunnels, being able to look after the injured in a clean environment was a treat. Everyone on the St. Thomas staff was accustomed to long hours and little sleep, but news that the RAF was beating the Germans in the air, meant that there might be a day, or night when the staff could get seven of hours of uninterrupted dream time. Cathy thought about her mother and sister back in Admiral, and understood why she couldn't write and or tell them where she was or what she was doing. Once this madness was over, there would be time to reunite with her family. Looking around at all the misery and suffering, where people had no idea if their relatives were alive or dead, having to remain incognito was not a great price to pay.

To the north, the war was being fought differently. Arvid was introduced to the Scientist who he was sent to assist. A mist drifted in over the Firth of Forth as Arvid joined his crew in the tunnel. The 'device' was loaded into the rear boat. It was about the size of a steamer trunk, and quite heavy. Five men would ride in the advance boat, with the Scientist Joshua McIntosh, Arvid and two heavily armed Royal Marines riding in the rear boat. It was still quite dark as the expedition left the security of the tunnel and sped away to the Isle of May. Within the hour, they beached the boats and began packing the device up to a shed a short distance from the dock. Ordering five of the Marines to disperse to various locations in the hill to guard against surprise visitors, Arvid opened the door of the dilapidated shack and stepped inside, With another card given him by Major Lithgow, Arvid slipped it into a slot in the rear wall. Like magic, an access panel slid back, exposing a staircase leading down in the bowels of the island. Packing the box down the winding staircase, three flights down, they arrived at a large steel blast door. Using the card once again, the door unlocked.

It opened up into a laboratory, with various pieces of equipment placed along the walls. Banks of lights turned on automatically. Unlocking the lid, it took two Marines to lift the electronic contraption and place the device on a table. Joshua hooked up cables to a strange looking piece of equipment with a video screen prominently affixed on top. This was far ahead anything he had seen during his tour of the Trenton surveillance bunker. This was a radar system far ahead of the units shown him by the technicians in Canada. With the device connected, Joshua turned it on.

Arvid could hear the intake of air as the Marines saw the boats at the dock.. Somewhere outside this cement hole in the ground, were cameras mounted in strategic locations. Selecting a camera, that portrayed a scene to the east of the Island. Joshua pulled up a chair and sat down.

"Now we wait. You chaps should make yourselves a coffee, We may be here for a while. There is a water closet in the next room." With that, the two guards, placed their weapons against a wall and loosened their flack jackets. Pulling up chairs around a table, they began to play cards. It was a surreal scene, and Arvid, although he knew what the device would do, wondered why there had to be such a concern about safety. Within the hour, the answer was forthcoming. A sound echoed through the room, and everyone gathered around the video screen. Joshua sat at the controls and watched as the aircraft hove into sight. Enlarging the view, it was possible to see the pilot, even though the plane was some ten miles distant. Controlling the crosshairs, Joshua zeroed in on one engine. Pushing a button on the device's panel, the propellor slowed, then turned lazily, as Joshua followed the plane's descent. Adjusting the focus, everyone in the room took a breath, as they realized that the crew was going to get wet. Refocussing on another aircraft, Joshua took aim at the Heinkel bomber. With dual engines, it took two shots to completely disable the plane. It also caused the pilot and bombardier to bail. There was no gun involved. No bullets, no gunshot to startle the many birds that swarm the Island. This was an electronic beam that shorted out any electronics on the aircraft. It was deadly and accurate, This was a test, a proof of concept. As the planes dropped one by one, Joshua shut off the device.

"When their scientists discover several of their planes went into the ocean without being hit with anti aircraft fire, they will zero in on this island. We have proven what we wanted to, so we'll button this place up and take the device with us." Joshua said, as he walked over to the refrigerator. Arvid turned to join him when a Marine came out of the bathroom carrying a .45 aimed directly at his fellow Marine.

"You won't be taking that anywhere," he said, and immediately shot his partner, who was reaching for his weapon. with three slugs penetrating his vest. The shooter checked his watch. "sit down Commander. By the way, why are you here? You aren't a member of the Home Guard, or even the Air Force. You're not a scientist or politician. Hell, you aren't even British." then, stepping over his comrade's' body, waved the .45 at Joshua, "both of of you." checking his watch, he added, "sit down and don't move. We've got a few minutes to wait." Arvid and his scientist friend sat as directed. There was the noticeable smell of death in the room, and the Marine holding the gun was becoming nervous.

"What's In it for you? You doing this because you love the Führer, or what?" Arvid asked, watching for an opening to distract the spy. The Marine laughed.

"No. Nothing as dramatic as that. When all this bullshit is over, I'll be relaxing in Argentina on a farm with a lovely Senorita and a whole batch of kids. I really don't give a damn about Germany, but when they take over this Country, I get paid and I'm on the next boat to a warm climate with sexy women." The Marine checked his watch again, "Joshua, you might want to turn on your cameras above ground." Joshua crossed over to the video screen and flicked some switches.

Selecting various cameras angles, it was apparent that a squad of German commandos had arrived by dinghy and were engaging the Royal Marines in a fire fight. The deck gun from an offshore submarine was peppering the trapped defenders, while the advancing SS used hand grenades to drive the Marines from their hiding places. It was painful to watch. Whenever a Marine broke loose, he was chopped down by automatic fire from the sub sitting just offshore.

Finally, there was no more resistance, and a camera located in the shack showed that the invaders had come prepared for a fight. Within minutes, they were outside the blast door. The killer Marine walked over to the cement barrier, and then pointing his gun directly at Joshua, said, "Open the door!" Joshua hesitated, then pushed the device from the table onto the concrete floor. The fragile case split wide open and hundreds of electronic pieces spilled out like confetti. The Marine was enraged and pulled the trigger four times, running out of bullets. Joshua's eyes opened wide, grabbed his chest and slumped to the floor beside his destroyed masterpiece. It was the moment Arvid had been waiting for. The Marine stood holding the gun, with an empty chamber, aimed at the dead Scientist, unsure of what to do next. The device was ruined, and his comrades were just outside the door, waiting to congratulate him for a job well done. Arvid charged him, hitting him hard, driving the smaller man into the wall, forcing all the air from his lungs. Hitting him repeatedly in the face until there was no more resistance, Arvid allowed the killer to drop. The Commander was now alone in the cement bunker, with a squad of German SS waiting for the access door to open. Crossing to the radio, Arvid opened a channel to Major Lithgow. After some confusion, the Major was located and picked up the microphone.

"Major. This is Arvid. We are under attack by a submarine and a squad of SS. Everyone is dead.

The spy is dead, but the attackers are at the blast door waiting to get in. Any way you can help?"

There was silence, but finally Major Lithgow replied. "Leave it with me, Commander." That was all he said. Arvid was left hanging on the microphone, wondering if perhaps the Major was in on the treason. With all the bodies beginning to gas in the enclosed space, Arvid anxiously surveyed the myriad of knobs and switches on the control panel, finally discovering one that was labeled 'Air.'

Taking a chance, he turned it on. From somewhere in the complex, a hum was heard. Imperceptibly, Arvid could sense a movement of air across his face. It was working.

Time dragged on, and the banging was becoming louder. It was quite possible, that the invaders were preparing to blow the door. If that happened, the resulting concussion in the enclosed space would kill him. Arvid was about to call the Major once again, but turning to the camera controls, he zeroed in on the submarine anchored just offshore. It suddenly blew up. The crew manning the deck gun flew in many directions. The banging on the door stopped. Selecting another camera angle, he could see a British destroyer coming into view. It was like watching a B movie in one of the theaters in downtown Regina. The SS invaders swarmed out of the shack and were met with withering fire from a Spitfire targeting anything that moved on land. Within minutes it was over. Bodies of both Royal Marines and German SS littered the hillside. The radio cracked to life.

"Hello Commander. Are you there?" It was Major Lithgow. Arvid sat at the desk and responded.

"Yes. I'm here, Nicely done, Major. I'm going to chance opening the door, so if I'm not out in five minutes, you'll know I made a mistake." Arvid commented, knowing that the SS were not known to giving up so easily. Taking a side arm from one of the dead Marines, Arvid slid the card into its receptacle. The solid slab of concrete began to move, and for a moment, his worst fears were put to rest, when suddenly he was pushed backward by a large, armed German Special Forces who aimed his gun directly at Arvid. The man began shouting and pulled the trigger of his Luger, but nothing happened. There was a split second of confusion, as the German looked at his malfunctioning weapon, but Arvid did not hesitate. The American made .45 performed perfectly. Arvid was able to get off four shots before the German hit the ground. As he collected his thoughts, Arvid sat on the floor, gun aimed at the doorway, waiting for the next attack, but it never came. Looking around the room, he was stunned by the what had happened in such a short period of time. The 'device' was ruined, its creator dead, two Royal Marines and a German SS special Forces left their blood, all in an effort to gain a leg up over their opponent. War, indeed, was Hell, and he could testify to that as he waited for someone friendly to arrive. Finally, an hour later, a group of royal Marines came into the bunker, which, by that time, was getting pretty ripe. Thankful to be spelled off by the new arrivals, he retrieved one of the boats on the beach, and declining an offer for assistance, Arvid spent a leisurely three hours motoring back to the command center. Thinking about what the Marine traitor said about retiring to Argentina with a farm, it was puzzling as to how the Germans knew they would be at the bunker at that particular time. Arriving in the tunnel, a Marine was there to tie up the boat as Arid stepped out. Major Lithgow met him within three steps.

"Well, you made it. Come on in the office. I've got to know what happened on the island. This was supposed to be top secret stuff." the Major commented, as the two entered one of the enclosed cubicles. Arvid nodded his head.

"The Germans had a team of specialists ready to pounce when we got to the island. They must have had a few days warning of our activity. There has to be a breach here in the office." Arvid suggested, knowing that he was suggesting the Major had slipped up. Major Lithgow reached into a drawer, withdrawing a sealed folder. He handed it to Arvid. Sliding the 'eyes only' band from the dossier, he opened it. There, staring back at him was the face of the Marine.

As Arvid studied the file, the Major's Adjutant came in and handed her boss a message. Major Lithgow read the note twice, then threw it on his desk. "Well, now we have another clue to the mystery of how our little secret was discovered. Our dive team inspected the German sub that we sunk off the Island. It's going to take some time before we get inside. It's in 170 feet of water, so we'll leave it for now. It's not going anywhere, but, that SS chap you shot in the bunker proved valuable. He was the Commandant of that squad. Sergeant McCaffrey found a message in a pocket. It appears that the Germans knew about the movement of the device five days ago. They had time to assemble an assault team and be picked up in Norway by the Sub. Interestingly enough, Joshua arrived here five days ago with the device. So, your supposition about a leak here in the Command Center is well founded. It's distressing to think that someone I work with every day is a German spy. Do you have any suggestions.?" the Major asked, taking back the file.

"When he arrived, where did he stay, Major?" Arvid asked, sensing a solution to this puzzle.

"Everyone here stays in the hotel. You stay there. You can see how handy it is being this close to work during these trying times. Do you think the place is bugged with microphones? That thought occurred to me, so I'll have our Royal Military Police do another sweep of the rooms." The Major replied, picking up the phone. Arvid held up his hand. "Not just yet. We don't want the infiltrator to know that you suspect someone in the hotel. Let me do some snooping first."

The Major put the phone back on its cradle. He nodded acceptance of the plan. It would keep things quiet and not alert the spy, giving him or her chance to cover any mistakes. Arvid stood and saluted. It was becoming as natural as saying hello. Returning the salute, the Major smiled.

"We'll make a certified Brit out of you yet, Commander Romanov. Go see what you can discover with that massive brain of yours." Closing the door behind him, Arvid crossed to the entrance of the bogus Records room. Going through the routine of opening the filing cabinet to access the hotel hallway seemed a little childish, but he was in no mood to argue about minor irritants. Reaching his room, he was finally able to use the bathroom. Relief truly comes in many ways.

Making full use of the shower, he allowed his mind to wander through the manic happening of the day. Finally, as evening arrived, he was more than ready to eat. Ordering a simple meal from the kitchen, he waited for the girls to deliver. Arvid was surprised when an older gentleman arrived at the door. He was obviously part of the old establishment, with mustache and decidedly Scottish accent. Taking the tray from the server, Arvid was curious.

"What happened to the young girls who served me yesterday?" he asked, sounding like a pervert disappointed by the substitution. The old gentleman smiled, and nodded his head.

"Aye. They wanted to come again tonight, but the Chef needed them to serve at the dining room.

Some big time mucky muck having a meeting. I'll tell you asked about them. I'm sure they'll be thrilled to pieces." he replied, sarcastically. Arvid laughed. He was too tired to best the Scotsman and his dry humor.

"Thank you, uh," Arvid felt stupid not knowing what to say to the distinguished old gentleman.

"Cory. Cory McTavish. I hear you're a Canadian, " he asked, picking up a napkin from the floor.

"Yes. I come from the prairies. Too bad there is a war on, right now. This is probably a nice place when the bullets and bombs stop flying." Arvid commented sitting down to taste the hot coffee. Cory opened the door. " If you need anything else, Commander, just give me call. I think you're alright!" he added as closed the door. Arvid thought about the last words. It was an odd thing to say. Digging into a meal of fish and chips, his mind went blank. It was time for bed.

It was two in the morning when Arvid awoke and sat upright in bed. The napkin on the floor. How did it get there. Getting up, he crossed over to the small safe embedded in the wall. Removing the files given him by Major Lithgow, he thumbed through the pages slowly. Page number ten and eleven were misplaced. They were reversed. Someone had taken the files apart and put them back together in haste. He sat on the couch and stared at the 'eyes only' documents. The thief could not know the combination, that was renewed each time the safe is closed. It meant that the safe isn't safe, at all. Opening it again, he ran his hand around the rear panel. It felt rough and uneven. Taking a small piece toilet paper, Arvid lit it, allowing it to burn out, causing smoke. Holding it against the back panel, the smoke was drawn immediately out through a crack in the rear. Anything left in it was accessible from the rear. Joshua's plans for the use of the device had obviously been discovered and passed on to the Germans. Arvid was faced with a dilemma. How could he discover who was taking the secret files from a supposedly, secure wall safe.

He was now certain that the information sent to the Germans originated right here in this place. Morning came slowly, but daylight finally arrived, and with it, came another bombing raid by the German luftwaffe.

The day was warm and wet. As Tzeitel got up and went downstairs to make breakfast, she looked in on Leo. Her grandson was growing at an astonishing rate, and at four years old looked more like eight. Patricia was already up and offered her mother-in-law a fresh cup.

"I just looked in on Leo. He sure is getting big." Tzeitel commented, as she took a carton of eggs from the fridge, " he'll be out herding the cattle pretty soon." Patricia smiled. It was true. Her son was growing up quickly, but with Arvid away doing work for the government, there was no way to send him a photo. As Patricia and Tzeitel sat and listened to the rain, the sound of a vehicle splashing in driveway brought them both to the kitchen window. They were both surprised to see Petrov get out of a brown government car and dodged raindrops as he ran to the back porch. Tzeitel was there to meet her husband. Patricia could see how much love there was between the rugged older Romanov and her mother-in-law. Her thoughts immediately went to Arvid. Without word of his location, Patricia did not know if he was nearby or in eastern Canada.

In three steps, Petrov crossed to his daughter-in law, giving her a vigorous bear hug. It was a very warm reception.

"How long are you going to be home?" Tzeitiel asked, as she prepared breakfast for her husband.

Petrov reached out and took Tzeitel's hand. "I have to be back in Regina in two days. I'm meeting with the pork and beef producers for shipments overseas. I don't know if either of you would be interested, but I heard that Arvid is doing well with his new assignment. I can't tell you where he is, but he's healthy. As you've probably heard on radio, the Germans have been bombing cities in England. We've got to keep sending food and material over to help them out. I've been told that Kate is helping out the Military now, so she's in good hands and safe," Petrov hated to lie about his children, but due to strict secrecy rules imposed by the government, he would be punished for releasing any information about the whereabouts of either Arvid or Cathy, "how's Leo?" he asked, desperately wanting to change the subject. Tzeitel could see there would be no more information forthcoming from her husband. She was content to know that if he was not concerned, then it was fruitless for them to worry. The day passed without any more mention of the war or its consequences. The next day, the weather was beautiful and Petrov was intent on checking the fences. Not bothering to saddle up Blaze, who was now 15 years old, and showing her age, Petrov got on and placed Leo on the horse in front of him. Patricia, having no experience with horses, could see that the senior Romanov knew how to handle the animal as they rode off down into the valley. Tzeitel put her arm around her daughter-in-law, assuring her that Petrov was a good horseman. Returning to the house, Patrica could not shake the feeling of dread.

As lunch hour approached, Patrica went outside to search for her son. From her vantage point, she could see the whole valley, but there was no sign of Petrov or Leo. Pacing back and forth, she was surprised to see Petrov riding quickly back up the hill toward her. As Blaze came closer, Patrica noticed that Leo was missing. As Petrov pulled up to the fence, he jumped from the horse. He was out of breath. "Where is Leo?" Patricia screamed, seeing the look of panic on Petrov'e face.

"I don't know. We dismounted to check a broken wire and let the horse drink. We were there for only five minutes, but when I turned around, Leo was gone. I looked for him everywhere around the area, and the creek isn't deep enough to drown in. I thought he would come home. I'll go out and look for him again. He will probably show up here. He's pretty smart, and certainly big enough to know where he's going. " As Petrov spoke to Patricia, Tzeitiel came out, alerted by her daughter-in-law's scream.

"What's the matter?" she asked, seeing the look on Petrov's face. This was obviously serious.

"Leo is missing!" Petrov replied, as he remounted Blaze, "I'm going back down to the creek."

he added, expertly turning the horse around on the spot. Both Tzeitel and Patricia stood and watched as Petrov disappeared into the valley.

"What are we going to do?" Patricia asked, her mind filled with all the wild thoughts of death.

""We'll put on our boots and search around here. Leo is a pretty smart boy, and he's got long legs. I'm sure he just decided to walk home." Tzeitel replied, not too convincingly. Nodding acceptance,

Patricia followed her mother-n-law into the house. Moments later, they were back out, and separating, they walked out into the fields surrounding the Romanov house site. Minutes became an hour. Petrov returned, angry with himself for losing his grandson. Patricia climbed the hill behind the house, wading through chest deep grass and wheat. Suddenly, she stumbled and fell down, scraping her arm on a metal object. Clearing away the stubborn grass, Patricia discovered a metal cross. A shiver went down her spine. She appeared to be in a graveyard. Getting to her feet, she felt lost. Placing one foot in front of another, she moved slowly forward until she arrived at a pile of overgrown rubble. There was a cold, strange mist swirling around the rotted lumber, and it was only desperation that drove her legs to move forward. Parting a growth of brush, she was shocked to see Leo sitting on a large wooden beam adjacent to the rubble. It took a moment for her brain to accept the fact that her son was smiling. He seemed quite alive and well. She looked down at her arm. It was bleeding, so she knew that this was not a dream. Kneeling down to hug her four year old, she began to cry.

"What happened to you, Leo? Where did you go? Your Grampa was looking for you."

Her son shrugged and seemed quite nonchalant about his disappearance.

"I got off the horse with Grampa and was watching him fix the fence, when a man came along and picked me up. I don't know how I got here. I don't know where I am." Leo said, without emotion or surprise. "how did you find me mommy?" he asked, finally. Patricia was beginning to realize that she had been directed to his place. She looked into her son's eyes and could see that the experience had not changed or frightened him. He just accepted it as another life event.

Looking around at the overgrown bush and piles of wood, It appeared to be the remains of an old building. Taking Leo by the hand, Patricia felt that cold mist again, and following her trail through the tall grass, hurried to get away from this unwelcoming part of the Romanov property. Reaching the fence, she followed it until she finally saw the familiar outline of the house. Patricia felt a great relief to be back home. She was about to enter, when Petrov rode up on Blaze. Jumping from the horse, he ran to his daughter-in-law, picking up Leo, swung him around, hugging the laughing 4 year old. "Where did you find him?" Petrov asked, carrying the boy through the gate and handing him back to his mother. There was great joy in his movements as he went back out to attend to Blaze.

"He was up at some old building on the hill. He was just sitting there. He told me that some man picked him up while you were fixing the fence. Did you see anyone?" Patricia asked, puzzled at how her father-in-law didn't notice the man. Petrov stopped and walked back to Patricia. He was suddenly concerned.

"You found him up at the old church? You should never go up there, Patsy. It's dangerous. There are all kinds of nails and things you could step on." then kneeling down to Leo, Petrov asked. "you say a man picked you up and carried you up the hill. What did the man look like?" Patricia knelt down, placing her hand on Leo's shoulder. Leo looked from his mother to his Grampa. He became frightened at the sudden attention, but did not cry.

"He had a long beard and smelled real bad. I don't know how I got there. I think we flew," the 4 year old said, reprising his recollection of the strange event, "he put his hand on my head.."

"What happened then?" Petrov asked, interrupting his grandson, anxious to hear more.

"He heard Mommy coming and he went into the building." Leo replied, turning to see his grandmother and Dorothy joining them on the path. Petrov stood and took his wife's hand.

"It's OK. Patsy found Leo up at the old church. He's alright. nothing happened." he said putting his arm around his wife. Dorothy began to sob, kneeling beside her nephew. "Don't ever go near that place again, Leo. It is a very bad place. Promise me" she said, kissing Leo on the forehead.

Leo was confused. All the grown ups were asking him to stay away from a place he didn't even know about or wanted to go. It wasn't his fault that he was there. Leo nodded his head.

""I told him that it was dangerous," Petrov said, " now let's go and have lunch. I suddenly feel like having a meal with my family." With that, Patricia took Leo by the hand, and as Petrov mounted Blaze, the women walked back down through the orchard to the house.

****

Cleaning up after the latest bombing raid, Cathy and three of the other Nurses on duty during the night surveyed the damage. It was a near miss. St. Thomas Hospital survived night after night of terror in the Wards. With injured civilians and pregnant women, Doctors were kept busy moving patients around as electricity and water stopped. As April turned to May, hit was unclear as to how long London could survive the constant fire and destruction. Cathy spent her off time with other workers from the Hospital searching through damaged buildings, looking for anyone who might be trapped and forgotten. It was a depressing and soul destroying task, but it brought the survivors together. Without any time for romance, Cathy and her fellow Nurses gathered in basement to toast another day. As the only place in the whole massive building that had proper sleeping quarters, the Nurses and Doctors could have some privacy, and even sleep. The discussion turned to what they would do when ever this insane conflict was over. With constant bombing and strafing by fighter planes, it was hard to even imagine life returning to normal.

The 5th of May, 1941 started with no night time bombing. There had been only one air raid siren, and then there was silence. Preparing for her shift, Cathy appreciated the first night of at least six hours sleep. Taking over from the weary night shift, there was a sense of optimism in the air. Even patients remarked at how quiet it was during the night. Cathy was about to change the bandages on a Corporal's missing leg, when there was commotion in the next ward. Quickly finishing the wrap, Cathy went to the entrance to see what caused the disturbance.

The Chief Surgeon was walking with a group of people who were dressed in civilian clothes. It seemed odd to have a tour of the facilities in the middle of a war. As the entourage approached, Nurse Gwyneth came up behind Cathy and whispered in her ear.

"It's a Royal Tour. The Queen decided to visit the wards while there was no air raids. I don't see King George. She must have come alone. " Cathy nodded and pulled back out of view.

"Who are those people around her? They don't look like Royals." Cathy asked, feeling excited about seeing Queen Elizabeth up close. As they came closer, there was no place for the two Nurses to hide. A tall, young man came up and stood beside them, as the Queen passed. She suddenly stopped and stuck out her hand. Cathy Romanov's heart just about stopped.

"I'm glad to see you two are on the job. I feel so much better to know that we have proper medical care for out injured soldiers and airmen," the Queen remarked, as she took Cathy's hand. "what's your name?" she asked, looking directly into Cathy's eyes. There was a moment when her mind went blank, but replied. "Cathy Romanov, you Majesty. " Queen Elizabeth smiled and nodded her head. " You don't have to say, 'your majesty'. Just, 'Mum', will do. That accent is Canadian, isn't it?"

Cathy was silent for a moment, then recovered enough to say, " Yes. I'm from Saskatchewan, Canada." The Queen smiled and suddenly, as the procession attempted to move, she held up her hand. "just a moment. The King and I were in Saskatchewan only two years ago. I really enjoyed our stay. My husband even rode a horse in the bucking contest. I think it was in a place called Saskatoon" then turning to the man standing beside Cathy, said, "I would like you to speak to me after we leave, Chris." The man nodded his head, and looked down at Cathy and smiled.

The Queen let go of Cathy's hand and moved along slowly through the ward, but every once in while, looked back in her direction. An hour later, as Lieutenant Cathy Romanov made her rounds, she was startled to find Chris waiting at the Nurse's Station. He stood beside her as she made out her reports. He stuck out his hand in an awkward fashion. Holding Cathy's hand while he spoke, she did not attempt to pull away. He was mesmerizing, with green eyes that bore through her defenses and melted her resistance.

"My name is Chris Peterson. My boss has asked me to invite you to tea." he said, unsure if he had the words came out in the correct order. As life went on around them, both Cathy and Chris seemed oblivious to the commotion. Cathy finally was able to absorb the question.

"You boss? You mean Queen Elizabeth? She wants me to come and have tea with her. You must think I'm really stupid to fall for a line like that." she replied, pulling her hand away from his.

Chris stood and stared at the young woman. He could not believe that anyone would pass up an opportunity to have tea with the Queen of England. He stepped back a pace, staring at Cathy as if she was a museum specimen. "You don't want to meet the Queen?" he asked, in disbelief.

Cathy was stunned for a moment. Was this man, with the green eyes and handsome face really serious? Was he actually asking a common person to go with him to meet the Queen? It seemed a little too much like a joke to be true. "How do I know this is for real?" Cathy asked, sounding like a teenager in a sleepover. Chris stepped back and picked up Cathy's hand again. He held it with both of his, and said quietly, "I know this sounds like a come-on, but it's true. The Queen has asked me to personally come and ask you to visit with her. If you can be ready tomorrow 9 a.m. at the front door, I'll pick you up. I know she really wants to talk to you. I guess she really had a good time in Canada. Can you make it?" Chris looked directly into Cathy's eyes. There was no way to say no. She closed her eyes, and nodded her head.

"OK. What should I wear?" she asked, still not believing that it was real. Chris laughed and took both her hands, lifting them in the air like ballerina, he spun her around and said, "it doesn't matter what you wear, you will still be beautiful." he said, giving her a hug. There was a moment when they both realized that this was more than a hug. Oblivious to her colleague's concern, Cathy laughed along with the Queen's bodyguard. As she walked with him to the entrance, they hesitated as they separated, and Cathy waved as Chris walked to the waiting Land Rover.

The rest of the day passed in a blur. Another night without sirens or Heinkels bombing the largest city in England. Borrowing a plain dress from another Nurse, Cathy was anxious to see if Chris would be true to his word. At exactly 9: a.m., a large black car pulled up to the curb in front of St. Thomas Hospital. Her fellow Nurses stood in the doorway, watching one of their own being picked up by a Royal limousine. Chris opened the door as

Cathy slid into the back seat. As the vehicle pulled away from the curb, Cathy could see the damage the bombing had caused from different viewpoint. It was startling to see how much damage the Germans had caused.

A few minutes later, the Limo pulled through the guarded gates of Buckingham Palace. Pulling up to a rear entrance, Chris jumped out and opened the door. Taking Cathy by the hand, he led her through the massive hallways of the ancient building, finally arriving at small, cozy room with low ceiling and the smell of food. Several attendants were busy setting a small table and placing utensils for the visitor. Chris held her hand, leading her to a chair that she guessed would be hundreds of years old. It all seemed surreal. As she stood by the chair, not knowing the protocol when visiting the most powerful regent In the world, the tensions was eased as Queen Elizabeth entered, followed by two women, who seemed to flutter around their boss like butterflies. Waving them away, Queen Mum came up to Cathy and hugged her. It was a shock to the attending staff to have their Queen show such a personal touch to a commoner. Cathy took a second, but reciprocated. It was a touching moment, both physically and emotionally. Motioning for Cathy and Chris to sit, they both did as requested. Settling down to face each other, it became a matter of many hands placing cups, saucers and plates of foods for her Majesty and guest. The Queen motioned one of her attendants to approach. Speaking softly, she instructed everyone to leave the room. It was an unusual request. Never before had she been left alone with a stranger, without at least two of her guards present. Chris remained seated. As the crew filed from the room, puzzled at the change of protocol, they were even more surprised to have King George enter and sit in a corner chair. Looking around the room, the Queen was satisfied her request had been obeyed.

Summoning her husband to join them at the table, he did so, immediately. Patting his hand, she looked at him and smiled.

"I want to introduce you to a relative of yours, sweetheart. This is Catherine Romanov. The great grand niece of Nicholas. Her granddad her was Nicholas's brother. We did a terrible thing in not allowing Nicholas and his family to come to England in 1917. I feel a responsibility, being your wife and knowing that we could have helped." A strange look appeared on the King's face.

He nodded, and Cathy could see that he was truly affected by having to explain his family's failure.

"I'm sorry. It was so many years ago, but history would be entirely different if the Bolsheviks had not murdered your great Uncle. I first learned of your family's connection when we were in Saskatchewan. We stopped at a town called Shaunavon. The local officials gave us water, I believe. While we were being introduced, I met your father, Petrov, and did some investigating. He did not even know he was related to Czar Nicholas. He may still not know. When my wife discovered that you were in St. Thomas, we had to meet you. My wife has something she wishes to speak to you about. I'll stop talking now, because I'm not good at it. " he said, handing the conversation over to the Queen.

"First things first," she said, as she reached for sandwich, "let's eat." Cathy could hardly move. Discovering she was related to Tsar Nicholas was a stunning revelation. With trembling hand she picked up a small, crustless sandwich, and felt she was completely out of her element. She was having tea with the Queen and King George. Looking over at Chris, Cathy was trying understand why Chris had to be with her in the room. She deduced that Chris was the Queen's personal bodyguard. After a few minutes talking about the lack of bombs falling in the past two days, the Queen turned to Chris and nodded. "I guess it's time to get to the whole purpose of your visit. Because you are family, Catherine, I know you can be trusted." It was a shock when the Queen began to speak French. It took a few seconds to shift from English to French. As Cathy responded in French, the Queen looked over her husband and smiled. After a few more minutes of questions and answers, the discussion shifted back to English.

"I was pleased when I heard you spoke French as well as English." Queen Elizabeth commented as she handed another sandwich to Cathy. Where did you learn? In Montreal?"

"Yes. I did most of my internship in Montreal General, so it was just much easier to learn the language than have things explained twice. I know it's not Parisienne French, but the people don't seem to mind the Quebecois accent." Cathy explained, laughing at the thought of her experiences with Frenchmen who talked behind her back, "it comes in handy sometimes." she added.

The Queen laughed at the mention of naughty Frenchmen.

"Well, I told my husband that you would be a good fit for our little escapade." then turning to her husband, she she said, " why don't you have those special cookies brought in, dear." King George nodded his head and rapped on the door beside him. Moments later a young girl entered carrying a tray of freshly baked chocolate chip cookies. The girl went directly to Chris and offered the tray to him. Speaking in German, she held the tray for a moment. Chris took a few cookies from the plate, then, in fluent German, began carrying on a conversation with the blushing Baker's assistant.

King George, although not terribly fluent in his native language, joined in, thanking the girl, who curtsied in the presence of the King and Queen, then left. As the door closed, the Queen laughed, "Very well done, Captain. I think we chose rather well, if I do say so, myself."

Leaning forward, it was time to get serious about the reason for the Cathy and Chris to be in the room with the King and Queen of the British Empire. Taking a sip of tea, the Queen wiped her lips.

Taking Cathy's hand, Elizabeth took a moment, then said, "We have an important mission we would like you to undertake. We have discussed it with Chris, and he agrees that you would be the perfect choice for this particular assignment. Please sit back and enjoy your tea while my husband and I outline what it is we would like you to do. There is, in Morocco, a scientist who we believe, no, we know is in distress. We need him here in England to finish a project he began before the war started. Being Canadian, you probably aren't aware of the extent of the Nazi's hold on France. The French have capitulated, and are cooperating with the Germans to enter Africa by means of Algeria and have chosen Morocco as the gateway. We believe he is in the town of Rabat, living under an assumed name, and may be injured. Since the Vichy control the country, the French are preventing anyone from leaving Morocco. We believe you, accompanied by Chris acting as your husband, can travel to Rabat and find our man and get him back home where he belongs." The Queen took a sip of tea, casting a look over at King George, who nodded his head in approval.

Cathy thought abut the situation she was in. She was being asked to do espionage work for England and the war effort, Looking at Chris, she could see that he had already agreed to the scheme.

"You want me to marry Chris?" Cathy asked, almost choking on the words, "or just make believe." Chris smiled at the suggestion. He was drinking the only coffee in the room.

"Is that thought that so terrible?" he asked, laughing as he did, " even for King and Country?"

The Queen and King both laughed. "I would ask my oldest daughter, but she is only 15, and it might raise a few eyebrows on Fleet Street." the Queen said, "believe me, Catherine, if there was some other solution, we would use it. You and Chris will be taken to the Morocco by boat and dropped off on the beach just south of Rabat. You will have Canadian Passports in case you are stopped, because you are a Nurse, you will be subjected to questioning, but allowed to travel, since you a non-belligerent. You and your husband are just tourists looking for quiet vacation."

The Queen seemed to believe that Chris and Cathy could just go to a foreign Country and kidnap a man and leave. "Chris can take care of most situations, and my advice is to keep your heads down and try to work below the radar, so to speak." the King interjected, walking over to the table and taking a sandwich back to his corner chair, " we need this fellow back here to finish a job he started. It's imperative he gets back to England. We would like you to leave in the next three days. That will give you time to adjust your schedule at the Hospital. If anyone asks, just tell them you are being transferred to another facility. Chris will pick you up and take you to the boat. It will take a day to get to Morocco and we must arrive at night. Do you think you can help?" King George asked, finally.

Cathy Romanov sat for a moment, then looking over at Chris, said, " If i'm going to marry you, the least I should know is your last name." Chris took Cathy's hand in his. I guess you didn't hear me at the Hospital. "Well, Mrs. Peterson, we've been married for, " and he looked over at the King, " three years?" King George nodded his head.

"Three years tomorrow, and never had a fight." A slight smile appeared on Cathy's face, giving everyone permission to laugh at the insanity of the plan. Queen Elizabeth sat back and breathed a sigh of relief. "That's it, then. I hope you and your husband have a good vacation, at my expense.

Try to enjoy yourselves, but remember your main objective. Bring our scientist home." The Queen stood, and King George banged on the door. It immediately opened and the room was flooded with help of all shapes and sizes. Cathy Romanov could see that living in Buckingham Palace would be just a series of meetings and ceremony. She was still smarting from the fact that she and King George were not so distant relatives. It gave some credence to the reason to help Britain win the war. She had a vested interest in having England survive. On the trip back to St. Thomas, Chris reached over and held Cathy's hand. "Don't worry.

I won't let anything happen to you." he said, and almost ran into a troop carrier ferrying soldiers to the docks.

****

To the north, in the small compound situated along the Firth of forth, there was a buzz in the command center as Arvid entered. Stopping at Charlotte's desk, he leaned over and quietly asked, " What's up?" The Lieutenant looked up and Arvid could see tears in her eyes. Others in the office turned to Arvid, as if expecting him to have answers.

"Major Lithgow is dead. He was shot by a sniper least night as he got into his Land Rover. The Provosts are searching the area now for any clues. They think it might have been a German infiltrator. It might have had something to do with the attack you were involved with on the Isle of May. There is someone coming from Whitehall to investigate. Just be careful, Commander. The same person may be trying to take revenge for the German's mistake on the Island. I don't know what the top secret project was supposed to accomplish, because it's not my business, but you were part of it, so be careful. We wouldn't want to lose you too." Charlotte said, placing her hand on his. It was a revealing moment. Arvid looked around at the others in the Office. They were studying him for any reaction to the news. Arvid walked to the front and stood by the white board.

" It's unfortunate that the Major was murdered, and I feel bad for his family, but we have a job to do. This kind of brutal killing is why we have to put a stop to the Nazis as soon as possible. Two days ago, with the downing of six Heinkel bombers, we proved to the Germans that the British people will not just lay down and play dead. The Major's death is just more proof that we are causing the enemy a great deal of grief. I'm here to testify that, as long as there is breath in our bodies, we will not run off and hide, but face these killers, and beat them at their own game.

The tide is about to turn, so keep the faith, and let's find out more about these murdering bastards."

There was an embarrassing silence, then loud applause from the workers, both uniformed and civilian. Arvid was taken aback. He didn't realize, until that moment, how deeply the events in the Isle of May bunker had affected him. Nodding his head, he went into the Major's Office, followed immediately by the Major's Adjutant. Arvid sat down in the Major's chair, and was immediately handed a sheaf of papers.

"These are the morning intelligence reports, Commander. I guess you will be in charge until we're told differently. I'm glad you're here. You give everyone confidence. Thank you."

Arvid could see that the unexpected death of her Boss was a massive blow. Taking the papers from her hand, Arvid smiled. "Thank you, Mary. Things are happening quickly now, and we have to be on top of everything, no matter how small the clue might be, let me know. I'll be here with you until I'm told to leave." he remarked, returning a salute by the faithful Scot.

Looking over the 'eyes only' information, he could see that the hit on the Heinkels may have caused a shift in the German's aircraft activity. Reports from Norwegian patriots Indicated that the Luftwaffe were withdrawing aircraft and logistics from airfields in Norway and Sweden. They appeared to be moving toward the Russian border to the east. With no bombs dropping overnight, it was possible that Goering had given up on trying to beat England into the sea. With his increased losses, it was proving too expensive to maintain flights over the water. Arvid's thoughts returned to Joshua's stolen secret papers in the hotel safe. It was more than possible that the Major's death was connected to whoever stole and read the plans. Digesting all the information on the documents, Arvid passed them through the shredder. He was about to go back into the tunnel, when a very large uniformed man entered the office, and snapped a crips salute. Returning the salute, Arvid sat on the edge of the desk. It was a tactic he noticed most commanding Officers used to denote a certain confidence.

"Good day, Commander. My name is Lance Corporal McPhee. We have been sent here from Whitehall to investigate the death of Major Lithgow. I've been told to report our findings to you, sir."

Arvid nodded, as if this was routine. "That's very good, Corporal. What did you discover?"

"Well, sir. The Major was killed with single shot to the head. The slug appears to be from a 303 Enfield. By reconstructing the angle. It appears that the shot was fired from the third floor of the hotel. We can't identify the exact point, but we can get within four windows." Corporal laid a drawing on the desk, pointing to a rendering of the hotel's facade. Arvid studied it for a moment, then made an executive decision.

"Corporal. How many men do you have?" Arvid asked, studying the drawing.

"I brought ten men with me, sir." McPhee replied, sensing a trail to follow like a bloodhound.

"Good. See if you can conscript twenty more, and assemble them away from here. When you're ready, come and get me. They won't need rifles, just side arms and crowbars." The look on the Corporal's face was priceless. Arvid smiled. This was going to be payback. Snapping another salute, McPhee spun around and exited the room. Within the hour, he returned with an eagerness that bordered on fanaticism. Following Corporal McPhee through the office, Arvid gave a thumbs up, signifying to the workers that something big was going to take place.

Meeting the Provost Marshall, his ten Provost and 23 Army recruits in a nearby warehouse, Arvid had to be the Commander. Arvid looked out over the assembled crew and spoke loudly enough to be heard by all who waited their assignment.

"Yesterday, a good man was murdered by someone who shot him like coward. Not face to face, but in the back like a thief in the night. We're are going to find the person and, as well, discover how military secrets were obtained. Corporal McPhee will separate you into three equal teams. Each team will tear the walls open to expose any hidden passageways. I know they exist, but it's up to you to find them. Now, I leave you to your C.O. to turn you loose." Arvid stepped aside and watched the big man take charge. As he watched McPhee, Arvid could see the similarity to his son Leo. Big boned and solid like a tree trunk, Arvid could see how Leo might look as he got older.

Minutes later, the wrecking crew descended on the hotel. Confused by the sudden entry by all the crowbar packing men, the desk clerk tried to intervene, but was merely pushed aside. In the confusion, guests, who had no connection to he military, grabbed their belongings, but could not get by the three female armed guards posted at the entrance. Everyone exiting was required show identification, that was logged in and recorded. There were no exceptions. Starting at the suspected third floor window, it was quickly discovered that the shooter had been waiting in the room for more than a day. This was a carefully planned attack. A small mark was found where the shooter had erected a tripod. With the location discovered, it was on to the next part of the plan.

With a contractor's eye, one of the soldier's pointed to where the hidden cavities might be built into the walls, going from floor with the Corporal, the carpenter showed the wrecking crew what to look for. Once the pattern was established, it took no time for a hidden hallway to be discovered leading to all the rooms in the hotel. It was built into the walls when the hotel was built some 70 years before. With all three floors being accessible to peeping Toms or to all the 'safes', the hotel was just a means to, either blackmail or steal from guests.

There would be no way of knowing how many people had been compromised over the years. One benefit of the unannounced raid, was the attempt by an employee to escape through a heating vent. She was stopped by a very diligent soldier, who held the would-be escapee until Arvid and the Corporal arrived. Arvid was surprised to find that it was one of the girls who delivered his meal.

Taking her to a room, while the crew continued to dismantle the hotel, McPhee and Arvid could see that she was going to be uncooperative. Arvid was now aware that her playful demeanor was simply an act. This girl was a seasoned spy. She had been trained by professionals.

"OK, Hazel, you can stop the act now," Arvid said, as he sat her roughly into a chair. " I know that you have been stealing secrets from the wall safes. As a prisoner of war, you will be treated with as much compassion as required. Now that I've told you, it's up to you how much torment you can take. First of all, what's your name?" Arvid was prepared to spend as much time or pain was required to procure answers. He looked over at the Corporal. He was not about to interfere.

"None of your business. If you want to put me in jail, go ahead. I'm not afraid of Churchill."

"No. I don't think I will put you in jail. I'll keep you here in the hotel for a day, and then let you go. The Corporal here will let it be known that you spilled your guts and told us everything. When word gets out that you cooperated fully with the British, your friends in the SS will make certain you will be handsomely honored. Perhaps with a bullet or maybe a barracks party with twenty of your fellow male Nazis. So, sweetheart, you don't have to say a word. You have already been a big help. We're going to leave you to think about your future, and in case you try to exit by the window, I've already asked our carpenter to board it up." As Arvid spoke, the light suddenly disappeared when a sheet of wood was placed over the opening. There was now only one way of escape, but the hundred pound young lady would have to get past two very determined armed guards standing at the door. There was a silence as 'Hazel' contemplated her future. Seeing the enclosed space was beginning to have the desired affect,

Arvid motioned to McPhee to leave her alone with her thoughts. Ensuring the prisoner saw the two Provost guards standing just outside the door, Arvid and the Corporal left 'Hazel' to her fate.

"What 's going to happen if she has a cyanide pill in her teeth? McPhee asked, as they walked to the front entrance. Arvid smiled. "I don't really give a damn if she does. She's a goddam spy, and whatever happens to her is not my concern. We know now that Joshua was successful, even though he died doing his job. The Nazis are worried. We took down six of the German bombers with his device, and they retaliated by killing the Major. This is a blow to their plans. This hotel housed all the command center employees. Just think how much information they have gained from being able to listen in on conversations and access documents placed in their phony safes. You did good, Corporal. You can a call off the troops now. I'm declaring this place off limits."

As Corporal McPhee looked around at destroyed walls and rooms, he laughed. "I've got to admit. this has been the most fun I've had since I joined the Army. Thanks for the opportunity to make a difference. It's frustrating, sometimes, to have to follow the rules. Are you Canadians always this crazy?" then realizing he was speaking to his superior office, he blushed, "I'm sorry, sir, I just meant.."

"It's alright Corporal, sometimes it just makes sense to bend the rules" They both laughed and shook hands, as the troops assembled for their final orders.

****

May 8, 1941. With only one air raid during the night, St. Thomas was reasonably quiet.

Cathy got her overnight bag ready to leave for her next assignment. Lying to the Chief Surgeon was painful, but, being asked by the Queen of England to perform a task in support of the war effort, it was an assignment she could not refuse. Waiting in the vestibule of the Hospital, Catherine Romanov wondered how she got to this point in her life. The news that she was related to Czar Nicholas of Russia, and that the entire family had been murdered by Bolsheviks, was shocking. She read about the event when she attended University, and when some fellow students asked her if she was related, she answered, no. It was quite possible her father did not make the connection either.

Finally, the Land Rover arrived and she ran down the steps to her destiny. Getting in, she was surprised to see Chris driving.

"Where are we going, driver?" she asked, seeing Chris smiling. She was beginning to appreciate him and his easy going nature. He was tall and well built, like her brother, Arvid, but Cathy knew that Arvid had a dark side that could be deadly. She hoped Chris Peterson would prove to be as resourceful as King George intimated.

"They have a plane waiting in Northolt. We can fly from there to the boat." Chris replied, reaching across to hold Cathy's hand. She did not pull away. It was comforting to know that someone really cared about her, so far away from home. Twenty minutes later, a short distance from London in a small place called South Ruislip, they drove right out onto the tarmac. A plane was idling as they approached. It wasn't a passenger plane. It appeared to be a fighter aircraft.

"We're going in this?" she asked, incredulous, where am I going to sit?" she shouted. Chris put his arm around her and led her to a group of men standing beside the plane. One of them took her bag, and climbing a ladder, placed it in the rear comportment. Another airman fixed her with a parachute, making certain it was secure. "See this?" he asked, pointing to a wooden handle. "if you have to bail out, wait until you're free of the plane, pull this and hang on." he said in Cathy's ear. She watched as Chris put on a similar 'chute, and shook hands with the ground crew.

"Who's going to fly this thing?" she asked, trying to understand the procedure.

"Captain Peterson. Don't worry, he hasn't crashed a plane yet....... this week," the man replied, laughing. Taking Cathy by the hand, he helped her up the ladder and as she climbed into the rear compartment, he assisted hooking up her safety harness. " if you do run into trouble, pull this lever. It will release the canopy. Good luck, and have a nice flight with the Royal Air Force." he added, laughing. As the ground crew member closed the canopy, she watched as Chris climbed into the cockpit ahead. He looked back and gave Cathy a 'thumbs up'. She returned the gesture.

Within a minute, the engine on the Fairey Fulmar roared to life and instantly the plane began to move over the ground. Picking up a headset hanging on a hook, she placed them over her ears, if only to cover the sound of the exhaust. Chris's voice was now in her head.

"We're going Castletown. We can't talk to anyone until we get there. We're on radio silence. This is just for you and I at the moment, " he said, as the plane rose into the sky. They were not that far off the ground. "it's a low level flight to stay out of the radar. The less people know where we are, the better. How do you feel, Lieutenant?" The question was unexpected. Çathy was becoming more interested in Captain Peterson as time went by. He seemed to be full of surprises. She recalled more of King George's words. "Chris can take care of most situations" This was definitely a situation.

"I'm fine, Captain. Where are we going?" Can we fly to our destination?" she asked, hoping that this conversation was truly private.

"We're going to Castletown. They just improved the airstrip, and it's close to the wharf. Just sit back and relax. We'll be there in ten minutes. Enjoy the scenery." Cathy took the advice and looked at the ground they were traveling over. There were signs of bomb damage in places, with houses and factories in ruin. This was random bombing. The purpose was to break the sprit

133

of the British, but it was doing exactly the opposite. Resolve was growing. Even with the injured soldiers and airmen in St. Johns Hospital, they couldn't wait to get back out and delivery a beating on the Germans.

Chris Peterson was off by three minutes, but as the plane circled the runway, Cathy could see boats moored at a nearby wharf. She could not see anything big enough to go across the ocean to Morocco. As the Fairey Fulmar landed, many hands came out to meet the passenger. Climbing down the ladder, someone grabbed the parachute. Studying it, the mechanic laughed. "Good job you didn't have to use this, Mum, he said, showing to his fellow ground crew, " theres no chute in it.

Cathy looked over at Chris, who showed her his chute. "It didn't matter about the parachute. We were only flying a 1000 feet, so there wouldn't be time to open it and land without breaking your back. It was only there to make you feel safe." he said, trying to make it sound like an apology.

For a moment, Cathy was about to tear a strip off his Chris's hide, but looked around at the men who were there to make the area and planes safe, and she just laughed.

"Well, it worked. It was nice trip and I'm glad I'm here. Now what?" she asked, as Chris took her by hand, leading her to a small shack that was being used as a communications center.

Once inside, a small woman in civilian clothes, handed Cathy and Chris their new Passports.

"We have clothes for you, and two small suitcases. There is nothing in the clothes or suitcases that could be construed as spycraft, so if you are stopped and searched, they will find nothing to incriminate you. Dr. Kravitz is believed to still be in Rabat. He may be injured. That is the reason we are sending you, Lieutenant." and directing her attention to Chris, "we are sending you to protect the Lieutenant. We have given you 10,000 Francs, which you can trade for whatever they are using for currency, at the moment. As Mr. and Mrs. Peterson, you will have to have a plausible background. We have made up a file for you to read. After you learn it, burn it!"

Chris looked at Cathy and shrugged. This was getting more complicated all the time. "when do we leave?" Chris asked, looking out at the setting sun. The woman, who never offered her name, checked her watch. "You'll be boarding the boat in another hour. The Captain knows nothing about your mission. He was told that the lieutenant has relatives in Morocco, and you want to visit before the war makes it impossible. Although Canadians are part of the British Empire, the French do not consider Canadians enemies of France. It's just the Vichy, who have sucked up to Hitler under Marshall Petain. Morrocco is still mainly a free zone, but as the Germans take more of Algeria, Morocco is going to be overrun by Nazis. That's why it's imperative we move now to extricate Dr. Kravitz before he is captured by the Germans." The anonymous woman sat back down and pulled out a camera. Turning on a desk lamp, she aimed it at Mr. And Mrs. Peterson, she snapped several shots. "Just in case Churchill asks if we're doing our job. " she said, putting the camera back in a drawer, " he's kind of anxious to get Kravitz out of Morocco. Now, go change you clothes. You are a couple of newlyweds who are just out for a holiday." As she spoke, she handed both Cathy and Chris a handful of French francs, " here is some seed money. If you need more, we'll get it to you somehow, because we can't trust the Banks now. " Feeling the briefing was over, Cathy picked up the bundle of clothing and retired to a washroom. Chris changed in front of the Mission Chief, much to her delight.

The time had arrived to board the fishing boat. Cathy was nervous when she saw the size of the vessel that was to transfer them across the Celtic Sea and out into the Atlantic Ocean. The large bearded man stuck out his hand as they crossed over the gunwale and onto the weather-beaten deck, "My name is Captain Cortez. I can see by the look on your face, Mrs., that you don't believe we will make out of the harbor. This boat has been modified to look exactly the way. It is less than a year old. It is equipped with the latest in electronic surveillance and has dual tanks for extended range. To anyone looking at it, it will appear to be exactly as you believed at first glance. An old fishing boat that has seen better times. We have a cabin for you, as well as for my crew of three. Now, if you will go below and stow your gear, we'll be off." Cathy could see that Captain Cortez was a 'no nonsense' sailor with more years of experience than her years on earth.

"Thank you Captain," Chris said, as he guided his 'wife' down the companionway to the cabin area. The satisfying sound of a large diesel engine meant that the Cosmo 11, carrying Mr. and Mrs. Peterson, was under way. Cathy could see, upon entering the small cabin, that she and Chris would get to know each other quickly. With only one double bed and a washroom down the hall, the night spent at sea would be an experience for both of them. Sitting on the bed, Chris looked at Cathy and smiled. "Well, Mrs., here we are on our honeymoon aboard the cruise ship that your mother planned for us. It's going to take two nights to get to Rabat, so if you want a divorce, speak up, because soon we'll be in international waters, and it will be too late." He was smiling as he spoke. Cathy sat in a chair across from the man with whom she had been paired. Studying his face, she realized that things could be worse. Chris was quite handsome, and she could see that if she had to spend time with someone in a room on the ocean, he would be a good choice. Queen Elizabeth and King George had chosen well. After an hour of travel, there was a knock on the door.

"Excuse me, Señor, we are having a meal in the galley. Would you like to join us. Soon we will be into heavier seas and the Cook will not be able to serve." He was looking at Cathy, but directing the question to Chris. Chris looked over at Cathy and offered his hand. Together, they followed the crew member to the small galley where another man was seated. Sitting on a bench, they were treated to a bowl of soup and large chunks of buttered bread. Sitting in close quarters, Cathy felt secure with these men around her. It was an experience she completely enjoyed.

Later, as they lay side by side on the bed, they both shared their early life experiences.

"Where did you learn to speak German so well?" Cathy asked, staring at the ceiling.

"My mother was German. My father was in the Merchant Marines. When he was away, which was most of the time, we would speak German in the house. My mother hated the English that most of the locals spoke. It was some kind of pidgin English, that was hard for her to understand. My mother was killed last year in an air raid, and my father was on a ship sunk by a German U boat. So, as you can see, I have a score to settle with the Nazis. Now, go to sleep. We are going to have a busy day tomorrow." he whispered as he put his arm around her and pulled her close.

The sound of Chris's voice had a calming effect, and as sleep finally claimed them, the fear of being harmed had disappeared from Cathy's mind, and she also appreciated his arm holding her from falling out of the small, and increasingly cozy bed. The next day on the open ocean, the occasional German plane would fly over, at times doubling back for another look. The Cosmo 11 could travel at twice the speed, but Captain Cortez did not want to draw attention to the fishing boat's hidden talents. As they passed the 36th degree latitude, there was considerable ship traffic entering and leaving the Gibraltar strait. The morning was dawning bright and beautiful, and the heat made itself known This was not the cool of a London mist, it was just off the coast of Africa, and Captain Cortez watched the skies constantly for spotter planes. At 11 a.m. on the morning of the 12th, the Captain made note of a plane dropping down for a better look at the Cosmo 11.

Shouting orders in Portuguese to a member of his crew, the crew member immediately took Chris and Cathy below, leading them to a row of lockers. Opening one, he reached for coveralls. Picking two that would fit, he handed them to Cathy and her puzzled 'husband'. Dressing quickly, the crew member took Cathy to the engine room, where he placed a bit of grease on her face. Handing her gloves, he said, "Stay here, Look busy." Hurrying back to Chris, he led the big Brit to the bow and handed him a hawser. 'Look busy!" then returned to the wheel house to be by his Captain's side.

Within minutes, the sea parted and a large sail of a submarine rose from the surface, causing the Cosmo 11 to rock from side to side. A voice came from the German sub.

The Cosmo11 was ordered to stop. Complying with orders issued in Spanish, Captain Cortez shut down the engine and drifted in the swells. Moments later, a hawser was thrown from the deck of the Sub., while Chris and a fellow crew member fastened to the Cosmo's cleats. The German vessel was enormous next to the Cosmo 11. Several Nazis stood on deck with guns at the ready.

A very officious SS Officer stepped aboard the fishing vessel, nearly falling into the sea in the process. Assisted by three armed submariners, the Officer pulled Captain Cortez out onto the deck.

"Where are you going?" What is your purpose here?" the Officer asked, motioning for his underlings to search the ship. As the three went below decks, the Officer inspected the ship's log.

"I am going to Casablanca and picking up supplies and fuel. We have permission to fish offshore.

What is you want? Do you want a portion of my catch at the end of the week? We have been permitted to fish for three weeks." the Captain replied, trying to keep the Officer from spotting the white skinned Englishman holding the bow rope improperly.

"I don't want your stinking fish. All you Greaseballs make me sick. We have had reports of a spy ship in these waters. Do you have any weapons on board?" The Officer kept a hand on his Luger, but didn't take it from its holster. Captain Cortez shook his head.

"We have a small rifle to shoot sharks that end up in our nets and destroy them, but other than that, we don't need guns." and checking his watch, added "we must make high tide at 6 pm in Rabat so we can reach the fuel depot."

Down below decks, the submariners checked all the rooms for passengers, and finally came to the engine room. Opening the hatch, they looked in to see someone with a pipe wrench on a valve. Watching for a moment, the German closed the hatch and returned with his companions to the surface, grabbing several slices of bread on their way through the galley. The Cook did not resist.

Arriving back on deck, they reported nothing special on board. Satisfied he had frightened the Portuguese into submission, the Officer nodded to the three men to board the Sub. Within minutes, large amounts of air and water boiled around the Cosmo 11, and the submarine vanished beneath the waves. His passenger approached the Captain, but Cortez would not look at him.

"Just go about your business. The Submarine has not gone away. The Captain is watching us with his periscope. He wants to see us celebrate. Just go and coil some rope or something. When we get underway again, Raul will teach you the proper way to hold a hawser." Chris turned away and made himself look a real seaman. He was, after all, a pilot, not a sailor.

Later in the afternoon, as the coast of Morocco hove into view, it was time for Cathy and Chris to get ready. They did not know how they were going to find the Doctor. Checking the time and charts, Captain Cortez was satisfied that the tide was sufficient to ease the Cosmo 11 into Rabat harbor, past the breakwaters and into the wharf for fuel. Still wearing their coveralls, the Petersons, carrying a large bucket containing their luggage between them, were led to a shed by the Captain. Inside, they stripped the overalls and with civil clothes underneath, were shown to a stairway leading down to a walkway. Bidding goodbye to the Captain, Cathy and Chris made their way ashore along the dock to the town. Dressed in western style clothes, it soon became evident that they would have to blend in, rather than be the object of suspicion. Finding a Cab, they asked to be driven to clothing shop. The Moroccan driver was most helpful to the 'Americans'. Not bothering to correct the error, the Cab dropped them at a small shop on Sidi Sahraoui. As they got out of the cab, Chris could see a man on a bicycle watching them carefully. Paying off the grateful driver, Cathy and her man entered the store. The owner was surprised to see foreigners in his small shop. Gracious, nonetheless, he showed them clothing that would allow them to somewhat blend into the population. A half hour later, they exited, after causing much happiness in the shop owner's family.

The money given by the mission chief was greatly appreciated by a Moroccan who was afraid of the upcoming war landing on the streets of Rabat.

Walking along the street, they were no longer stared at by the locals. As they turned a corner, the bicycle man approached them.

"Would you like a guide for the city?" he asked, speaking with a very pronounced Arabian accent.

"No thank you," Chris replied as they stepped around the persistent individual. He did not a take the hint. "But I can see you are searching for something." he added, as he walked beside them. He was noisy enough to attract attention from others as they walked along looking in windows.

Then quietly he said, "I think I know what you seek, Lieutenant." Cathy missed a step and stumbled. She put out her hand to stop her fall, resting it on the stranger's shoulder.

"What do you know?" she whispered, as Chris helped her to a park bench. The man held on to her hand, slipping a note into it. "I have been told you were coming. The Vichy are holding your man in a compound in Casablanca. He has been injured. You must be very careful." he whispered as he pretended to pick up change dropped by Chris. Backing away, expressing his love of Mohamed and the blessed Quran, the man slipped into the passing foot traffic and disappeared. Cathy did not open the note immediately, but pulled her kaftan around her, and looked into her hand as she unfolded the paper. An address was written in strange script. She looked at Chris. "how do you feel about going to Casablanca?" she whispered, as Chris took her by the arm, looking for another Cab. Ten minutes of bargaining proved to be expensive, but as the old Chrysler pulled out onto the road south, both Cathy Romanov and Chris Peterson knew that the most dangerous part of their mission was ahead in the Vichy controlled town of Casablanca.

****

On the Firth of Forth in Scotland, Commander Arvid Romanov watched as an old Land Rover pulled to a stop in front of the Command center. After all the problems in the past month that ensued from trashing the hotel, and authorizing divers to enter the German sub that sunk near the Isle of May, Arvid Romanov was happy to hear that Whitehall had picked someone else to look after the Forth and its attendant problems. As a Civilian drafted into the Military, he was not comfortable with having to make decisions about the radar installation at Drone Hill, or about aircraft at Drem.

He knew he was filling in until someone with RAF credentials could take over, so he was being relieved by an RAF lifer. Major Carter. Dressed in a crisp new uniform, the older man walked casually to the door as the Land Rover drove back through the nearby lumber yard. Waiting at the door, Arvid was happy to turn over the command of the center to the British again. Saluting Major Carter, Arvid could see that this officer was a 'by the book ' lifetime military.

"Good day, Commander," he said as he walked with the Canadian, " I understand you have had your fill of spies and such here. Well, Commander, we'll show these Nazis that they can't play silly buggers with the Queen's finest. I hear you have been called to Whitehall. I'm sure you'll be placed somewhere at little less stressful." Arvid was puzzled by Major Carter's attitude.

"I'm sure you'll find everyone here helpful." Arvid commented, as they arrived at Charlotte's desk.

The Major looked at Lithgow's former Adjutant and shrugged. "Well, we will run this place like a professional. It will take no time to correct this wild west attitude that has crept into the Royal Air Force and Army. Thank you for your help, Commander, but I think I'm capable of taking it from here." With those words, and a sloppy, unprofessional salute, Arvid was dismissed. Charlotte looked at him and shrugged. His time at the Forth command center was over. Collecting his duffel bag, Arvid walked away from the arrogant Major and made his way to the parking lot under cover in a nearby warehouse. The message from Whitehall was short and to the point. He was to be at Westminster in London in 24 hours. Walking into the darkened building, he could see a mechanic working on a Lorry. Three Land Rovers, a flatbed and two old Humbers. The mechanic slid out from beneath the Lorry, stood and saluted. "Good day, sir. What can I do for you?"

"I'm supposed to pick up a vehicle here. Do you have one that will make as far as London?" Arvid asked, leaning against the fender of the unwashed Humber. It was an ugly looking vehicle, but as long as it kept running, it was good enough, compared to some of vehicles he had driven over the rough roads of Saskatchewan. The mechanic got in the Humber and started it. It rumbled to life.

Saluting again as he exited the car, the mechanic smiled. "There you are, sir. One of Britain's finest. It's full of petrol and should make it to London without problems." Arvid nodded his head, and returned the salute. Getting into the tank-like auto, he was surprised at the feel of the power as he exited the warehouse. This was going to an experience. Checking the map given him by

142

Charlotte, Arvid made his way through Edinburgh, searching for the road south. Arriving a stop sign, he was about to make the turn when the back doors opened, and two men got in.

One immediately stuck a military issue .45 against his head. Checking the rear view mirror, Arvid could see both men wore masks, and appeared to be some type of militia.

"Take the next right and head north. We're going for a little drive." The accent was definitely Scottish. Arvid did as instructed. The British issue revolver in the holster on his hip would be of little use against semi automatic pistol, even if he could reach and use it.

Guiding him with a prod of the gun to his neck, Arvid drove carefully, unaccustomed to driving on the left side of the road. After few missed turns, they headed east to a town called Dundee. With 24 hours allowed to arrive at Whitehall, he would not be missed immediately. Another hour of navigating the winding road, he was directed to the dock area. Moving slowly along the wharf, he was told to stop at an old freighter. Tempted to reach for his weapon, he was thwarted when one of his captors reached over the seat and removed the six shooter. Walking with a gun at his back, Arvid was forced to climb the ladder on the side of the rusted ship. Reaching the deck, they entered a passageway and then down to, what appeared to be a supply room. A table in the middle of the floor was equipped with a chain and handcuffs. This was not a good sign. Pushing their captive into the chair, they grabbed Arvid's arms and clicked on the Military Police style cuffs.

Finally, they removed their hoods. One was young while the other was grey haired and bearded.

They pulled up chairs from the wall and leaned on the table. They studied Arvid like a specimen.

Arvid was puzzled, but when the door opened, it became clear that this was going to be a painful session. The man was dressed in Russian garb from the Steppes. Unlike his fellow kidnappers, he seemed to be Mongol. He stood between his henchmen, who moved to give him room.

"I am finally pleased to meet, Mr. Romanov. My name is Vladimir. When I first heard your name, I was unsure if you were the one I wanted, but looking at you, I can see you were a good choice."

"What do you want?" Arvid was trying to understand what this bizarre abduction was about. "are you German? Do you think I have some kind of state secrets?" He looked at the other two who seemed to be following their leader's words. Vladimir laughed.

"I don't give a shit about the Germans. I don't really care if the Americans enter the fight, or England wins the war. I am Russian. We have a history that reaches far back beyond the Hitlers of this world. In 1918, we got rid of the monarchy. We believed that killing the Czar would free us from royal domination, and for 24 years we have lived as Lenin wanted. I am Bulshevik, and proud of it. When I heard that a relative of the Romanovs was still alive, I knew you had to be eliminated." Vladimir walked around behind Arvid and placed a hand on Arvid's neck.

"What are you talking about. Just because my name is Romanov, doesn't mean I have anything to do with the Tsar, 24 years ago." Arvid argued, "I'm a Canadian. Born in Saskatchewan. What the hell do I have to do with the Bulsheviks?" Arvid was beginning to see that the Officer's uniform he was wearing was not the reason for his kidnapping. The man released his grip and returned to face his prize captive.

"We have information that your grandfather was the Czar's brother."

The words hit Arvid like a sledgehammer. Is this what the killer who was pinned under the car in 1935 meant when he said to check with his father. Petrov Romanov did not seem to know his father's early life or reveal any secrets about Peter Romanov. It was quite possible that Peter was trying to shield Petrov from any connection to the people who murdered his brother. Moving to Canada may have been the only way to isolate the Romanovs from the crazy Marxists who killed the Tsar and his entire family. Arvid sat and pondered his future.

"What are you going to do me?" Kill me?" Arvid asked. The question seemed to cause the two henchmen to look up at their leader. It appeared to be a problem that was also on their minds.

"I have been ordered to take you to Moscow. My superiors want to see you in person. I have been told that the very nursemaid who birthed your grandfather can identify you. She is 97 years old, and will be the last person who can prove that you are a Romanov." There seemed to a relief of tension in the room. They were not going to kill the prisoner. It was not clear in Arvid's mind how a woman who was helping with the Tsar's birth, would know if he was related to a baby 74 years later, but did not argue. It would mean he would not die in the bowels of a rusted old ship in the harbor of Dundee, Scotland. Vladimir walked to the door. "Release the Canadian and put him in number two cabin. I will go talk to the Captain and get this boat moving. Make certain he has food and water. We have to deliver him to our Comrades in good shape." The henchmen nodded understanding and unlocked Arvid's handcuffs.

"Let's go. Don't do anything stupid, and you will survive another day, now, move." the older man whispered, advice Arvid was keen to follow. With two guns at his back, heroics would prove fatal.

****

Far to the south, Lieutenant Cathy Romanov and Captain Chris Peterson could see the smoke from outdoor kitchens as they neared Casablanca.

The driver, thankfully, did not question his passengers, feeling with Germans taking over Morocco, the safest path to getting home at night, was to just do his job and not ask questions. After some confusion, they arrived at a small hotel located in the Vichy controlled quarter of Casablanca. The Cab driver, with great flourish, took the two pieces of luggage to the front desk. It was important for both Mr. and Mrs. Peterson to be seen as simply tourists. Paying the Cab driver an exorbitant amount, in full view of the Desk Clerk, Cathy spoke to the Clerk in French. He was more than happy to accommodate the free spending Canadians, explaining that he had a cousin living in a town called Quebec.

"After these animals leave our country, I plan on emigrating to Canada and hopefully never see sand or Muslims again." he admitted, taking the French Francs with a glee that was impossible to hide. A small boy came from the back room and struggled to take two suitcases to the second floor.

Slipping the Clerk's son another ten Francs, the newlyweds were shown the amenities. Running water, doors that opened out onto a terrace. The weather was beautiful but hot, and changing into more sensible clothing, it was time to locate the address on the paper Cathy had already destroyed. Finding a map in a side table, they studied it, trying to understand the convoluted numbers and names written in both English, French and Arabic. Finding a driver willing to take the two visitors on a tour of the city, required lying to a very official Vichy Officer who was suspicious of the pair's intentions, until Cathy explained the death of her father in a construction accident. She wanted to visit the site while before they left for South Africa. Using all her considerable charm and persuasion, the Commandant agreed to allow them to visit a street next to the Avenue de Force Auxilliare. The Cab driver offered to pick them up within the hour. Dropped off on the corner of the street, it became obvious that this was a military area, with German and French vehicles parked at odd angles in line along the laneway. It was chilling to see German Officers standing in an alcove, smoking and discussing important matters.

"We'll have to find out where the Doctor is being held. This is the right address, but he could be in any one of the buildings. We can't just go up and ask the Gestapo where the prisoner is." Cathy mused, as they stayed out of sight.

Chris smiled. "Why not? These guys are trained to take orders from the Fuhrer. We'll come back here tonight, but first, we need a vehicle. Let's go back to the hotel and do a little more planning. Besides, I'm hungry, and I heard there is a place called Rick's Place where we might make a deal.

It is apparently a joint run by an Expat. American." With the decision made, they had the grateful taxi driver return them to their hotel. As night fell, Cathy and Chris arrived at the bar where there seemed to be a good number of American, French and Moroccans enjoying the freedom from the constant inspection by the German Gestapo. Although there were a few Germans in uniform, they seemed to be unconcerned with the arrival of two more celebrants. Sitting at the bar, the bartender took an instant interest in the new attractive woman who spoke French with an accent. Nursing two drinks, it wasn't long before a denizen came and sat beside Cathy.

"You new here? I can show you guys around the city." he said, eyeing the bottle of Scotch whisky placed before the pair. Chris took the bottle, and motioning to the bartender, filled the man's glass.

There was sign of life in the man's eyes, as he sipped on God's nectar.

"We need a vehicle. Can you get us a car. We want to tour the city tomorrow, but the Taxi drivers are afraid of the Gestapo. Think you can find one. We can pay you." Chris added, refilling the man's glass. The man put the glass to his forehead, feeling the cool against his fevered skin.

"Sure. I'll talk to Rick. He's got a couple old wrecks he keeps to chauffeur his women to work. When do you want it?" he asked, emptying the contents once again. Cathy could see the definite signs of alcohol poisoning on his skin. The man nodded then turned and wandered in to another part of the Bar room.

"What do you think? Think he will remember what he was supposed to do?" Cathy asked.

"It doesn't matter. We've got job to do." he was about to continue when a man in a rumpled, but expensive, suit approached and stood beside the bartender. Studying Cathy and Chris for a long minute. he asked. "You the couple who want to rent one of my automobiles?" It was obvious that this was Rick, and there would be no double dealing. As Chris was about to speak, three Gestapo Officers entered, and pulling two customers from their seats, sat down, expecting instant service.

Rick watched the reaction of both Cathy and Chris to the arrival of the Germans.

"You guys are not just visitors, are you?" a chill went down Cathy's spine. Did Rick see something that showed his hatred of the Nazis in Chris's reaction. There was moment when no one spoke.

"Alright. I'll rent you a car. It looks like you have something besides sightseeing in mind, but I don't care. " and turning his head, motioned for a Waiter to come close, "see what the Germans want, and after you serve them, go pick up the Chevy out back and make sure it's got gas in it." The young Arab nodded his head and went directly to the table.

"How long do you need it for? Whatever you have in mind, when you're finished with it, just leave it someplace with the keys on the right rear tire. That'll be 5000 Francs." he said, turning to the Bartender, adding, "get these people a seat at a table. They deserve a good meal. We try to look after our friends." Rick added, "and good luck with whatever you have in mind." Cathy handed Rick 5000 Francs, which he just shoved in his pocket, like loose change.

The evening was turning into a pleasant experience, even having to listen to the German Officers, who got louder as they drank free liquor delivered by the frightened Arab Waiter. Finishing their excellent meal, Mr. and Mrs. Peterson waved to Rick as they left, finding the old Chevy parked on the street at the front entrance of the Café. Driving back to the hotel, Chris kept his eye on the rear view mirror. Dropping Cathy off at the hotel, Chris reached over and kissed his 'wife'. "Get ready to leave when I get back. Have the luggage ready. We're leaving here tonight." Cathy stepped from the car and nodded. The kiss was a nice touch, and appreciated.

Assembling everything, as instructed, Cathy took the two suitcases down and waited in the shadows. Although the night was warm, she was shivering.

Within twenty minutes, she froze as she saw a German Officer drive up to the door. She tried to hide, but the SS officer waved her to the vehicle. She couldn't believe the transformation. It was Chris. With perfectly fitting SS uniform and hat at just the angle, her 'husband' was now a German Officer. Not asking any questions, she got in and smiled at her driver. He was certainly a good looking German Officer. Driving to the Compound, Chris drove right up to the door. There seemed to be no one attending the gate. Pulling up to the guard post, Chris stopped and got out.

Opening the door, there was a brief struggle, and Chris reappeared. Suddenly another German soldier appeared. He seemed confused as Chris addressed him in very strict language. With much apologizing, the soldier led his Commanding Officer toward another building. Chris motioned Cathy to join him, as they walked toward a small building at the rear of the compound. Opening the door. Cathy stepped in behind Chris and the confused guard. One sharp blow to the chest, and the German fell to the floor.

Cathy quickly checked the guard's pulse. Looking up at Chris, she said, "He's dead!" Chris nodded approval. In the corner, another man, older and seemingly incoherent, reached up, looking for help.

"Dr. Kravitz? We've come to take you home." Cathy said, wrapping the frail man in a blanket. Moments later, stepping over the body of the dead guard, they loaded the Doctor into the Chevy and drove out of the compound just as another vehicle rounded the corner. It was filled the guard detail who were just arriving for their shift. Cathy sat in the rear seat with her patient, as Chris drove west out of Casablanca to the Anfa airstrip. Driving through the night, Chris watched the mirror for any sign of a pursuit. Cathy did her best to keep the Doctor from wanting to jump from the vehicle. It was obvious he had been drugged. Probably some type of sodium pentathol. Minutes later, Chris drove onto the darkened runway. Several aircraft were parked in a line. Stopping at a Fokker trimotor, Chris opened the hatch and climbed in. Moments later, he was back at the Chevy. Helping Cathy, Chris lifted the delirious patient into the plane. Cathy entered after him trying to find a place, in the dark, to lay the thrashing man.

"I'll hold him down, Cathy. You go get the luggage!" Chris said, trying to control the Doctor's arms.

Within a minute, Cathy was back, throwing the luggage into the cavernous interior, allowing Chris to enter the cockpit. The sound of an engine starting was a wake up call for the four guards who stumbled to the door, trying to see in the darkness, who was stealing one of their planes. In their haste to get dressed, one of the men knocked over an oil lamp, setting fire to the building. In the Fokker, Chris had finally started the second engine providing enough thrust to get the aircraft moving. As he aimed at the airstrip, a huge ball of fire erupted at the far end of airport. With only two motors pulling the Fokker forward, it was with some relief that the third finally coughed and came to life. There was now enough power to lift the aircraft free of the ground. A bullet buzzed past his nose. With hands full, he could not immediately respond, but with the Fokker under control, he pulled the Luger and fired out the open window. Seconds later the Trimotor lifted from the earth and was airborne. Below, he could see, by the light of the burning building, another vehicle pulling onto the airstrip. Several people were shooting in the air, but the plane was now far enough away, there would be no danger.

"How's your patient, Cathy?" Chris shouted, as he banked away from Casablanca. He would have to stay out over the Atlantic to avoid any land based weapons. Although Morocco was still a French protectorate, the Germans were moving in heavy guns and equipment in their rush to take over Algeria, which made setting down in Morocco a very bad idea. As the engines droned on, Chris checked the fuel tanks. Although the Fokker was built for long distance, it needed fuel in the tanks to do that. Without enough fuel to reach the Tenerife, and with the German controlling the Mediterranean around Spain, Chris decided on reaching Faro in Portugal. Although Portugal was neutral, he was flying a German plane dressed as a German Officer. In the darkness, it was only following compass readings that would allow him to hit Portugal rather than Spain. Calculating the distance in his head, Chris felt that he had enough fuel to make it as far as Faro, but the Trimotor would be sucking fumes. He could shut down one motor, but that would increase the load on the other motors, causing them to use more fuel. It would be a gamble. Using the radio would alert the Germans to his position. Cathy, having held the Doctor until he calmed down, feared that the large gash on the Doctor's head, possibly from a gun butt, may have caused a concussion. Doctor Kravitz would need proper medical attention soon, or the whole exercise would have been for naught. As light brightened the eastern sky. The outline of Portugal's southern coast became clear. With fuel dangerously low, there would be only one shot at finding a runway near Faro. Chatter on the radio proved that the theft of a plane in Casablanca did not go unnoticed. Flying low to avoid any radar, the land mass grew large in the windscreen. With the glass shot out on the left side window, the constant buffeting was causing Chris to lose concentration at a time when it was most important. Cathy came up into the cockpit.

"How is the Doctor? Is he going to make it?" Chris asked, as Cathy sat in the co-pilots' seat.

"I think he's going to be alright. We have to get him to a hospital as soon as we can. Where are we?" The Fokker was now over land and even at 120 mph, it seemed that they were moving much too slow. "Take the wheel. I've got to change my clothes. If we're in Portugal, I'll be shot. According to the radio, There is a shoot to kill order by the Luftwaffe on us." With that, Chris got up and disappeared into the back. Cathy was now tasked with keeping the plane in a straight line. No easy feat with a brutal onshore wind from the Atlantic. She could see houses and farms below, but had no idea what country they belonged to. A few minutes later, Chris returned, dressed in a pants and shirt, but no shoes. "OK, Kiddo, let's see where we are. Pulling back on the wheel, the Fokker rose in altitude quite quickly. Minutes later the whole expense on land was visible. Moments later, a small airstrip came into view, just as number one motor cut out. They were out of gas.

"you had better go back and make sure the Doctor doesn't move too much if the landing isn't textbook." Chris said laughing. But before Cathy left, he grabbed her by the arm and brought her close, and kissed her. She kissed him back. Now anxious to get back on the ground, Chris circled the airstrip, noticing a horse and wagon moving slowly across the airfield. The farmer was stopped. looking up, then realized he was on the runway. As number three engine cut out, there was only one chance to land the brick with wings. Lining up into the wind, Chris eased the Trimotor down and felt the wheels touch mother earth. The short runway was not built for a Trimotor, but other than taking out a few shrubs in the adjacent field, the landing was a success. There was just silence as the main motor stopped. It was now up to God to save them. Walking back through the fuselage, he stopped as Cathy held up her hand. For a moment they were as one human body.

Opening the side hatch, Chris jumped out onto solid ground. The one farmer had become many.

Armed with pitch forks and shovels, they approached the aircraft. Chris held up his hands in surrender. As they came closer, he could see they were as curious as he. There was a definite chance that they would attack, but suddenly they stopped and put down their weapons. Chris turned and looked back at the plane. Cathy was standing beside the plane.

A woman made her way through the gathering crowd, passing Chris and crossing directly to Cathy. After a few words in French, it was determined that they were, indeed in Portugal. Moments later, the farmers had placed the Doctor in the wagon, and like a procession to Church, men, women and children walked with the wagon into town. Hand in hand, Lieutenant Cathy Romanov and Captain Cristopher Peterson walked with them.

****

On a freighter making its way across the North Sea, Arvid Romanov sat on a bunk in his cabin, contemplating his fate. By noon the next day, he was supposed to arrive at Whitehall in Westminster for a new assignment, but being kidnapped by Bolsheviks was not something anyone had planned on. As the cabin door opened, two men stood abreast, guns in hand, ready for an escape attempt. Another man, smaller in stature entered carrying a tray of food and a bottle schnapps. He placed it on the floor beside Arvid, nodded to the captive, smiled and turned and left, The door closed, and that was the meal for the day. It would take the entire night and next day for the Cargo ship to arrive at its destination. When the door opened once again, the two gunmen prodded Arvid across the gangplank to a waiting car. By the signage, it would appear they had arrived in Oslo, Norway. A short ride in a Van brought the trio to a rail way station. Boarding the train along with several hundred German soldiers,

Arvid could see that there was a mass exodus from Oslo to the interior. Arriving in Stockholm by 3 p.m., everyone vacated the train cars, boarding another freighter. Arvid did not appear to be noticing, but kept note of platoon and division numbers. Chained to a deck chair, German soldiers passed by, spitting on him, but the two gunmen were quick to put an end to any attempt to harm the prisoner, who was still dressed in a British Uniform. Several hours later, as night fell, the troop ship arrived in Helsinki, Finland where all the Germans disembarked, leaving only the Captain and crew to continue on. By midnight, it was obvious that the small cargo vessel had reached its destination. Leningrad, in the Soviet Union was busy with military vehicles. There was a feeling of immanent danger, but the three men who guided Arvid through the streets to a warehouse area, were fixated on doing their job. Entering, he was surprised to see rows of boxes.

Although not understanding Russian script, the containers seemed to dried foodstuff. With a gun in his back, he was pushed toward an office at the rear of the warehouse. Entering the room, he was pushed into a chair. Expecting to be handcuffed again, Arvid put his hands behind his back.

The bearded man waved his hand. "Don't bother. We know you aren't going to escape."

"Why am I here?" Arvid asked, wondering why anyone would go to all the trouble to kidnap a Commander of the British Military from Scotland and transport him all the way to Leningrad. The excuse given seemed was quite far fetched. To meet a 97 year old woman who could identify him as a Romanov, seemed like someone's dream. After some time, his guards were becoming agitated. Checking their watches, the proposed meeting was apparently behind schedule.

Finally, as the guards were about to change shifts, the door opened, and a small, winkled old woman entered. After the usual greetings, the woman walked around Arvid, inspecting him like a possible purchase at a slave market. Saying something to the guards, they relayed the message.

"She wants you to take off your shirt." the one man said, waving his rifle at the Commander.

Reluctantly, Arvid stood and pulled off his government issue jacket and shirt. The old woman put her hand on his back, then lifted his arm. After a moment, she smiled, and out of the view of the guards, winked. Putting his arm down, she patted his shoulder. Speaking to the guard, the guard was convinced. "Looks like you win the prize, Commander. Every Romanov has a small wart under their arm on their arm pit. That makes you a true Romanov. Now that we know we have a real relative of the Czar, we have to wait for a decision from our Boss We are going to keep you on ice until we get word about what to do with you" The old woman walked back and forth, studying Arvid more slowly, then spoke to the guard.

An argument ensued, with voices being raised, until finally the woman shook her head, issued some type of Russian curse, and left the room. There was a discussion between two of the Bolsheviks, until finally, one grabbed Arvid by the hair, pulling him up to his feet.

"I want to shoot you right now, but I guess it is not my decision to make. Come, we have a cell waiting for you. I think it is a waste of time, but there are others who have control of our lives." Pushing Arvid through the open door, he was led to a back door and out into the street. As Arvid buttoned his shirt, he could see there was much activity along Bobylskaya road. A short drive in a rattling old Van brought them to a house set apart from others on a street in the outskirts of Leningrad. Walking around to the rear of the building, Arvid was pushed into a basement room. It was like an apartment set aside for in-laws. "You will stay here until we receive instructions. First, take a bath. You stink." the bearded man shouted as he closed the door. Arvid could hear the men laugh as they went into the back door of the floor above. Arvid took the advice. If he was going to be shot, at least he would die without the smell of Russian cigarettes in his nostrils.

****

1300 miles to the south, Major General Sutherland stepped out of his office and spoke to his Lieutenant. " Have you heard anything from Commander Romanov? He was supposed to be here by now. Major Lithgow had a great deal of faith in him, and I would like to brief him on his next mission. Let me know the minute he arrives. We haven't much time to waste." Lieutenant Grisholm saluted and nodded his head, "Yes sir. I'll make another enquiry at the Firth of Forth.

Swinging around to the radio, he contacted the command center in Edinburgh. Writing down the information, he became alarmed. Crossing to the Major General's door, he knocked, then entered.

"Sir. It seems that Commander Romanov's vehicle was discovered by a plane spotter in a forested area north of Dundee Scotland. It had been burned. There was no body. What do you make of that, sir?" Major General Sutherland took the paper from his Assistant and studied it.

"Why weren't we notified of this when they found it. This information is six hours old. Who's in charge up there?" The lieutenant could see his commanding officer was not pleased.

"A Major Carter, sir. He just took over from Commander Romanov. You remember, you placed Commander Romanov in charge after that dreadful shooting of Major Lithgow. Apparently Major Carter felt that, because the Commander was Canadian, that it was not his concern. What do you want me to do, sir?" Lieutenant Grisholm asked, seeing the fury building in Major General's face.

"Get that nitwit Carter on the phone, and I don't care if it's too inconvenient for him, I want to talk to him personally, and make certain the call is scrambled. I don't want the Nazis to see what kind of idiots we have running the show here in England." Within minutes, Major Carter felt the wrath of Major General Sutherland's fury. "I want you to find Commander Romanov. You have no idea how important that Canadian is to the war effort. I speak for Churchill when I tell you this. Find out what happened to Commander Romanov, or you will be reduced to wrapping fish in newspapers. Do you understand?" With the message delivered, Major Carter was put on notice. Within the hour, evidence from witnesses stated that the Humber Snipe had been seen on the wharf in Dundee. The Harbor Master, who was also the Fire Marshall, recalled the Freighter Grundig V1 flying a Norwegian flag, departed shortly thereafter.

With all the information gathering apparatus available at Whitehall, the search was on for the missing Canadian Commander. Reports from a British Patrol boat operating in the North Sea, described shadowing the freighter Grundig V1 for several miles. It docked in Oslo. Another report from Norwegian partisans in Olso confirmed that a British Officer was loaded aboard a train heading for Stockholm. A Conductor on board the train reported seeing the Officer being guarded by Russians. He was afraid there would be problems with the large number of German soldiers, but as they left the train, the British Officer was still alive. Major General studied the information.

"Why would they be taking the Commander to the Soviet Union?" he asked, seeing the trail being traced onto a map. Another analyst joined Sutherland at the large rendering.

"Does he have any information that they can retrieve through torture?" he asked, not understanding why there was such an interest in the 30 year old Canadian. The Major General nodded.

"Commander Romanov has a photographic memory. He picks up things up that you and I would deem irrelevant and stores them in that big brain. If they have him anywhere where he can see, they have just committed an error. It's like carrying around a movie camera. If they don't kill him, anything he has seen in his travels will be worth its weight in TNT., besides, if he is important enough for the Soviets to kidnap, he is certainly important enough for us to rescue." The analyst caught the hint and went back to work, taking all the bits of information being fed into the system.

****

Back In Admiral, Saskatchewan, Petrov was finally able to return to the farm. With war heating up in Europe, shipments of grain and fuel increased dramatically, so that Petrov's job, as overseer, became even more important. Canada was now building tanks and aircraft for the war. There was no shortage of work. After a week relaxing in Admiral, it was time to return to work. Meeting with C.D. Howe in Ottawa, Petrov learned that Cathy had been instrumental in retrieving a nuclear scientist from German hands. Although most of the details were top secret, he was content to learn that she returned to England safely, and had resumed her nursing duties. There was still no word concerning the disappearance of Arvid. In a meeting with the Prime Minister, the importance of finding his son was brought up by MacKenzie King himself..

"Don't worry, Petrov, the British have assured me that they know where Arvid is, and have people on the ground keeping an eye of his condition. The Germans are planning something, I can feel it.

We've got the tanks ready to roll, and De Havilland is ramping up production of planes. C.D. tells me that the four engine Lancaster proved to be a winner. We've been flying them over the pond now for the past two months. Now in July, production is ramping up even more. I'm counting on you to get the shipments organized. How is Tzeitel? I know it's hard being separated from the family, but if we keep pumping out the supplies they need in

England, we can beat the Germans and give Hitler the boot." The words by the Prime Minister were comforting, but Petrov's mind kept returning to Leo's disappearance. Now, Arvid was missing as well. The Prime Minister's belief that he was safe was not much comfort, with his last words still ringing in Petrov's ear. "Arvid is a smart lad, I'm sure he's doing just fine"

****

Across the Atlantic, in the basement of a house in Leningrad, Arvid was becoming concerned for his safety. He had not seen or heard from his captives for two days. In the meantime, the single meal per day was also missing. Bars on the lone window and the metal door appeared to block the only way out.. Still in uniform, he would be a target for those who were looking to kill him, but It was time to leave this prison. There was no door knob or handle on the inside, so he could only guess at where the latch would be. Using the steel handle of a frying pan, Arvid began to pry at the metal sheet covering the door panel. Making progress, his blood froze as he heard voices approaching.

Breaking a leg off the kitchen table, he waited for whoever was now trying to break down the door.

Finally the door burst open, and three men with weapons rushed in. Arvid felt like a caveman facing three armed gorillas, and waited for the attack. A large bearded man stepped forward.

"Commander, come quickly. We haven't much time. Here, put this on." he said throwing an old leather coat to him. " we've got to get out of here before the bombs start falling." Arvid put on the bomber jacket. As the men filed back outside, Arvid was aware of people running. Shadows moved through the night, with people shouting. "Where are we going?" Arvid asked, following the men down to the water's edge, he climbed into the rubber dinghy, and took the oar handed him.

"We are with Special Forces. We were ordered to pick you up tonight." the leader replied, as they paddled quickly out onto the center of the bay. Arvid could not see a ship, and began to wonder if this was how he was going to die. Within minutes they bumped into a black, half submerged steel form. "OK, Commander, climb through the hatch. We've got to get out of here, now."

Arvid crawled onto the vessel and dropped down into the hold. Another man saluted as he took a seat along the wall. Moments later, his three rescuers joined him, and closing the hatch, felt the strange craft begin to move. There was a distinct hum, and the sound of water brushing again the hull. He was in a submarine. Closing various valves, it was obvious that they would be underwater and invisible from the surface. As everyone settled into their respective seats, the leader turned to Arvid and laughed.

"I can see by the look on your face, that you don't believe what just happened. My name is Sergeant Carol. Johnny, Jock and I were chosen to find you and get you out of Leningrad." the Sergeant said, motioning to the others, Mickey is the Captain of the vessel. Right, Mickey?"

The man at the controls looked back and smiled. "it's his job to keep from running into anything hard. We'll be in this for about 4 hours, with any luck." the Sergeant added, drinking from a flask.

"How did you find me?" Arvid asked, as the mini sub rocked back and forth.

"We got word from one our people in Leningrad. Some old lady said she knew where you were, and felt that you were going to be killed if you were taken to Moscow. It took a bit of searching, but you were right where she said you were. We had to do it tonight. Tomorrow would have been too late. It's June 21st. The Germans are going to invade Russia. They have a million and half soldiers and thousands of planes ready to Blitz the Country. You wouldn't stand a chance." Sergeant Carol adding, " this is first time we've used this Mini sub. Churchill wanted to see if it would do the job. If it does, we could build a hundred of these things and beat the Germans at their own game. Isn't that right, Mickey?" Sergeant Carol shouted, as noise from outside the hull drew louder.

"How do you know where you're going?" Arvid asked, not having any experience in underwater boating. "I was hoping you knew where we were going, sir." Mickey replied. After the laughter died down, he added, " we have a ship out in the Baltic and all I have to do is listen to the ping. It changes frequency from left to right, so as long as I keep the ping in my earphones, we're on track.

It's going to take about five hours to get out of the Gulf of Finland and reach the boat, so sit back and relax, Commander. I'm sorry we don't have any on board entertainment. for you." Mickey looked back at the Sergeant, who reached into a container, pulling out a bottle of milk. Offering it to Arvid, he said "No problem keeping anything cold in this steel tube. Milk is the only thing the Admiral will let us drink. He wants to make certain we come back. The Germans and Russians have schnapps or vodka, but this is the British Navy, so God save the King" he laughed as he held up his bottle to toast the success of locating and saving Commander Romanov. As the hours ticked by, other sounds rumbled through the hull of the mini sub. At times, it sounded as if the propeller of a large ship was going to slice the sub wide open, but as quickly as it appeared, the threat vanished. Finally, Arid could hear the sound of rushing water change to just a trickle. Mickey turned to speak to Sergeant Carol.

"The Captain said we have about ten minutes to surface and scuttle, so are we ready, fellow mariners?" Mickey said as he blew the ballast. The little sub rocked back and forth as it breached the surface. Lining up, with Arvid in the middle, the crew exited the hatch and were pulled up onto the deck of a large Norwegian fishing boat. The Captain welcomed his fellow Navy Special Services comrades, as well as Commander Romanov.

Turning to Sergeant Carol, he said, "Set the timer for ten minutes," Sergeant Carol disappeared back down into the sub, and moments later, came back out, sealing the hatch. As the boat moved away from the slowly sinking mini sub, Arvid felt a sense of loss. It had allowed him to escape certain death at the hands of fanatical Bolsheviks, but knew that having the sub fall into the hands of either the Germans or Soviets would be handing them a technical advantage. Somewhere in the night to the rear of the boat, there was a dull thud as the explosives did their job. The Cook aboard the fishing boat was happy to have his customers back, and it was a happy crew who dug into a meal of fish and fries, knowing that there were still many miles to travel before the Maersk 14 was out of the Baltic Sea. Weaving through the shallow shoals and rock protrusions, the was a sense of dread as chatter on the radio proved that there was something extraordinary happening in the area. Waves of bombers flew overhead, heading east. Some were coming from Sylt, a German airstrip on an island on the coast of Denmark. "Looks like Whitehall called it, Commander. They wanted you out of Leningrad before the shit hit the fan." Putting in for fuel in Ronne, the special Forces members transformed into deckhands, while Arvid spent his time as sous Chef in the Galley. Having topped off the tanks, the crew were about to cast off the bow lines, when a German Officer, with three armed soldiers arrived on the dock. Screaming orders, the departure was halted. Jumping onto the deck, he walked up to the Captain and began to interrogate him about his purpose for being in Ronne. The Special Forces began to move around the deck in a defensive position. One soldier went down below, walking through the passageway, checking all the rooms. When he arrived at the Galley, he poked his gun barrel into the Cook's ribs.

Looking over at Arvid, he pointed the barrel into Arvid's face. Speaking in German, he asked for Arvid's papers. Arvid smiled, grabbed the gun from the surprised German, and struck him in the face with a blow that made the Cook wince. The sound of breaking bone was evident, and the Cook grabbed him, driving a knife deep into his back, preventing the man from falling onto the hot stove top. The deed was done. The German soldier was dead. Arvid took his rifle, moving cautiously through the passageway to the stairs leading to the deck. Mickey looked down at Arvid, and realizing the whole search was going to blow up into a gun fight, he stepped behind the nearest Soldier, and in one swift move, reached under his helmet, professionally breaking the German's neck. Sergeant Carol took out the remaining Wehrmacht gunman, leaving the Officer in shock, staring at the Captain. Before he had a change to reach for his Luger, the Captain drove a knife into the man's neck, causing blood to pour out onto the deck. Within minutes, the bodies of the dead Germans were thrown overboard, and the Maersk 14 was motoring slowly out of the Ronne harbor.

There was no mention of the incident, and other than washing the blood from the deck planks, the crew went back to watching for any approaching vessels. Finally, after navigating through narrow passages toward the open sea, when the Maersk turned the corner at Skagen, there was a breath of relief. In the mist of a June morning, the Captain set a course for Scotland. After a hot meal, and fresh coffee, a routine was established to keep a lookout for U boats, Arvid was not anxious to spend any more time in a lifeboat. Twenty three hours later, the Isle of May appeared off the bow of the Maersk 14. Within the hour, Arvid was back at the Command Center, being welcomed by Charlotte and very contrite Major Carter.

****

Tzeitel could smell the dirt. With sun heating up the soil, she thought back to when she first met Petrov. Unlike her father, Petrov was a young man who could get things done. The Romanov name was already well known and respected in the area. Petrov's father, Peter, was a learned man, who enjoyed music and art, but knew how to work. The work ethic was passed on to his son, Petrov built more grain elevators, convinced the CPR to extend their line through the land where grain was grown. Those were exciting days, With Arvid, Catherine, who hated the name Kate, Abigail... Tzeitel stopped and studied the flower in her hand. The fact that Abby was still missing was the event that changed her husband. Even having Dorothy stay at home did not alter the loss of Abigail for Petrov. Tzeitel wiped a tear away, causing a streak of mud to appear under her eye. The happy sound of laughter brought her back to the task at hand. Patricia, with Leo in hand were allowing the long grass to tickle their bare legs.

" What are you doing, Gramma?" Patricia asked, as they sat down beside the matriarch.

"Just planting a few more of these lilacs. They won't flower for years, but they should make a nice hedge along the trail. Did you two find anything exciting?" she asked, handing Leo a small bush to plant. Patrica sat down in the dirt beside her son. "Looks like the town was busy today. The war has certainly made a difference in how much money there is around. I see the Sinclairs have a new car. They said they had to buy it now, because the car companies might have to stop building cars and start making planes and tanks. I wish I could hear where Arvid is. I guess no news is good news. Grampa should be coming home pretty soon. It's been a month since he was here. Do you miss him, Gramma?" Patrica asked, knowing it was a stupid question.

""Oh yes, of course, but I know he has an important job to do, so I don't pressure him. He knows a lot of people in government, so if anything happened to either Arvid or Cathy, he would know.

The Prime Minister trusts him, so I don't worry like I used to." Tzeitel said, putting on a brave face for her daughter-in-law, " Dorothy should be home from school next week. It will nice to have both of you to talk to." Patricia could see the pain of having all her children away from the nest was stressful, never knowing when they would get that awful telegram from Ottawa. Some of the families around Admiral had already received that terrible news. Some of the farm boys that joined up just to get away from farm work, would never drive a tractor, or bale hay again.

"Let's go in and have a tea and a fresh baked muffin." Tzeitel suggested, Shaking the dirt from her apron. Together, holding Leo's hands, Patricia and her mother-in-law left the gardening for another day. Just being together on the farm was reward enough for the two women who loved the same man.

****

Casualties from the fighting in North Africa were being be brought for long term care at St. John's Hospital. Cathy could see that her secret trip to Morocco was executed in the nick of time. The Germans were pressuring the Vichy to tighten security as British troops crossed in Tunisia, and fighting was becoming intense. As June 1941 came to a close, Britain was gearing up to take the fight to Germany. With the Soviet Union under a siege by German troops, pressure on England had been lessened, but still suffering from the various campaigns launched to keep Germany from gaining access to the oil fields of Africa. As she started her shift, Cathy was approached by a Queen's gentleman. She recognized him from her visit with the King and Queen.

"Excuse me, Lieutenant. But I have come to fetch you for the King. I have spoken to the Chief Surgeon, and he has graciously allowed you to take the time you need." the Queen's Gentleman stood back, as if giving Cathy to make up her mind. When asked by the the King and Queen of England to attend a meeting, there would be no declining the request.

"Yes. Certainly. Do you want to go right now?" she asked, hoping that it didn't entail packing a suitcase. The man smiled. "No. If you need time to organize, I can wait." he said apologetically.

Feeling that this was not going to a spying mission, Cathy shrugged, and said, "OK. I'm ready. Let's go." With that the

Gentleman offered his arm to Cathy. It was a strange feeling to be escorted to a limousine parked at the entrance to the Hospital, while her fellow Nurse and Doctors looked on as they started their shifts. Driving through the rubble left from bombings earlier In the year Cathy wondered what the Queen had in mind for her. Arriving at the rear of Buckingham Palace, she was warmed by the acknowledgment of staff as she passed through the rear door and into the lower hallway. It was all familiar now. As the Gentleman led the way, Cathy could see she was heading to a different part of the huge Palace than during her las visit.. The Gentleman stopped at a door, and knocked. A voice from inside bid her to enter. It was a large sitting room. The Queen, dressed in a simple skirt, stood in the doorway opening onto the garden below. The Queen turned and beckoned Cathy to join her. Queen said nothing for a moment, then turned to Cathy and smiled. "I'm glad you could make it, Catherine." she said, taking Cathy by the arm. Crossing to a small table, she motioned her guest to sit. A young girl quickly set a tray with tea and cookies in front of the Monarch. Cathy looked up at the server, who seemed nervous in front of her.

"Thank you," Cathy said, and immediately regretted it. was not her place to speak to the Palace help. She looked over at the Queen, who smiled. "Yes, thank you Charmaine. I'd would like you to meet a relative of mine. Catherine Romanov. You will be seeing more of her around here, so please be kind to her. Now go tell my husband that Catherine has arrived." The girl curtsied and hurried off on her mission. Cathy sat back and enjoyed a perfect cup of tea. As they sat and looked at one another, Elizabeth finally spoke. "My husband wants to visit some of the members of the military, and I want to visit the bombed out areas to see for myself what the Nazis did to our Country. " Cathy could see that her days at St. John's Hospital were over. As she took a cookie offered by the Queen, a door opened from the side wall. King George entered, still doing up his shirt. Elizabeth immediately stood, causing Cathy to panic, and placed her cup on the table, It rattled to the floor and broke. Panic had turned to apoplexy. Queen Elizabeth laughed. "Sit down Catherine. I've got to fix my husband's shirt. He can never seem to get tucked in at the back." As Cathy stood looking down at the shattered bits of royal pottery, she had the urge to find a rug to crawl under. Minutes later, with the king's shirt under control, Charmaine was summoned to clean up the brown cup. Cathy knelt to help the young girl, and as they picked up the smaller pieces, King George offered a comment... "I guess we'll have to use the cheaper China with Kate around." he said. There was a moment of silence, then everyone in the room broke into gales of laughter. Tears rolled down the Queens's cheeks, as Cathy and Charmaine hugged one another. It was an inauspicious beginning to Cathy's residence in Buckingham Palace.

The next few weeks were filled with visits out into the hinterland of England, seeing the devastation wrought by German bombing and strafing. Cathy was never too far away from the King and Queen as they toured houses and factories being rebuilt to provide goods and materiel for the soldiers, sailors and airmen who were being beaten by a larger and better equipped foe. America had not entered into the war, but allowed some goods to be transported across the Atlantic, which helped in Britain's survival. Being with the King's party, it meant Cathy had to keep back from being noticed. Blending in with the Security and Gentlemen, she was careful to always be near King George if anything were to happen. The time spent in Buckingham Palace was filled with hours spent with the queen's young daughters, when they came back for a visit. The King sent them away to Scotland to keep them safe from the worst of the bombing in London, but with the eastern front taking Hitler's attention, being in England's largest city was no longer a death sentence. Cathy enjoyed her time with the Elizabeth and Margaret, learning that Elizabeth preferred to be called Alexandra, but since the Queen made the rules, it was used only when the girls were by themselves. Although 13 year their senior, Alexandra and Margaret treated Cathy like an older sister. Discussing dresses, make up and boys, the Queen was happy with the choice of her husband's distant Cousin as her daughters' companion. The fact that Cathy was a Registered Nurse, a Lieutenant in the Canadian Army and a Romanov were all a bonus.

****

Back in the Firth of Forth Command Center, it was time for Arvid to complete the journey he started ten days before. This time, he would be flown to Northolt from RAF Drem so there would be no chance of a repeat performance by fanatic Bolsheviks. Arriving at the airstrip just outside of London, Arvid was picked up and driven directly to Whitehall. This was a no-nonsense facility where serious decisions were made concerning the entire war. With Churchill paying a visit from time to time, there was a feeling that only the brightest and best entered the basement door.

Major General Sutherland saluted, then shook Arvid's hand. "I'm glad you're finally here, Commander. We've got a job I think you can help us with. My Lieutenant will show you around, and once you see how this place operates, you will be taken to Bletchley Park. When you get there, you will see exactly what we're up against. So, go with Lieutenant Grisholm, absorb much as you can, and in an hour, I'll have someone take you Bletchley." Arvid nodded understanding, and with a snap salute, the Major General returned to his office, while Arvin followed the Lieutenant as he explained how Whitehall worked. As they went up to the second floor, Arvid heard his name being called.

"Arvid Romanov. So you finally made it. I was getting little worried when I heard the Bolsheviks had you." It was Winston Churchill, who was doing up his pants as he exited the washroom. "I told your Prime Minister that I would take care of you. I also didn't want to explain to your father that the bloody Bolsheviks had added to their crimes against humanity. Did Sutherland tell you about Bletchley Park?" he asked, as he straightened out his waist coat, "I think you will be a good fit over here. We've got some pretty smart people doing some great work, but we can always use another few brain cells." Arvid looked over at Lieutenant Grisholm and caught him smiling.

"Yes sir. I don't know what I can do, but I guess I'll find out when we get there." Arvid replied, feeling that with Churchill's faith in him, there would be nothing that was impossible to achieve. It was that kind of faith that the people of Britain had in Winston Churchill. Anything could be accomplished. With a nod and grunt, Churchill turned and left the Commander and Lieutenant to solve any problems a world war can generate.

After seeing the map rooms and Command Center, Lieutenant Grisholm walked with Arvid out the back to the garage where they found a Second Lieutenant waiting beside a car, with the engine already running.

"Here's your ride, Commander. The Lieutenant Cavanaugh will take you to Bletchley Park. They'll fix you up with accommodations. Good luck, Commander. I think you'll find a challenge that suits you."

With a salute, Lieutenant Grisholm turned and went back into Whitehall.

The ride north to Bletchley took over an hour, having to pass through several checkpoints, but 45 miles north of Whitehall, Lieutenant Cavanaugh pulled up to the rear door of a beautiful old mansion, which seemed like a strange place to have a top secret coding facility.

A rather large Provost Guard opened the door for Arvid as the brown Humber Snipe stopped. There was no salute, no talking, but Arvid was led to a basement door. The Provost opened it and Arvid stepped in. Immediately upon entering, he was greeted by a small man with glasses and a note pad. He shook Arvid's hand.

"Hello. My name is Prentice. I'm glad you finally made it. Come on upstairs. We've got a room set aside for you. I'm sure you want to wash up. You're just in time for lunch with the others." Arvid followed the little man upstairs to the second floor, stopping just long enough to look into the dining room. Three men were sitting at the table, while another one was lighting a pipe. They looked up and waved. Continuing on up to a bedroom, Arvid was pleased to see that he had a water closet connected the room. Washing and changing his socks, he went back downstairs to meet the other occupants of this odd place. Prentice pulled out a chair for Arvid, causing the others to stop what they were doing. Arvid felt self-conscious as one of the other mathematicians walked over and shook his hand. "Name's McCandless. That little genius over there is Hugh Montgmery. The fellow already savoring the egg salad is Peter, and that ugly little chap in the corner with the pipe is Alexander, and we mustn't forget that fellow in the corner who seems to be off fighting his own war, that is Alan Turing. Prentice told us we were getting a new partner in this endeavor. You must have some special gift that Winnie feels we need. How much do you know about what we do here?" McCandless asked, looking over at Prentice. Arvid could see he wasn't that he wasn't exactly welcome in this tight knit group. " I know that you are having a problem solving the enigma code.

I know it can be broken. It's all a matter of finding a pattern. If you will allow me, I would like to help you crack the cypher." Arvid said, looking around the room for some sign of friendship. Alan Turing stood up and walked over to study Arvid up close. "What is 421 times 53?" Turing asked, watching Arvid's face for any sign of confusion. Arvid shook his head.

"I have no idea, but I'm sure you do, which means my knowing the answer is unnecessary. But I do know that you took eight steps to reach me, you have a slight limp in your right leg, and you are left handed. The shirt you're wearing has two buttons missing, you have adjusted your belt due weight loss, probably due to to your lack of regular meal times, and I can spot any deviation in a pattern, however slight." Alan stood staring at Arvid for a long moment, then smiled. "You'll do, " he said, then turned and went back to the desk in the corner of the room. After the interrogation, Prentice broke the silence. "Ok, fellows. Eat up and get back to work. We have a war to win."

Sitting down to sandwiches and soup, brought into the room by a young woman, who seemed to stand up against McCandless's shoulder as she set the platters down on the table. McCandless looked up at her and it was obvious that, if any rules were going to be broken in this secret place, it would McCandless who would break them. After a short meal, everyone followed Turing into the next room.

Arvid was surprised to see the confusion in the way papers and files wire strewn about. In the middle of the room stood a strange looking device made up of wheels and wires. Alan Turing went immediately to work on the machine. Seeing Arvid's expression, McCandless stood next to Arvid, his arms folded as if explaining a construction site. "That's Alan's baby. It was originally dreamed up by a Pole, but we ended up with it, Alan figures he can improve the design to make it more efficient. As you know, the Germans send out communiques hourly to their troops using the enigma machine. It is so efficient and complicated that there are 150 million possibilities for each letter in the message. To make matters worse, every day, the code changes, so that when we get close to understanding the message, it changes completely. We are always behind trying to read the results. Here, " McCandless said, handing Arvid a stack of messages received for that day, " see if you can make any sense out these." Arvid took the pages, and finding an uncluttered space, began to sort through the daily correspondence. A roomful of women next door copied everything that was downloaded from the airwaves. The Germans were so confident of their system that they broadcast over shortwave to their army, navy and Luftwaffe by Morse code. Without a way to decipher the dots and dashes, it was just gibberish. Arvid looked over at Turing. The briefing by Major General Sutherland prepared him to overlook the idiosyncrasies of the mathematician who was chosen by Churchill to find a solution to the enigma device. Arvid could appreciate the dedication and single mindedness of Turing. Many days with long hours of testing and rejection of results wore on the whole team. After a short sleep, it was in the middle of the night that Arvid awoke, sitting upright in bed, There was something about the messages. The next morning, Arvid went down to the work room. Alan Turing was already there, running the machine, cursing the results. He looked over at Arvid, angry with the failure of his years of work. Arvid stood beside him.

"I think I might have something for you, " Arvid said, waiting for a moment of calm.

"I don't think you understand the complexity of the device." Turing said, not looking at Arvid.

"You're right. I don't understand the intricacies of your machine, but I do understand patterns. Picking up a handful of the scripts prepared by the women computers in the adjacent building, he laid out a series of sheets in a row. Turing was now taking an interest. Arvid began to explain.

"When the women deliver the messages, they are in the order received from the radio transmissions, but I find every third message is not in order. When I look at the order, I see the Germans are not sending the messages, one, two, three, four. If you move the third message to the front, take the second message to the fourth. and fourth to the second, I discovered that the pattern repeats itself every time. If you reverse the message, then they make sense. I don't speak German, but I see the pattern like it is cast in stone." Alan Turing stood and stared the papers laid out before him on the deal. McCandless, Hugh and Alexander joined them.

"What's up?" McCandless asked, seeing Turing and Arvid lost in thought.

"Work with Arvid and sort these messages into their proper order. When you're finished, we're going to try the machine again" Turing said, going back to the large device that was patiently clicking away. It took an hour to sort a stack of the day's deliveries into a new pile. When ready, they set up to read and translate the morse code into letters. As the letters were entered into the device, the machine began to digest every one separately. Watching the wheels spin, it was without emotion that the words were churned out like teletype. Moments later, the machine stopped. Taking the results, Turing gave them to his crew who were ready to translate the jumble of letters into something intelligible. Amazingly, commands, latitudes, longitudes appeared on the blackboard. There was suddenly silence in the room, as the import of what they were seeing struck home. They had cracked the enigma device. It would allow Britain to know what the Germans were doing as soon after the command was sent. After all the disappointment and doubt, the machine was finally doing what it was supposed to do. It was just a matter of feeding the information in the proper order. McCandless turned away from the board and crossed over to the door. "we've got to go and tell the girls that we've cracked it. They'll really be happy after all the misery we've put them through over the past year. " he said, "we can stop the Nazis cold."

Alan Turing put up his hand. "Stop!. You can't tell anyone that the machine works. If the Germans discover we've cracked their code, they'll change the system, them we'll have start all over again."

McCandless put his hand on the door handle, then stopped. He could see the logic in Turing's words.

"How are we going to do this?" Hugh asked, sitting at a desk piled high with unsorted messages.

Alexander shrugged. "Do we tell Prentice?" he asked, wondering how far the secret could be spread. Arvid walked over the machine. He was not involved in the politics of Bletchley Park.

This was beyond his reach. Alan Turing was the leader of the group, and it was up to Turing to make the decision. After a short discussion, it was decided to go next door and retrieve a new stack of messages from the computer girls. An hour later, the group had reorganized the stack and began to feed the information into the waiting machine. It didn't take long for the device to sort out the letters into a legible line of information. It worked perfectly. They had done it. They had the answer. Shutting off the machine, they turned out the lights and locked the room. Alan Turing went directly to Whitehall. His visit with Major General Sutherland brought Winston Churchill into the discussion.

Without drawing a connection to the success at Bletchley Park, it was decided that not every action by the Germans would be prevented. It was a difficult decision to allow some people to die, rather than alert the Nazis to the fact that their every command was being translated. The High Command of the British Military had to pick and choose who would live and who would die. It was not up to Alan Turing, Arvid Romanov, McCandless, Hugh or Alexander to play God. Their job was to hand over the information derived from the spinning wheels. Hugh and Alexander became morose, McCandless felt no remorse, Alan Turing looked upon it as simple logic, but Arvid Romanov began to feel the weight of what he was doing. By the summer of 1942, he knew that he had seen and done enough. His request to be let go from the group and return to civilian life was accepted. He was told that he was still under the Official Secrets Act. As a Canadian citizen, he was subject to the same penalty for revealing any mention of Ultra, the name given to the code breaking program.

Boarding a Lancaster, he was transported back to Gander. From Gander, Arvid took the train to Port aux Basque. Hopping aboard a Portuguese fishing boat, he arrived in North Sydney, having been treated to Cognac by the friendly fishermen. Finally, he was back on Canadian soil.

A four day train ride west across Canada gave Arvid Romanov an opportunity to see the whole Country in a relaxed setting. No longer wearing his Military uniform, he was just another passenger, so he was able to appreciate conversations between soldiers and sailors on leave.

When he heard talk of the German submarines causing all the death and destruction, the guilt returned. He knew of many occasions when a ship or tank crew were heading into danger, but alerting them to the danger would be proof that the British had solved the enigma dilemma.

He had not spoken to his family for almost three years, and as the train stopped at Gull lake, Arvid was filled with a strange fear. He had been disconnected from normal life for so long that he didn't know how to act. Standing on the platform, carrying his duffel bag, he recognized faces from Admiral and Scotsguard, but with a growth of hair on his face, no one came to say hello. He felt like a stranger in a strange land. Finally, he heard a voice from the past.

"Arvid. Arvid Romanov. Is that you?" It was Charlie Vogel. A farmer with a large section to the east of Admiral, he was in Gull Lake to pick up his daughter who was returning from school in Swift Current. Charlie stuck out his hand. "Good to see you, Arvid. I hear you've been in Ottawa. How is everything with those big shots who spend all our money?" Arvid had to adjust his reply to suit the story that the government wanted disseminated. He wanted to tell his neighbor the truth, but had to remember the oath of secrecy he took when he joined Alan Turing's team. Climbing into the new Chevrolet four door automobile, Arvid had to smile. It had been quite a while since he had ridden in an American car. Land Rovers, Lorries and old British autos that were somewhat shy of amenities.

"It looks like you're surviving the war, alright, Charlie.'" Arvid commented, turning around to look at the man's daughter. Celia was fresh faced and healthy. After watching young children searching through rubble to find missing parents, or lining up to receive meager rations after the bombing blitz, it was like landing on another planet.

"Yeah. The price of wheat is holding, and the government guarantees have been good. Pretty good crop this year. By the way, I haven't seen your father for a while. Do you ever get together in Ottawa?" Arvid closed his eyes. He had to come up with a reasonable lie.

"We worked in different areas. Ottawa is pretty busy with all the war activity. Lots of hush hush stuff that most people don't hear about. It's going to be good to get home." Arvid said, hoping to change the subject. He looked over at Charlie Vogel and could see he wasn't interested.

"I left Dorothy in Swift Current, " Mr. Romanov, "she said she was going to drive home." Celia said, as if it was common knowledge. Arvid turned and looked at the girl and frowned.

"She's going to drive home? She can drive?" he asked. Incredulous. His baby sister seemed too young to drive. The war had played tricks on their lives. When he left for service in the army, Dorothy was only 18. He thought about that for a minute and began to smile. She was a grown woman. attending University, she was no longer his little sister. "she's got a car?" which sounded like a stupid question.

"Yeah. Your Dad bought her a little Chevy convertible. It made her kind of popular at University."

Arvid could hear a bit of jealousy creeping into Celia's description of her best friend's boy magnet.

Charlie stopped at the entrance to Admiral. Arvid shook his hand, said goodbye to Celia, threw the duffel bag over his shoulder, and walked into town. A pick up truck passed, and waved to the bearded stranger. The town was busy. The war had brought business back to the mechanic shop, grocery store and Post Office. Several people passed and waved. As Arvid climbed the hill to the house, he could smell the lilacs and see the top of the roof. Finally he stood at the back door, looking into the kitchen. His mother was busy washing dishes, and Patricia was having a sandwich with Leo. Leo looked up, and without waiting to clear the dish away, caught the table cloth in his arm, dragging it off the table, crashing all the dishes to the floor. He ran to Arvid, who opened the door and swept the 7 year old up into his arms. Arvid strained to pick the young boy up. He was going to be a big lad. Tzeitel turned and dropped a dish, while Patricia jumped up and ran to Arvid, arms outstretched. This is a what it felt like to finally make it home. Putting Leo down, he held Patricia close. "Fancy looking beard, Mr. Romanov." Tzeitel joined in on the communal hug.

The afternoon was a time of renewal. It wasn't until late afternoon that Arvid remembered what Celia said about Dorothy "she said she was going to drive home." She should have arrived by now. Several phone calls discovered Henry Anderson saw Dorothy on the side of the road just outside of Admiral. Arvid was curious, and taking the farm truck drove to Anderson's farm.

"Yeah. I saw her standing beside that little Chevy Petrov bought for her. Neat little car." Henry recalled, ' I had truck full of feed, so I had to drop it off home. I got rid of it, then went back to see if she needed a hand. She was so close to home that I figured she would walk into town. When I got back to the spot, the car was gone. I figured she got it started and drove home. She's not there?" Henry asked, feeling badly for not stopping the first time. Arvid was now concerned. Thanking Henry for the information, he drove back to the spot Henry described. He could see tracks where the car had pulled off the road. There were two sets of footprints. A man and a woman. Had she met someone? Arvid drove home, expecting to see the convertible in the driveway. But it was not there.

Tzeitel was on the phone when Arvid entered the kitchen. She was crying. Patricia also had tears in her eyes. Leo was confused by the sudden unhappiness in the house.

"What's the problem?" he asked standing beside his mother. She held up her hand to pause the conversation. Arvid crossed to his wife. "What's the problem?" he asked again.

"Your father is coming home. The RCMP found Dorothy's car in McGilley's pond. Arnold McGilley found it when he went down to water the horses. There was no sign of Dorothy." A chill went through Arvid. Abigail disappeared without a trace, now his little sister was missing.

"McGilley's pond is only a mile from here, so she must be close." Arvid reasoned, "I'm going down there to see if I can get any more information. How is Papa getting here?" Arvid asked, changing his boots. The last known location of Petrov Romanov was Edmonton, so he would drive back to Admiral. It would take several hours. Arvid would have to take lead until his father arrived.

Staff Sergeant McLure was just coming out of the water. As a Diver, he was able to search the bottom of the pond for any more evidence, but taking off his gear, he shook his head.

"The Chevy was driven into the pond. It looks like the driver jumped before it went in. There is no way anyone could have accidentally driven off the road, through the gate and into the lake. The car was deliberately ditched. Your sister was not driving. We hear that Charlie Vogel saw her talking to a man near Admiral. We got a pretty good description of him, so we're putting out a sketch. He must on foot. I just wish we had dogs in the Swift Current Detachment. You know the area better anyone. Can you think of anywhere Dorothy could be? Somewhere between the Admiral Cemetery and here." Sergeant McLure placed his diving gear in the trunk of the Dodge, and picked up his two-way. A Constable was in another vehicle patrolling the local grid roads, but reported no obvious disturbance or strangers. Thanking the Sergeant for his help, Arvid took the farm truck and dove back to the Cemetery. The tracks he noticed earlier had been trampled on and were no longer visible. Whoever the male prints belonged to, knew where Dorothy was. He felt an instant hatred for the man who would take his little sister. Petrov arrived late that night. He was angry and confused. Seeing his son for the first time in two and half years should have been a reason to celebrate. Instead, it felt like a time to mourn.

"How can someone just disappear like that?" the senior Romanov asked, knowing that it was not only possible, but happened to Abigail, "I shouldn't have bought the convertible, but Dorothy loved that car, and I thought it would make it easier to get around while she was in University." he reasoned, stopping when he realize he used the word 'was'. " Arvid was shocked when his father sat down in his usual chair, and began to sob uncontrollably.

Petrov Romanov never recovered from the loss of another daughter. He withdrew from his government activities and spent his time walking the fields around Admiral. Tzeitel did her best to bring him back to life, but two years later, Petrov Romanov died of a broken heart. With the death of her husband, Tzeitel gave up as well. Even seeing photos on the front page of newspapers showing Cathy walking next to the King and Queen as they toured sites in Britain, did not bring cheer to her face. It was as if the switch had been turned off. Tzeitel Romanov died a year later. It was now up to Arvid to take over the reigns of the Romanov business. With oil leases and drilling operations expanding into Saskatchewan, grain elevators, large farm holdings, and two Hotels to manage, Arvid had to shake the guilt he felt about complicity in the Ultra project at Bletchley Park.

In 1945, World War 2 came to an end. Millions of people had died, towns and cities destroyed.

Thousands of ships and their crews were now at the bottom of the sea, and it was difficult for Arvid to see how his help in solving the enigma code did anything to shorten the war.

With war ended, and the family together, once again, there was laughter in the house. Leo was growing into a handsome, and brutally strong young man. Arvid could see that, although he himself had killed men simply using his fist, his son could snap a man's neck without effort. He was more athletic and moved with ease. Although Blaze had died at the age 18, another horse was purchased as a colt. Together, Leo and Siren grew into an inseparable pair. Arvid could see that his son would be the perfect manager for the farm end of the Romanov business empire. He rode Siren to see the other sections under cultivation. The local farmers could expect that when Leo said something was going to be rectified, it was done. Within days of his 17th birthday, he was given the task of overhauling the four grain elevators.

Arvid was surprised when his son decided to tear down on the oldest elevators, choosing to have trucks haul to the closest one. It was a decision that saved the Romanovs thousands of dollars.

Leo Romanov was to be respected, or else. As a dedicated horse rider, Leo competed in many competitions where his mother had to cover her eyes. Patricia could see that trying to stop a runaway freight train would be easier than talking her son out of competing to be the best.

By 1960, Leo had taken over more responsibility from Arvid. With the town of Admiral suffering from the ease of shopping elsewhere, it was becoming a ghost town. Roads had improved so that locals could drive to Swift Current or Shaunavon, bypassing the local machine shop or grocery store. Soon, even the cemetery was unused. With so few residents, there was no one left to die. Arvid could see that Leo was becoming restless. At twenty-three years of age, he was anxious to get married and start a family. Patricia was equally interested in having grandchildren. Arvid could see that his son had a different attitude when it came to dealing with the Romanov business partners. Arvid recalled the days when Petrov would make deals with people who were less than honest, and chose to forgive them their trespasses. Arvid took the same tack. Leo, on the other hand, being more aggressive and hands on, would physically lift the offenders off the floor, at times frightening everyone in the area. It was a tactic that worked remarkably well. He soon gained a reputation as someone who was fair, until he wasn't. Scheduling a trip to Calgary to negotiate a new contract with an oil company, Arvid invited Leo to join him. Leo, in his usual uncompromising fashion, suggested he take Siren to ride in the Calgary Stampede. Although it would mean driving to Alberta towing a trailer, Leo purchased a new 1961 Ford pickup for the occasion. As father and son waved goodbye to Patricia and the housekeeper, there was a sense of adventure in the trip. By the afternoon, they had reached the Calgary office building where a meeting had been scheduled. With no time to go to the fair grounds and make arrangements to board Siren for the next few days, Leo parked truck and trailer on the main street in front of the building. Arvid, although nervous about leaving a new truck and trailer parked at the curb, allowed Leo to lead the way. Running a finger down the list of tenants, they discovered the outfit wasn't as large they had been led to believe. Finding the large glass doors, a pretty young lady was surprised to have a client actually visit her boss. Arvid and Leo were let into a plush office on the second floor. After cordial handshakes all around, the three men sat down to discuss a new lease on property owned by the Romanovs. Bruce Cloutier, after offering both Romanovs a cigar, which they refused, settled back in his chair to lay out his terms for the future drilling schedule.

"I'm going to need a fifteen percent increase in my fee in order to facilitate the changes you require," he said, leafing through the papers on the desk, "handling these smaller accounts takes lot of valuable time away from my more, ah, prominent clients." Bruce Cloutier looked up at his visitors. He could see a smile was forming on Leo Romanov's lips.

"May I borrow your phone?" Leo asked, and without waiting for a response, he dialed a number. Sitting back, he looked quite comfortable, Leo was looking directly at Bruce Cloutier.

"Hello, Armand. Yeah, it's me. Tell me, what is this," picking up a page with a letter head, "Cloutier Consulting Ltd. worth?" There was a moment when Bruce Cloutier's face drained of color. " OK. Buy it. I'm tired of playing around with these guys". Moments later, nodding his head, Leo hung up the phone, and said, "don't go away, I'll be right back." Arvid watched as his son left the office. There was a definite silence, and the receptionist came to the door to ask if they would like a coffee. Moments later, screams were heard from somewhere near the building entrance. Shouts and laughter emanated from beyond the office door.

It was a satisfying sight to finally see the wet nose of Leo's horse poke through the office door. Riding over to the desk. Siren pushed Bruce Cloutier out of his chair. Terrified, the man made a break for the bathroom attached to the office. With the precision of a barrel racer, Siren stopped the panicked executive, pushing him against the wall. Leo leaned over the saddle to speak to Bruce Cloutier, who was now a captive audience.

"Pack your things. You are no longer employed here. I've been checking your work orders for the past two years. You have been padding the service charges, and in some instances, the drilling wasn't even started, yet you charged us for a dry well. Now, get out!" There was undertone of violence in the way Leo spoke. Bruce Cloutier, as well as Arvid, could feel it. Backing away, Leo allowed the frightened man to collect his brief case and name tag, and with some difficulty, slipped past the ample rump of Siren, and without speaking to his Secretary, disappeared down the stairs.

As Leo took his horse back through the outer office, he stopped at the desk.

"What's your name?" Leo asked, reverting to his natural tone. The woman took a moment to answer, but finally she replied. " My name is Ruth Caruthers sir." Leo patted Siren's neck.

"Well, Miss Caruthers, take a week off, with pay, and be prepared to come back next Monday. You'll be working for the

Romanovs, from now on, if you like." Leo smiled. He could feel there was a connection between them. Ruth reached out and stroked Siren's nose.

"Thank you, Mr. Romanov. " she whispered, " I'll be happy to work for someone who appreciates honesty. I've always been afraid that Bruce would go too far. By the way, I like your horse."

"Thank you Miss Caruthers. My name is Leo. That handsome gentleman behind me is my Dad. Just lock up after we leave, and enjoy you time off. We will be busy after the Stampede." With that, both Arvid and Leo left the woman to wonder if she could handle her new employers as she watched the horse expertly descend the stairs to the front entrance.

The next day, after arranging board for Siren, Arvid and Leo became spectators at the Fair.

It had been many years since the two of them enjoyed time off from the many various ventures that made up the Romanov business empire. After taking in the bucking and roping, they were sitting in the restaurant, when Leo looked through the crowd and saw a familiar face. "I'll be back,!" Leo said as he disappeared into the crowd. Moments later, he returned with Ruth Caruthers. Arvid could see that his son was hooked, and not only that, had very good taste. He was pleased that Leo chose someone of Ruth Caruthers mindset. He watched as Leo grew and became eligible, there were many girls who wanted to be with the big galoot, but they were only looking for a life away from farming. Sitting across from Ruth, Arvid could see she was just as happy to be with Leo. The next day, Leo was booked to do some calf roping. It would be a chance to show the world how nimble Siren was. If Leo was nervous, it didn't show. Placing his hat firmly over his forehead, he and Siren were ready. Arvid watched as, time and again, other contestants missed the calf, or fell off their horse. The competition wasn't that talented, but Leo was riding to impress a pretty young girl who believed that world revolved around him. Arvid had to admit, because of his size and strength, Leo made roping and tying a calf look easy. By the end of the day, he and Ruth celebrated his first place finish. Returning home together, Arvid and Patricia fell in love with Ruth. Maggie, the housekeeper, seemed pleased that the latest addition to the household, did not require any extra care. Closing the office in Calgary, Leo had a large trailer brought onto the farm property. Liquidating Bruce Cloutier's business, it was folded into a new company in which Ruth was named CEO. Arvid was impressed with Ruth's business acumen. The value of that portion of Romanov holdings increased quickly.

The wedding was small but well attended by locals and government hacks who wanted to show the Romanovs that they were friends of the large corporate family. By 1963, Arvid was 50 years old, and could see that Leo and Ruth had taken control of the many oil and farm projects he began after Petrov died. It was a surprise when Leo drove up beside Arvid as he walked to the store. Since trucks and cars had become numerous, and the Province of Saskatchewan began to maintain roads throughout the area, business in the general store and welding shop had all but dried up.

With his father in the truck, Leo drove down to the end of the street, parking in front of the vacant Romanov Hotel. It looked quite forlorn. Gone were the days when the CPR crews stayed in the rooms and drank themselves stupid. For the past five years, since the last train stopped in Admiral, the building had suffered from weather and local kids throwing rocks, just to see glass break.

"Well, Papa, what do you want to do? Spend some money and fix it up, or tear it down?"

Arvid got out and walked around to the back of the building. Grass was growing through the porch, and birds had taken full use of the dry nesting areas in the upstairs rooms. He stood at the back door, looking inside. Recalling the time he and Patrica made love on the couch in the foyer. It probably accounted for Leo. It was definitely beyond repair, and the Romanovs would be liable for anyone hurt in the derelict building. Leo joined him on the porch.

"Well, what do you think? Fix it or tear it down?' Leo asked, as they walked carefully over the dirt covered floor. Broken windows allowed the constant wind to bring in a great deal of Saskatchewan, which covered everything with a layer of sand. Arvid started up the stairs, but stopped halfway up. "Did you hear that?" Arvid asked, as Leo waited at the bottom.

"Hear what? All I hear is the wind." Leo replied, starting up the stairs to join his father. Arvid continued up the stairs to the landing and peered into a bedroom to the left. He stopped, just about knocking Leo off the stairs. "Who the Hell is that?" he asked, not expecting an answer.

"Who?" Leo asked, not quite understanding Arvid's sudden state of panic.

"Upstairs, in the bedroom. There's a little boy about ten or eleven years old. He looks like an orphan. He's got no shoes. What is he doing here? How did he get in? He didn't leave any tracks."

"Let me pass. I want to see this." Leo said, as he squeezed past his father and continued on to the the top floor. Walking directly into the bedroom, he stood in the middle, looking around for any sign of a human, large or small. There was nothing, not even footprints. He wondered if perhaps his father was suffering from some type of hallucination. Walking through the rest of the rooms, he could see gophers and birds had taken ownership of the cupboards and dressers. The beds were completely shredded, their stuffing used for warm nests in the winter. Returning to his father, Leo shook his head. " Nothing up there but dust and rot. Let's go into the bar and see if anything is salvageable. Crossing the porch, the large oak door was missing, and inside, the scene was even worse than the living quarters. The refrigerator doors had been ripped from their hinges, and the once shiny counter was covered with dirt and cobwebs. Several glasses, intact, were lying on the floor. Arvid walked across the room to the kitchen. He looked in and suddenly backed out.

Arvid's unexpected movement caused Leo to stumble.

"He's in the kitchen!" Arvid whispered, his voice low and gravelly, like a drunk on Sunday morning.

"Who is?" Leo asked, becoming concerned by his father's strange behavior.

"That little boy. How did he get down here from upstairs? He's got no shoes. He'll cut his feet!" Arvid turned and entered the kitchen in an obvious effort to keep the little boy from injury. As he entered, he stood and looked around at the stove, sink, pots and pans that were once clean and new. They once provided meals for hungry CP section crews, but they were now dirty and useless. There was no one in the kitchen. The little boy with no shoes was not there. Leo joined his father. He could see there was something troubling the senior Romanov.

"He was here. He was right here." Arvid repeated, pointing to a spot on the floor. I'm not crazy!"

Leo nodded his head. This was unlike his father. "Come on. Let's get out of here. I'll get a crew together and we'll get rid of these memories." Leo added, as he led Arvid out of the old building and back to the truck. Preferring to go the long way around back to the house, Leo hoped the fresh air would blow away the last few minutes of confusion. Reaching the house, Leo could see that his father was still back in the hotel kitchen. Whatever he saw still stuck in his mind. Entering the house, Patricia could tell by her husband's vacant stare that all was not right. Sitting him down, she placed a fresh cup of coffee under his nose. Slowly, he came back to the present, but his first words were very telling. "I saw him. I don't know who he was, but I saw him. Do you think it's some kind of message?" Arvid asked, in a subdued tone, like a sleepwalker might remember his midnight wanderings. Patricia put her arm around Arvid and kissed him on the cheek. She looked over at Leo, who just shrugged. Feeling his father was too young to get alzheimers like old man Vogel, Leo was even more concerned about the vision Arvid claims he saw. Twice.

"What do you think is happening to your Dad?" Ruth asked, as she folded the bedsheets. Leo moved his boots into a corner. He did not answer immediately. His father's performance in the hotel was puzzling. What could the little boy with no shoes represent? As he put on a clean shirt, he looked in the mirror. It was time to get out on Siren and check the fences. He also had to round up a crew to demolish the hotel. Crossing to his wife, Leo wrapped his arms around her and held her tight. She was three months along and just starting to fill out. As their first child, he knew his mother would be a big help. Ruth got along with Patricia like a sister. Leaving the house, Leo went immediately to the horse barn. Siren ran back and forth in the field.

Waiting at the barn door, Leo smiled as his black stallion galloped toward him. It would be good to get back into shape. Minutes later, saddled up and astride the excited animal, Leo rode along the CP tracks. Weeds growing through the ties and rust appearing on the rails, it was a reminder that fewer trains were moving along the southern route. Looking up at the three Romanov Grain terminals, only one was being used. With the local roads improving, farmers were trucking grain to the large terminals where they knew they would get their money sooner. As he slowly moved along the right-of-way, a simple thought became a flood of ideas. An hour later, Leo returned to the barn. Having ridden Siren hard enough to produce a sweat, it was time for a rub down and water.

Checking his hooves for any bits of rock from the ride along the rail line, Leo could see that the run was a what Siren needed to loosen him up. With a final check of the stallion legs, Leo turned him loose into the field. As the horse galloped and bucked, Leo's mind once again turned to his new project. Finding his father in the pump house, Leo was anxious to share the idea.

"I was just rode past our elevators down at the tracks. We're only using one of them now. The Grain Growers are trucking their products to the main elevators on the main road now. I think we should tear it down and sell off the lumber." Leo watched Arvid's face for any sign of rejection.

"I guess if they're not in use, they may as well come down. What if we get a bumper crop? What happens then? " Arvid asked, turning toward his son. Leo could see that his father was not really interested, one way or another.

"I'm going to shop around and see if there is an outfit that will build me a steel bin. We can make different sizes. That way, the farmers can select a size they need. What do you think?" Leo asked, hoping the idea would generate some type of interest in the senior Romanov.

"I don't care, son. " Arvid replied, returning to the water valve he was working on. Leo nodded his head. So, that was it. If Leo wanted to build metal silos, it was on his shoulders. Excited with the prospect of a new project, Leo entered the house and put an arm around his mother.

"The Romanovs are branching out, mama. I'm going to be gone for a couple of days, so you and Ruth can get together to talk babies." Leo kissed his mother on the cheek and rushed to get an overnight bag together. Ruth could see that her husband was on a roll. After her father-in-law's hallucinations in the hotel, it was good to see Leo concentrating on something else.

"When will you be back" she asked, as she helped assemble his clothes. Leo shrugged. He was still formulating a plan in his mind. As he walked to the car, he looked up and waved at both of the women in his life. Knowing the oil industry dealt with massive amounts of steel, Leo headed for Edmonton. Having the money and contacts, it was only a matter of days before a contract was let to produce steel grain bins. Several Engineers were interested in working for the Romanovs, but were surprised when they discovered that Leo had full control of the Company, and made all the decisions. Diagrams were submitted and rejected. Within four days, the first galvanized steel was being rolled for the construction of a gleaming new system for storing grain. Having lived in the business since he was born, he knew exactly what he wanted. Driving out to a vacant lot behind the pipeline company, he was surprised to see the new bin almost completed. It was beautiful. When placed on a concrete foundation, it would be rodent resistant and easily accessed right on the farmer's property. Leo felt a great deal of pride when the name Romanov was stenciled on the side. Arranging with the production company to handle manufacture, Leo would set up a sales team to peddle the new storage silos. On the way home, he felt the satisfaction of creating something that would, not only be profitable, but spread the Romanov name across the landscape.

As the summer months grew into fall, Ruth Romanov continued to grow larger. Arvid and Patricia doted on their son's pregnant wife. Doctor Neufeld was on call from Shaunavon, just in case.

February 12, 1965, Leo pulled into yard, with the Doctor in tow. Rushing into the bedroom, he was surprised at how quickly Ruth Romanov's condition had changed. She went into labor much sooner than expected. With Patricia's help, while both Arvid and Leo were chased from the room, A 6 pound baby boy was delivered to Ruth and Leo Romanov. There was great joy in the Romanov Household. A boy would guarantee the Romanov name would continue on. It was only a week later when it was suggested that Ruth and the baby be transferred to the Shaunavon Hospital. It was worrisome, but they were assured by the Doctors that it was just a minor infection, and they could take Alexander home by the end of the week. Arvid and Patricia visited Ruth as often as they could. Leo kept himself busy with new storage bin sales. The idea of keeping their seed safe at home struck a chord with farmers. Bins began appearing across Saskatchewan and Alberta. Leo tried not to think about his wife and son in the hospital as he drove to Swift Current to make deal with a farm equipment company to sell the bins locally.

Throughout the next year, Ruth was in and out of care, trying to keep Alexander alive, but six months after his amazing birth, Alexander Romanov was declared healthy. His color improved, and he became a happy baby. something the whole family could appreciate. Sometime during a night, when the moon was high and the nights were warm, someone stole into baby Alexander's room, and took him away. Although the RCMP conducted an investigation, and the Hospital apologized, another Romanov was gone. A witness who was smoking outside the rear entrance of the hospital, noticed a man with a beard packing something out into the nearby woods. Ruth went into a deep, dark depression. Arvid and Patricia could do or say nothing that would make it better. Leo found it difficult to speak to Ruth. She didn't want to discuss having other children, so Leo kept his distance, hoping that time would heal the deep wound. The Romanov house was not a happy place, but business did not care. Whether it was oil, construction, farming, ranching or sales, the family had responsibilities.

The town of Admiral was drifting into obscurity, but it did not matter to the family on the hill. One day, a new vehicle entered the driveway. A woman and man got out and walked up to the front door. Finding no answer, they went around the rear. Arvid and Patricia were concerned about the visitors as they came in from the trail. Entering the rear gate, they stopped. A woman ran up to Patricia, hugging her. Arvid could not believe his eyes. "Kate!" he shouted, as his sister hugged him. "the last time I saw you, you were walking with the Queen. Who is this fellow?" he asked, gesturing toward the man who stood back from the happy reunion. Cathy waved the big man forward. " Arvid, Patricia, I would like you to meet my husband, Christopher Peterson. We had to leave the kids in London because we had trouble getting passports for them." Chris and Arvid felt a bond. They both loved the same woman. Amid much laughter, the four entered the house. With over twenty years of gossip to absorb, talk dragged on into the night. It was a strange meeting when Patricia went upstairs to use the washroom and met Ruth, who was dressed in a bathrobe.

"Hello. Who are you?" Cathy asked, not quite understanding what had occurred in those missing years. Ruth did not answer, but just closed the door to Cathy's old bedroom. Puzzled, Cathy competed her business, then went downstairs to have the question answered.

The revelation that Arvid and Patricia had a son named Leo, and the resultant complication, caused Cathy's nursing instincts to come forth. Making two cups of tea, without any explanation, Cathy went back upstairs. Using the excuse to retrieve something hidden in her old room, Cathy gained entrance to the darkened pit of sorrow. Placing the tea on a night table, she sat across from Ruth and studied the 23 year old. Leo had good taste. Ruth was beautiful. Even in the dim light, she could make out features that would attract a Romanov. Sipping on her tea, Cathy asked, "how do you feel?" Ruth did not immediately respond, but did turn and look at Leo's Aunt. There was another moment of silence, then. Ruth said, "I've lost my baby. He was stolen from me. How do you think I feel.?" Cathy could see the young woman wanted to talk and waited until Ruth turned to face her.

"Losing a baby is painful. As a Nurse, I have had patients who lost more than one, but women are strong, I guess that's why God gave us so many eggs. Did they tell you what the baby died from?"

Ruth shook her head. "Don't you understand? Someone came into his room and stole him." Cathy sat back and studied her nephew's unhappy wife. This was more serious than death. This was theft of a life. "Have you any idea who would do a thing like that? Do you and Leo have enemies? What did the Police say. Did they investigate. Do they have any clues? What did they tell you." Cathy asked.

"Leo knows, the Police told him, but he wouldn't tell me. I don't know. I just know he's gone."

Cathy did not pursue the question any further. " Well, I have never met my nephew. What's Leo like?" Cathy asked, changing the subject, "if he's like every other Romanov, he'll be running the world. Where is he right now?" Ruth looked toward the window.

"I don't know. He said something about building bins, or something like that. I'm just too embarrassed to speak to him, He sleeps in the office apartment. I guess he'll never speak to me again. I don't blame him. I lost his son." Ruth said, then broke into tears again. Cathy could see Ruth was beginning to sort out the blame and punishment. It was good sign.

"Well, I've been in England for over twenty years, so I don't know what's been happening here. I don't even know where my brother was during the war. " Cathy admitted, feeling left out of part of the family's history. My father and mother died, and I didn't even get to bury them, so if you want company being miserable, I guess we both have reason to feel guilty about something. Come on downstairs. I want you to meet my husband." Cathy said, walking over to the window and raising the blind to allow light into Ruth's life again. Shading her eyes, Ruth was about to complain, but instead, took a sip of tea and hugged Cathy with a warmth reserved for a true friend. After selecting the right 'coming out' dress, and combing Ruth's beautiful blonde hair, it was time to make an entrance. Holding hands, Cathy and Ruth descended the stairs. Like a pair of long lost survivors, there was a group hug that felt sincere. As the laughter rang out in the kitchen, a car drove into the yard. Within minutes, Leo arrived, cursing the idiot who parked in the way.

It was a grateful Leo Romanov who saw his wife laughing and happy once again. The only awkward moment was when Chris asked Arvid what he did during the war.

Patricia solved the dilemma by saying that her husband was in Ottawa doing some secret stuff that he wasn't able to talk about. Chris could understand Arvid's reluctance to speak about things that occurred during those dark times. Arvid thought back to those days in Bletchley Park. A pang of guilt surged through him, but lasted only a minute.

"That was then, and this is now." Arvid said finally, offering a drink of whiskey reserved for an occasion such as this. "now let's forget about all that crap. When are you returning to wherever you came from?" he asked, holding his sister's hand. Chris spoke up. "We are going back to the airport in Swift Current. I'm delivering a plane to Alaska from the rebuilder in Virginia. I thought it would be nice if Cathy came along to visit you. From Alaska, we ferry it to Hawaii. Thankfully, Cathy has her pilot's license. The DC4 can be a bit of a bear to handle at times. From there, I don't know where we'll go. Now that Cathy is retired, we are in no hurry." he said, reaching over for his wife's hand, " as we drove here, we saw a bunch of round metal silos with Romanov on the side. Is that you?" Chris asked, looking at Arvid. He shook his head.

"No. Those are Leo's baby." The minute he said it, he knew it was a mistake, which was only exacerbated by looking quickly over at Ruth. There was a sudden silence in the kitchen, but Ruth reached over and took Cathy's hand. "No. I'm OK," she said, smiling, " I know now that it was God's way of showing me that was a test, and that I've got better things to come." With a possible hysterical outburst avoided, the atmosphere became even more jovial. Leo, who was leaning against the counter, walked over and kissed Ruth. She kissed him back.

With a choice of rooms, the Romanov house on the hill was filled with a family that had been divided, but was now somewhat complete. Arvid felt fortunate to see Cathy had survived the war, was married and had children. He still thought about his other sisters, who disappeared without so much as a 'by your leave'.

The next morning, with everyone helping prepare an outdoor breakfast, it was goodbye to Cathy and Chris. As his sister and her husband disappeared down the driveway, Arvid couldn't help but worry about what Leo and Ruth were going to do without a child to hold them together. The news that Cathy had two children, Edwin and Tracy, back in England caused Leo to raise his eyebrows. At the moment, there would be no one to carry on the Romanov name, and that was a concern. With the excitement over, it was time to get back to business.

With Ruth returning to her buoyant self, life began to feel normal in the Romanov household.

Patricia could see her husband was still troubled by seeing a little boy on his visit to the old Romanov hotel. There was nothing she could say that would change what he claimed he saw.

Making sandwiches, she looked out and saw Arvid walking with Leo's horse. It was a strange sight, since Siren was very difficult to handle, but the horse seemed to be following without any sign of protest. Patricia went to the back door to meet Arvid with his new friend.

"Well, this is a first. How did you manage to calm Siren down long enough to put a halter on him. Leo will be impressed" she laughed, as Arvid tied Siren to a post in the shade.

"He was out running loose, but the minute I called him, he came right to me." Arvid admitted, still not believing the change in the Stallion's disposition. As Patricia and Arvid admired the normally excitable stallion, Leo drove into the yard, and jumped out. He ran up to his parents. It was not an act normally connected with Leo. He looked at Siren, but seemed to be close to tears.

"Cathy's missing", blurting out the news as if it was poison, " the U.S. Navy is looking for the plane. They figure it went down somewhere between Alaska and Midway island. The Russians say they lost contact with it about 400 miles north of Midway islands. Both the Russians and the Americans are searching the route on the flight plan that Chris filed. So far, nothing."

Arvid sat on a bench nearby. After all the years during the war that either of them could have been killed, his sister dies in a plane that should have been retired long ago. He clenched his fists.

"What the hell were they doing in an old plane like that?" he asked. A question that that Leo tried to answer. " It had been restored for some billionaire from Hawaii. Chris picked it up in Virginia Beach and flew it to Swift Current. After leaving us, he took the plane to Anchorage, Alaska. Chris and Cathy spent a couple of days in Anchorage, then took off for Hawaii. They know he stopped at a small airstrip on Atka Island and refueled, then took off to Midway Island. "

Patricia began to cry. "Ruth is not going to take this well." she commented, with her hand on Arvid's shoulder. "Oh my God. What about their children back in England. I have no idea how to contact them. What are we going to do?" she asked, feeling helpless.

"Chris is pretty well known in the airplane business. The Police in Anchorage were already contacting next of kin" Leo said, shaking his head. " I learned all this from a CBC news broadcast. They figure it's exciting because it's like the search for Amelia Earhart. I hope it ends better."

The sudden silence was broken by bird chatter. The shock of losing an Aunt and sister, as well as her husband was something that would change the dynamic of the Romanov family.

"The DC4 is a four engine aircraft. It can lose two of them and still fly. Something catastrophic would have to happen to have it crash into the ocean." Arvid said, knowing from personal experience the capabilities of four engine airplanes. Leo nodded, knowing that his father was grasping at straws in order to keep from thinking the worst. Leo followed his father and mother into the house. They immediately went downstairs to the old office and spread out a map of the Pacific ocean. As they perused the various points where an aircraft may have landed, Ruth came down to see what all the action was about. When she saw the map spread out on the desk, she became suspicious. "What's going on? Are you buying an island in the Pacific? For Leo's sake, they had better have horses." she said, as Leo put his arm around her. The moment had arrived when he had to make a decision that may send his wife back into the misery of dealing with death.

"Chris and Cathy are missing. The Navy is out searching for them now. They probably landed on an island, somewhere," Leo said, " Chris has been flying for long time. I'm sure if there is any place to set down a plane, he'll find it. Don't worry, sweetheart. " Leo looked over at Patricia and Arvid. He knew that it was lame excuse, but they too were concerned that Ruth would not deal with Cathy's possible death very well. Ruth looked up at her husbanding smiled.

"It's OK, honey. Whatever happens is supposed to happen, but I think God is looking after Cathy."

There was a collective sigh of relief to know that the remaining Romanovs were going to stick together and face whatever happened, as a family.

The days passed, and every bit of news was analyzed and regurgitated. There was no sign of the DC4. Arvid spent his time walking the trail down to Notukue creek. Leo rode Siren and checked fences. Patricia and Ruth wandered down to the deserted town and speculated at how Cathy and Chris would fare living on a deserted Island in the Pacific. It was the only way to cope with such an odd and unexpected loss.

****

Finding a friendly Control Tower Operator at Anchorage, Chris was allowed to taxi the DC4 to a vacant hangar. The proximity to electricity would allow a local Aircraft Technician to work on the electrical system. On the trip from Swift Current to Anchorage, minor problems developed in the fuel delivery system. It would take a day to organize an AME and have it repaired. In the meantime, Chris and Cathy could explore the city. Since the rest of the journey would be over the ocean, Chris felt it safer to have another pilot experienced in ocean navigation. Cathy agreed. Being a co-pilot on a large four engined aircraft like the DC4 was a lot different than piloting a Cessna. With all the various gauges and instruments to constantly monitor, it would be wise to have another person with hands on the yoke. Finding accommodation in a nearby hotel, Chris immediately set out to find a competent co-pilot. Contacting the Pilot's Association in Anchorage, he was told to check the Bars and Hotels. There were several ex Air Force and Navy pilots who take on odd jobs, and are always happy to make a few extra bucks sitting in the right hand seat. With no other choice, Chris Peterson walked the area of 5th Ave and C street, checking in at all the drinking establishments. Finally, feeling that it was a lost cause, he stopped in at a corner Pub for a beer.

Sitting on a stool, Chris looked around at the nearly empty Bar and sipped on a Rheingold. If he couldn't find a co-pilot, his insurance policy would not cover any problem that arose during the flight. The Plane's owner would bury him in law suits, and his company would disappear in mass of paperwork and court costs. Reaching the bottom of the can, he put up his hand for another, when a man came though the door, walking directly over to him. He was not a young man, but stuck out his hand and sat down next to Chris. He needed a shave and shower, but he seemed to be reasonably sober. "I hear you need a co-pilot to Hawaii." he said,. "My name is Jacob Powers. I was a B17 pilot during the war, and have been working with government ever since. Flying into mining and fishing camps. Things are kind of slow right now, and if you need someone to sit in the right seat for the flight, I can do that. I've kept up my license." he added pulling out his wallet.

Chris studied Jacob as he laid out his recently renewed CME license, along with a medical document certifying him as fit to be a Pilot. He was apparently a recent graduate of the local dry out clinic, but with a schedule to keep, Jacob would be a legal co-pilot to take the DC4 across the miles of open ocean. "OK, Jacob. Where are you staying?" Chris asked, but without waiting for response, added, "I can arrange for you to stay out at the Pilot's trailer out at the airport." Taking out 200 dollars, he handed the money to Jacob. It was a gamble, but he had to know if his new co-pilot was serious about flying to Hawaii. Jacob took the money, and staring at the cash in his hand, several thoughts went through his mind. "OK. My name is Chris Peterson. Buy anything you need, then take a cab out the airport. Tell the Manager you'll be flying out in the morning with the DC4. I'll be out there around 9 a.m. and we'll get the bird fired up. It might take a minute to remember where all the switches and levers are, but together, we should be able to figure it out." Chris said, laughing. He could see Jacob was relieved that he would have a chance to familiarize himself with a new aircraft. He stuck out his hand, and shook Chris's, smiling as he did. He was going to be paid 1500 dollars for a twelve hour flight. Chris ordered another beer, and waved as Jacob left the Bar. The DC4 was that much closer to being delivered.

Returning to the Hotel, Chris found Cathy in an upbeat mood. Completing a call back to England, although complicated with the time difference and Operator's challenging accents, she was able to speak to Edwin, but Tracy was at work. "I told him we would call them again when we reach Hawaii. Ed sounded jealous, because it was raining and miserable in Southhamptom right now." Cathy said, looking forward to finally seeing the island paradise.

"I found a co-pilot. He's been around the block a couple of times, but I think he'll be alright once we get in the air. He's an old bomber pilot, so he shouldn't scare easily." Chris said, unpacking a pair of slacks for the flight. Feeling that they should be in Hawaii by the next evening, he was looking forward to a good meal at a steak house. They just don't make good T-bone in London.

The next morning dawned bright beautiful. Mountains in the distance shone with their snow caps reflecting the bright sunshine. The Cab ride out to the airport was mercifully short, as Chris felt an excitement about flying over the Pacific in the four engined aircraft. Checking in with the AME, he was told that the problem was simply a loose bus bar making intermittent contact. The rebuilders forgot to replace a bolt. Satisfied the problem had been rectified, Chris met a much cleaner and presentable Jacob Powers. After an Introduction to Cathy, the two men entered the cockpit, and sat in their respective seats. Cathy sat behind in the engineer's compartment, keeping an eye on gauges and instruments. She was actually glad to see Jacob in the right hand seat, as it was so much different than the smaller aircraft she helped Chris deliver. With four engines, there was a multitude of meters to watch. After a quick run-through of the basic controls, Chris was satisfied that Jacob knew what he was doing. After a warm up and taxi, the four engines were throttled up and the old plane began its roll out down the runway, seconds later, they were airborne, on their way to Hawaii. Climbing to an altitude selected by the FAA in Anchorage, Chris nudged the DC4 up to 22,000 feet. The DC4 fell into a constant drone produced by the Pratt and Whitney twin wasp engines that had all been rebuilt. Even with ear phones, Chris, Jacob and Cathy kept conversation to a minimum. Heading southwest, the archipelago of Alaska shrank from sight. The Douglas Corporation series 4 transport aircraft seemed to enjoy the open ocean with its constant layers of air, unlike the Rockies, or even the Appalachians, with their currents rising and falling. After five hours of flight, Cathy, as Navigator had pinpointed their location as eleven hundred miles west of Alaska, at a heading of 230° in attempt tp stay near land for as long as possible. Checking the gauges, she was alarmed to see the fuel tanks registering already one half depleted.

"Did you have the tanks filled when we were in Anchorage?" Cathy asked, hoping that she was mistaken. Chris turned to look at his wife. The tone of her voice was that of a concerned parent.

"Yeah. I had them topped off. Why? We should have a range of 4000 miles, even with this headwind." Chris commented. Looking over at Jacob, he turned around to see the fuel gauges more clearly. He nodded. "Your wife is right, Skipper, We've already used half of the fuel and we've gone only 1100 miles." Chris was silent for a moment.

"OK. We'll head north to Atka island. There is an old military landing strip and fuel station there. It will take us 2 hours out of our way, but we'll have full tanks." Banking to the right, Chris aimed the DC4 north to intercept the island. 95 minutes later, Atka island came into view. Lining up for the runway, he settled the big plane softly onto the pavement. Within seconds, a jeep approached with two very determined M.P.'s aboard. As Chris climbed down from the cockpit, the M'P's drew their weapons. Cathy could see the conversation, and within minutes, the jeep departed. Ten minutes later, a fuel truck parked next to the plane, and using a ladder, refilled the tanks of the DC4. An hour later, as Chris taxied to the end of runway, he was laughing. It was good sign.

"They heard from Anchorage that some idiot was going to take a plane all the way to Hawaii. I told them that the idiot pays well, and they filled us up. They said the fuel will just go to waste in the tanks. They get swapped out every month. They're only here to keep an eye on the Russians."

As he pushed throttles forward, the DC4 seemed anxious to complete its journey. Resetting the course at 170°, three hours later, and six hundred miles south, the plane was flying at 24,000 feet. "Do you want to take a break, Jacob?" Chris asked, "this plane has a washroom and sleeping quarters. The guy who owns it wanted to make sure his family could fly with him. " Jacob looked over at Cathy, and nodded.

"OK. I'll take off for an hour, then I'll spell you off, Skipper." There was general agreement that they were making good time, even with a headwind. Jacob unbuckled his seat harness and left the cockpit. "What do you think, Chris?' Cathy asked, seeing a look of concern on her husband's face.

"I just don't understand how we were not topped up in Anchorage. I've dealt with the outfit before, and never had a problem. Hell, the last plane I flew out of Alaska, I flew directly to Kamchatka Island. It's Russian, and they wanted the Cessna delivered. It was for one of the Commissars in Kamchatka, and the Americans wouldn't let him go to Anchorage to pick it up. I was returned to Atka island where I waited for two weeks before I was picked up when they changed the guard."

A little more than an hour later, Jacob returned. He seemed quite enthusiastic. As he climbed into the right seat, Chris squeezed past Cathy. "Are you hungry?" he asked, the refrigerator is hooked up, isn't it, Jacob?" Jacob nodded. "Yeah. It's got food in it. Ham sandwich was good with a cold coke."

Taking the obvious hint. Cathy took off her headset and joined Chris walking back to the living compartment at the rear. Cathy was impressed the owner did not spare any expense when converting this old war plane into living quarters. With a shower and toilet, it was quite luxurious,. Flying at 24,000 feet, the temptation was too great. Both Chris and Cathy succumbed to the lure of joining the 'mile high club'. With Jacob flying the plane, they were assured of complete privacy.

An hour and half later, refreshed and embarrassed, both Cathy and Chris resumed their positions in the cockpit.

"You two enjoy yourselves?" Jacob laughed, looking at the blushing man and wife. Cathy put on her headset and settled back to check the gauges. A moment of panic struck her. "What happened to our fuel? We're down below half!" she screamed, reaching over and shaking Chris's shoulder, He looked over at Jacob, then screamed. "You've been dumping our fuel. That's what happened before. You dumped our fuel. Are you crazy?" Chris was enraged. Reaching for the fuel dump switch, Jacob knocked Chris's hand away. " You and me are going to die together, Mr. Big Shot, and the insurance is going to look after my old lady and kid." Jacob said as Chris tried to shut off the switch, but he couldn't reach it. Cathy took off her headset and wrapped the wires around Jacob's neck, trying to strangle the mad man. He turned and punched Cathy in the face, sending her onto the floor of the cockpit. In that moment, Chris reached over and grabbed Jacob by the throat. The plane was now out of control. Dragging Jacob from the seat, Chris placed an arm around the man's neck, a maneuver taught in the military to completely incapacitate a struggling foe. It was now a struggle between an American aviator and one trained twenty five years ago by the RAF. As Jacob kicked and screamed, he reached for anything to use as a weapon against his larger opponent. Dragging Jacob out of the cockpit into the cabin. Chris screamed at Cathy. "Take control of the plane. Level it out!" The DC4 began to bank severely, throwing Chris and Jacob against the bulkhead. Jacob broke free, and began to kick at Chris. Cathy climbed into the left seat, and placed her hands on the controls. The wheel felt strange compared to her Cessna, but knew that unless she bought it out of the uncontrolled dive, they would crash into the ocean. Pulling back on the wheel, the big plane responded and moments later, leveled out. Reaching over, she shut off the fuel dump switch, She could hear the struggle behind her over the sound of the engines. With a level floor, Jacob ran at Chris with a knife he had taken from the plane's galley. Scrambling to avoid being skewered, Chris grabbed a pillow from the couch and managed to get a fist in Jacob's face. He could see blood on the man's face, but could see no cut. Chris realized that the knife had penetrated the pillow and sliced his hand. It had become a true fight to the death. Swinging a foot across Jacob's knees, the man's legs buckled. Chris could hear something break. It was a sickening sound, but it caused Jacob to fall on the floor. He struggled to get up, but in a moment of madness, Chris opened the cargo door.

He looked out and could see they were only a thousand feet above the ocean. As Jacob tried to get up, Chris grabbed him by the broken leg, dragging the screaming poser to the open hatch, and in one sweeping moment, threw Jacob out of the plane. He didn't even watch to see him fall. Closing the door, Chris rejoined Cathy at the controls.

"Where's Jacob?" she asked, seeing Chris's bleeding hand. He shook his head.

"He had to leave. How much fuel have we got left?" he asked checking the gauges. "looks like we've got enough to keep us flying until we crash." Chris said, laughing, "can you go back and see if you can find a rag to wrap my hand." he added, taking over control of the aircraft, we've got to gain altitude so we can see where we are." Cathy nodded, knowing that Chris could fly better with one hand than she could with two. Stepping back through the cabin, she could see the fight had been brutal, with blood and broken bits of furniture laying against the outside edge of the fuselage.

Searching through the medicine chest in the toilet area, Cathy found some mercurochrome and bandages. Hurrying back to the cockpit, she discovered a panel that read: Life Raft. Continuing onto the front, she sat and professionally bandaged the pilot's hand.

"Have you figured out where we are yet?" Cathy asked, watching for any indication of infection.

"As close as I can guess, that we are north of Midway. We can't let the engines die. The minute one goes out, we have to be ready to ditch while we can still control the beast. We've got enough for one more hour at this altitude, so we can cover another 200 miles, and glide another twenty."

The ocean below was changing in color. There were spots where Cathy could make out the bottom.

"I see the owner thought of putting a life raft on board." Cathy said, putting on the headset.

"Yes. An FAA requirement for any plane that can fly over the ocean. Gather up all the food and non-perishables you can get your hands on and get ready to ditch. I'll give you plenty of warning.

It all depends what kind dinghy the owner could afford." Nodding her head to acknowledge the task at hand, Cathy left the cockpit to attend to lifesaving activities.

Using a pillow slip, she went through the cupboards in the galley, taking anything that might come in handy in the middle of the Pacific. As she dragged the large yellow life raft bag from its compartment, she was careful to not pull the rip cord, otherwise they would have a fully inflated life raft inside the plane as it descended into the depths. The sound of the engines suddenly changed.

Number 4 had run out of fuel. Cathy ran to the cockpit.

"Now what?" she asked, as Chris began to make adjustments for a landing on the ocean.

"I've want to get close as possible to the surface before we run out of fuel completely. Go back and hang onto something solid. Is the raft ready to go?" Chris asked, as number 2 engine stopped.

"Yes, Scream at me before we hit the water." Cathy shouted over the roar of the last two engines.

Going back to the raft, she propped her back against bulkhead and waited for the sudden shock of the large aircraft hitting the water like a brick. Looking out a nearby window, she could see waves flashing by the fuselage. It seemed to take forever for the first sounds of water hitting the bottom of the plane.

"OK. Hang on!" Chris screamed as the DC4 hit the water tail down, and then dropped onto the body, its wings sliding over the ocean like a water skier. Finally, all forward motion ceased.

Chris ran back to join Cathy. "We've got a few minutes before we sink. With the fuel tanks empty, we'll float for a little bit. Going to the forward cargo door, and with a heave, opened it. The ocean was only a few feet below the opening, but the water had not yet entered. Grabbing the big yellow bag, he threw the raft out into waves and pulled the cord. Instantly, the bag exploded, as a huge yellow rubber raft filled with CO_2 and took shape. Taking Cathy by the hand, Chris threw her into the bouncing craft. Next, he threw the bag containing all the foodstuffs after her. With the plane beginning to sink, it was time to leave. Chris leapt into the raft and pushed it away from the sinking aircraft. Slowly, like a dead bird, with water filling the interior, the DC4 made its last flight beneath the surface. Chris and Cathy leaned over the edge of the raft and watched as the plane glided to a soft landing only 150 feet below. It looked like it was ready to fly again.

"Now what?" Cathy asked, as she sat in the big yellow inner tube. Chris worked his way over to the edge and released a rolled up compartment. Two paddles, a flare gun with shells, an emergency kit. Opening the kit, he found a compass. Smiling, he looked at Cathy. "Well, at least we'll know which way to go, even if we can't get there." Cathy opened the bag, and withdrew the bottled water. "I see the emergency kit has a water filter. I found six cans of peaches and four bottles of pop. The owner of the plane must have kids," she laughed as she organized the pantry. "let me have look at your hand. " she added, moving next to Chris as they bounced over the waves.

"It doesn't hurt, but I don't want to get any salt water on it just yet. We've got to rig this raft with a sail. I see it has a center divot and the mast and sail are in the compartment. I'm glad the owner didn't cut corners when he equipped this raft. With all the seamounts around us, we must be close to Midway. The winds around Midway are always changing, so if we are close to it, we might just run up on it. In the meantime, let's try one of those cans of peaches." Chris moved to be next to his wife, and knew that if he was going to be lost in the middle of the ocean, Cathy Romanov would be a perfect choice of companions.

****

Back in Admiral, Saskatchewan, Arvid tried to get the television to work properly. Standing outside, he fiddled with the antenna while Patricia issued orders. Finally, after much confusion and short tempers, they achieved a watchable picture. Settling in with a tea, both he and his wife became addicted to newscasts. Every once in a while, an announcer would mention the search in the north Pacific for the missing DC4. The owner of the plane was interviewed and was concerned that the plane had developed engine trouble. More investigative journalists dug deeper into the plane's history. Day after day, American Navy vessels crisscrossed the area. A sighting by a freighter heading to Alaska from China, reported that they saw a large, four engined aircraft passing over head flying on a 170° heading south. It was dumping fuel. It was not a good sign.

Why would Chris be dumping fuel? As days passed by, the news became less frequent, and Arvid had to resort to phone calls to friends in government circles. Because Chris Peterson was a British citizen flying an American plane over International waters, there was some reluctance by the Americans to spend much time on a lost cause. It was only a massive push by an intrigued public that convinced the Governor of Hawaii to continue the hunt for new 'Amelia Earhart'. Las Vegas Bookies were taking bets on the chances of finding the missing couple alive.

"I can't stand around just waiting for someone to do something." Leo said, as he entered the kitchen, "my Aunt and her husband are out on the ocean somewhere, and these idiots are arguing over whether or not they're important enough to rescue. I just got off the phone from the man who owns the plane they were in." he added, pouring a fresh coffee," he invited me to join him in a search. I'm leaving this afternoon to fly to Vancouver. From there, it's a direct flight to Hawaii. He owns a bunch of aircraft." Leo sat down and looked at his parents. They had become accustomed to Leo's direct action. He always jumped into action, sometimes before thinking it through, but in the end, achieved results. Patricia reached across the table and took her son's hand.

"Just be careful. We need you back home here, safe and sound." Patricia commented, looking over at her husband. Arvid could see the there would be no value in talking his son out of the trip.

Thinking back to World War 2 and his own participation in it, knew there were some things that had to be done, regardless of the danger. Placing his hand on Leo's shoulder, nodded his head as approval for the trip. Finishing his coffee, Leo stood and left to finish packing his overnight bag.

****

Out in the North Pacific, a large yellow rubber dinghy drifted slowly westward with a slight easterly breeze pushing on the small sail. With a tarp overhead to keep the ever present sun from cooking the occupants, one day passed into another. By the fifth day, after paddling for most of the night, the dinghy came to rest on the sandy shore of a seamount that protruded slightly from the surface.

Chris jumped out and dragged the raft up onto reasonably dry ground. At least they could walk a few feet, rather than paralyzed on the small rubber craft. The pleasure of semi solid ground was short-lived when Cathy screamed and jumped back into the raft. Lifting her feet, she looked at the bits of blood from bite marks. Chris joined seconds later.

"Sand crabs. Little bastards don't want us here." he screamed, cursing the thousands of snapping claws that appeared from beneath the wet sand, "we can follow the sand west." Grabbing the paddles, both he and Cathy began to cruise along the ribbon of sand stretching into the distance.

At least being this close to solid ground was encouraging. After two hours of chasing the seamount, their effort was rewarded by a grassy surface that seemed to be endless. Pulling the raft far up onto dry ground, it took a moment to realize they had arrived at a place where they would not drown. It was connected to the real world, and no sand crabs.

Walking through the sharp bladed grass, Chris and Cathy agreed that it was uncomfortable, but not as bad as losing skin from thousands of sand crabs. The island appeared to be a quarter mile long, ending in more ocean to the west. Seeing evidence of turtle activity, it was obvious they were in between egg-laying season, so wouldn't have to face the giant reptiles in their quest. A sudden blast of wind caused both Chris and Cathy to look toward the horizon. A massive dark cloud was approaching quickly from the west. A typhoon was on its way, in a hurry. With possible 80 mph winds, being trapped out on a sand island in the middle of the ocean was not the way to a secure future. Running back to the dinghy, Chris and Cathy began to dig in the sand like a turtle seeking to lay eggs. Looking up at the gathering storm, there would be little time to bury it deep enough to save the raft and supplies. With the first gusts of wind, sand began to swirl, making vision almost impossible. There was nothing to fasten the bow rope to, and hanging onto it might prove fatal.

Within minutes the main storm hit with a fury that seemed bent on transporting anything above ground into the surrounding ocean. Hanging onto each other, Cathy and Chris felt the dinghy ripped from their grasp. There was nothing they could do to save their only means of transportation. It vanished into the blinding maelstrom. As sand covered the two humans hunkered down behind a mound of grass and debris, it became apparent that the storm was lessening in speed. Within minutes, the rain came and drenched the sand that filled every body crevice. If misery had a name, it would be sand island. The hollow that saved them was now filling with water. Chris stood and helped Cathy to wash off the gritty coating. Looking to the east, they could see the funnel that almost carried them away, lifting water from the ocean becoming stronger as it moved. It was an instant collective decision to run into the water and rid themselves of their unwanted coating. Shedding clothes on the beach, both Chris and Cathy Peterson dove into the warm ocean. It was a moment of collective insanity, but felt so good after being buried in dirt and pummeled by a vicious wind. Swimming out into the deeper water, Chris could see a portion of the bow rope protruding from sand farther down the beach. Swimming to the spot, he discovered the bag of supplies hung up on a portion of a sunken vessel. Perhaps a relic from the war, it saved the vital bits of food in this desolate part of the world. Waving to Cathy, his joy was shattered when he saw the dorsal fin of a shark only feet away from his beloved. Shouting over the sound of waves crashing on the shore, Chris could only hope Cathy would look behind her as she swam toward him. Finally, hearing the frantic screams directed in her direction, she turned and saw the large fin of a Tiger shark ready to grab her leg. Releasing the bag of food, Chris swam directly to Cathy's side to frighten the shark, who was ready to secure a meal. Together, they swam into the shallower water while the shark's attention was diverted to the floating bag of food. With an anger that he could not control, Chris stood on the shore, screaming at the thief who was now, swimming out into the deep ocean, the bag of supplies locked firmly in his greedy mouth.

Laying on the warm sand, they were very relieved, but hungry survivors, now without transportation or sustenance. Reluctantly dressing, they knew it would be only days until they would be dead.

****

Arriving in Hawaii, Leo was met at the airport by a rather large man who stuck out his arm and shook Leo's hand vigorously.

"Glad you could make it, Mr. Romanov. I've got one of my PBY's ready to go. Are you hungry?" he asked, as he led his visitor to a waiting Army Jeep. A driver took Leo's bag, placing it on the front seat, as Leo and his jovial host climbed into the rear seat.

"My name is Arnold. Can I call you Leo? You don't mind?" he asked, as the Jeep drove into a fenced portion of the airport. The name on the sign was Blundell. Leo could see that Arnold Blundell loved older planes. As a multi-millionaire, he was able to buy up a good number of aircraft from various eras. Pulling into the shade of a large hangar, the Jeep parked beside a beautifully restored PBY Catalina. Following Arnold through the side hatch into the massive interior of the flying boat, he could easily see how this would be the perfect search vehicle to look for someone lost on the ocean. Leading Leo to the galley, Arnold introduced the pilot and co-pilot, who were both finishing off sandwiches and coffee.

"George and Hank have been with me for twenty-two years, and if Chris and your Aunt are out there, we'll find them. They calculated how far the DC4 should fly while dumping fuel. The report from the freighter placed the plane 45. 50 by 168. 40. with a heading of 170°. They refueled at Atka Island, so if they started dumping fuel at that point, they could have flown for another 1000 miles. That would place them just north east of the Midway Island chain.

Now, grab yourself a sandwich and coffee, and we'll get this bird in the air." Arnold said, sitting down in a leather chair obviously made especially to support his massive girth.

"I'd like to thank you for doing this, Arnold. My Dad is concerned about his sister. Not knowing what happened is worse than knowing." Leo said, taking advantage of the ready supply of food on board the Catalina. As he poured a coffee, the whine of the newly installed turbo prop engines on the old flying boat drew attention to the rest of the ancient plane.

"I've used Chris before to deliver planes for me all over the world. He's a Pilot's pilot. Something weird must have happened on board my DC4 to have him ditch the plane. Now sit back and relax for a few hours until we reach the islands. You can tilt the chair back and get some sleep. You couldn't have had much on your way here with all the party goers heading for Hawaii." Arnold stated, seeing Leo's eyes bloodshot from lack of rest. It didn't take long before the suggestion was acted upon, and Leo laid back and fell sound asleep.

He was awakened by Arnold. "We're over Midway, Leo. Time to get into one of the recy windows and start searching for any sign of your Aunt and my plane. We've got about three hours to search before we have to land and refuel." he said, pointing to a seat next to bubble on the side of the plane allowing a view below as well as to the side. Fitting himself into the starboard seat, he buckled up and began to scan the endless ocean beneath the PBY. After an hour of flying a grid north and south, there was a scream from the cockpit. Hank, the co-pilot had spotted something floating on the ocean. With the ability to land on the water, it was only a matter of minutes before the PBY was floating next to a yellow rubber dinghy. Opening the side cargo door, Hank and Leo dragged the torn life raft into the plane. Examining it closely, both Hank and Arnold came to the conclusion that it had been attacked by a shark. A chill went down Leo's spine. Could Cathy and Chris survived a plane crash, only to be killed by a shark? Arnold decided that the damage was done after the occupants had vacated the raft, as both safety bags had been taken. Checking the charts, it was assumed that the raft had traveled some thirty miles to the east.

"A typhoon passed by here two days ago." George commented, as he looked at his weather reports," it came out of the west and tracked Northeast until blowing itself out one hundred miles north of here. Revving the turboprops again, the large aircraft lifted from the surface and banked

West toward the sand islands. As they climbed to 5000 thousand feet, Hank screamed once again.

"There's your plane, Boss." adding, "it's just under the water about one hundred feet. It looks like it's intact. Should be an easy salvage." Arnold took his place in the recy window, and laughed.

"Damn, it looks good. I'll order up the salvage crew. They might be able to lift it out in one piece."

There was a happiness in his voice, until he realized that the two people on board the DC4 were still missing. Resuming their positions, everyone was fixated on the surface of the ocean. Twenty minutes later, it was George's time to scream. "There they are!" With the plane in a steep bank, Leo was able to see two people standing on a spit of land, waving as if their life depended on it.

His Aunt and her husband were still alive. It had been a good move to speak to Arnold Blundell.

Within minutes, the Catalina taxied up to the shoreline of the sand island, and two very weak but grateful people boarded and lay exhausted on the floor. Their clothes. were in tatters, but kneeling beside his Aunt, Leo could see that both Cathy and Chris would live to fly again.

While refueling at Midway, Chris and Cathy were given a cursory check by the island's Medical Officer. Other than dehydration and starvation, they were declared fit to continue on back to Hawaii.

After Chris explained the problem with his choice of co-pilots, Arnold laughed off the loss of the DC4, feeling it would be worth more after it was rebuilt. In fact, he was already contemplating building a permanent spot for it at his compound. He felt tourists would pay a fortune to see and touch the famous 'Amelia Earhart' lost plane.

****

By the summer of 1974, the Romanov house had become only one of three occupied homes in Admiral. With the community shutting down year by year, Arvid could see that farming was becoming an industry rather than a livelihood. With improvements in the local roads, and larger trucks, the use of Romanov grain elevators by the Wheat Pool were basically bypassed. Arvid inspected the terminals, and one by one, ordered them to be dismantled, leaving only one in Admiral. Sitting in his new truck, he thought back to the days when his family suffered through the depression and drought. He was startled when, out of the corner of his eye, he saw a shadow move into the front seat beside him. Turning his head, he found the small boy, dressed in white, with no shoes, sitting beside him. Anxious moments passed as they studied one another.

"Who are you?" Arvid asked, not expecting an answer. The boy turned away for a moment before answering. Arvid could feel his heart beating, and wondered if, perhaps, he was having a stroke.

"I've come to warn you. They will try again to kill you. They will not be happy until you and your family are dead. Please be careful. We will speak again." The boy's voice did not emanate from his mouth, but seemed to be understood as thoughts. Arvid was about to speak again, but the apparition dissolved like a wisp of smoke. Arvid hands gripped the steering wheel. Was he hallucinating? Starting the truck, he dove slowly back to the house on the hill. He was about to open the door, when Leo came and stood beside him, leaning against the hood. He was smiling.

"What are you smiling about? You sell another thousand bins?" Arvid asked, puzzled by his son's behavior. Leo shook his head.

"No. well, yes, but that's not the good news. Ruth is pregnant. She's due next May. Hard to believe, isn't it?" he said, laughing. Arvid shook Leo's hand. After the kidnapping of Alexander eight years before, Ruth felt she could not bear to lose another child so kept Leo away as much as possible.

"You aren't going to believe this, but she said she had a visit by a small boy who convinced her that it was time to have another Romanov. Maybe it was the little boy you saw in the hotel that day." Leo suggested, walking with his father into the house. Arvid did not mention his encounter with the boy only an hour before. Patricia, who was ecstatic with the news, promised to bake a huge cake for the occasion.

As the months passed, and Ruth began to show that she was, indeed, with child, a sense of excitement was present a meal time, with everyone knowing that this child would be protected against anyone who would try to harm him, or her. The winter of 1974 dissolved into an easy Spring of 1975. Grain prices were good and bins were emptied. Romanov oil leases and wells produced consistently, and land acquisitions proved that the economy in Alberta was unstoppable.

The 20th day of May was unusual in that it was raining. Leo returned home just in time for witness the birth of his daughter. Patricia called a Doctor from Shaunavon to assist in the birth, so when Leo arrived, the deed was done. Doctor Levinson patted Leo on the shoulder as he left the house.

Hurrying to the upstairs bedroom, he found Ruth holding a small pink human in her arms. There was a glow about her that he had not seen for years. He sat beside her and looked at the newest Romanov. It wasn't a son to carry on the Romanov name, but she was healthy and knew that she would be protected.

"What are we going to call her?" Ruth asked, offering the bundle of blankets to Leo.

"I think Cathy would be a good name. My Aunt is a survivor, and she will love her grand niece as much as we do." Leo said, looking into the eyes of his daughter. Handing the newest Cathy back to Ruth, the name seemed to strike a chord with everyone the room. There was a quiet determination that this Romanov would not be lost to a thief.

As months passed, Cathy Romanov grew and became the center of attention. Arvid would stand beside the crib and watch his granddaughter sleep. She was beautiful in his eyes and knew that no one would ever take her the way Alexander was stolen from their family. He thought back to those terrible days and recalled the little boy's warning. Whoever *they* were, may try again to harm him or Leo. The day the bearded man took Leo came to mind. The bearded man seen talking Dorothy before she disappeared. The Bolsheviks who kidnapped him at the start of Germany's attack on Russia, wanted him dead. He would not let that happen to this little girl.

By the age of three, Cathy was developing an interest in the land around the house on the hill. Panic arose when she crawled under the fence and wandered down the trail. Arvid and Patricia, along with Ruth became frantic as they searched the tall grass along the path down to Notukue Creek.

There was great relief when they discovered their lost little girl in the pump room trying to repair her tricycle. When told of his daughter's escape from the compound, Leo was, at first, angry, but saw how controlling the family had become in an effort to protect Cathy from harm. It was decided that he would take Ruth and Cathy with him when he toured the various Romanov properties so that his wife and daughter would see and learn more about the business end of the family.

It was on one such outings that the lives of the Romanovs changed forever. Stopping at a farm in Scotsguard, Leo walked up to the main barn, searching for the farmer and his wife. As he walked through the large, open building, he heard someone call his name. Turning to the sound, he saw a small, bearded man standing in the corner. The bodies of a man and woman lay in a pile of straw behind him. Leo was about run back to the truck for his rifle, but found he couldn't move. There was something holding him in place. The man walked towards him. He was smiling.

"Well, Mr. Romanov. I guess this is it. This is where it all comes to an end. As your wife and child wait for your return, they will be disappointed. I have worked toward this day, and here we are. You and I alone at last." As Leo watched, the man pulled a knife with a curved blade from his belt.

"Who are you? What do you want?" Leo asked, trying to move his legs. Moving closer, the assailant took the knife and made sweeping motions in the air, close to Leo's chest.

"I have been sent to do a job. It is a commission that I have taken seriously. Eliminating all Romanovs from the face of the earth. I have still more to do, but here and now, I intend to do what I have been told to do." Without warning, the man lunged at Leo, driving the curved blade deep into the chest of the young Romanov. He withdrew it and watched as Leo stood and looked down at his chest. He tried to understand what was happening. Again, the attacker stabbed Leo. As he did, Cathy ran into the barn looking for her father. She did not scream. The bearded man looked at Cathy Romanov and smiled. He withdrew the knife, wiping the blood off on Leo's sleeve as the young Romanov fell to the ground. Turning, the killer walked calmly out through the doors at the far end of the barn. Cathy approached her father, standing over him and holding his outstretched hand. He dropped his arm. Her father was dead.

The RCMP never questioned Cathy Romanov. Ruth Romanov was transferred to a hospital where she was kept under suicide watch. Cathy eventually returned to the House on the hill, where Arvid and Patricia mourned the loss of their only son, while trying to raise a little girl in a vacuum.

****

At the old church on the hill, Peter, Caroline and Ellen waited outside while their mother disappeared through the doors covered by gross spider webs. Several minutes passed, but suddenly, Cathy Spenser reappeared.

She seemed dazed and confused. Ellen ran to her mother and took her hand.

"What's the matter, mommy, what did you see?" she asked, as Cathy shook her head, as if to clear the cobwebs from her hair. She couldn't speak for a moment, but slowly, the importance of what she experienced allowed her to rejoin the present. She would need time to digest all that she had witnessed and experienced.

"Oh, it's just a messy old basement filled with spiders and creepy crawlies." Cathy replied, not entirely certain what she witnessed. Taking Ellen's hand, she walked back down to the house, Peter and Caroline following behind, talking about the bugs that were crawling on the fenceposts.

Once back in the house and settled in her kitchen, Cathy made sandwiches for her brood. She thought about her visit to the past. How was it possible to have lived her whole family's lives in just a few minutes. She now understood why she was moved to Woodstock. She had completely forgotten about her father's murder. It was as if the crime had been wiped from her memory by some mentalist. Armed with the knowledge of her past, Cathy Spenser was prepared to do battle with whoever was trying to eliminate the Romanov name from history. That evening, with the kids asleep upstairs, Cathy looked more closely at the records of the Romanov farm. Finding nearly illegible documents, the name Peter Romanov appeared on land titles from 1890. It was just as the dream sequence portrayed, everything started with his purchase of the property that was now hers.

Bills of Sale, receipts, dates, names. They were all here. Just as the story was told during those few minutes she was in the basement of the old church. As she put away all the papers, she heard a vehicle in the driveway. Curious as to who would visit at such a late hour, Cathy went upstairs to the back door. As the light came on, she could see it was her husband, Craig. She had mixed emotions. She suspected the trip to Japan was a ruse, but took Craig at his word. Opening the screen door, Craig walked right past her, placing his briefcase on the floor beside the table.

"Hi. How have you been?" he said, with the look of a condemned man.

"Fine. Did you have a good trip? Are you hungry?" she asked, watching Craig shift his weight, looking from side to side. He would not look directly at her. "OK. What's the matter. Craig?" Cathy asked, siting at the table. Finally, Craig sat down opposite. Rubbing his hands together like someone summoning courage, he said, " I would like a divorce," The words did not have the impact that Cathy thought they would, "I've been seeing someone else, and it's pretty serious. I don't belong here, you know that. This is your kind of life. I didn't go to Japan. I've been staying in Regina with…." he delayed saying his mistress's name, but finally said, "Joanne." After Craig blurted out the name of her replacement, Cathy smiled. Joanne. A young Secretary at the Engineering firm that Craig transferred to from Woodstock. She was pretty, but dumb as a sack full of hammer handles. Craig looked alarmed. He did not expect such a placid acceptance of a new lover. "Did you hear me?" he asked, "I'm going to move back to Ontario with Joanne. Please don't be angry. I'll provide for you and the kids, but I need my freedom from all this." he said, looking around the kitchen of the hundred year old house. Cathy nodded her head.

"No problem, Craig. And you can keep your money. I'll make out, somehow. Now, you can get back in your car and leave before the kids wake up and make your life even more miserable. Leave it to me to explain why you never came back from Japan. I'm sure I'll think of something." Cathy said, standing. Taking the hint, Craig grabbed his briefcase and went directly to the door. He was hurt more by Cathy's sublime acceptance of his infidelity, than if she had complained and screamed in anger. His ego was crushed. Like a whipped dog, he walked back out to his car, and without waiting for him to leave, Cathy went back into the house and made a fresh cup of tea. With millions in the bank, and knowledge of her past, she did not need Craig to get in the way. She had Romanov blood coursing through her veins, and could definitely look after herself and children.

Locking the doors and arming the surveillance system, Cathy went to bed, happy with the thought of running her own life. She felt a trifle sorry for Craig. He did not know what Joanne was after. Once she had her hooks legally planted into Craig's bank account, he would be wishing he knew more about farming. His leaving opened new avenues for the Romanov empire to grow. Her first order of business would be to drop the Spenser name for her and her children and rebrand as a Romanov. Closing her eyes, she vowed to visit the church basement again. There were things she didn't quite understand.

The next morning, when her brood was assembled for breakfast, Cathy announced the changes.

"Your father sent a message from Japan. He'll be staying a lot longer, but it won't matter. Today, we are going to Swift Current and buy some new clothes and bicycle for Ellen." A cheer went up from the three children, who began to love trips into town. It would be another chance to see the Pronghorns and Buffalo running across the prairie.

Within a month, Peter stopped asking about Craig, which pleased Cathy, and Caroline and Ellen never even mentioned their biological father. It was as if he never existed. With the help of Barry Gordon, Cathy updated some accounts, transferring others into a new company, over which she had control. Her name change went smoothly, and although Caroline wondered why she was no longer a Spenser, Peter and Ellen accepted that it was their mother's name, so it was fine. In fact, Peter became quite proud of the fact that the Romanov name was on the side of buildings and bins as they drove along the road. He finally stopped pointing the fact out to his siblings, but Cathy could watch him in the mirror and he would mouth the name on each bin. As summer turned to fall, the school, with only eight students remaining, was scheduled to close. Peter and Caroline would have to travel by bus to Shaunavon. Making arrangements with the School Board, Cathy was able to keep the two oldest Romanovs for home schooling. Caroline was growing quickly, and although having never ridden a horse before, was determined to have her own horse. With the horse barn unused for at least twenty years, she began a regimen of cleaning it out. Having been allowed to see the past and her father Leo with his apparent love of horses, Cathy was content to allow Caroline to pick out just the right animal. It was a big day when the dealer brought a pony in a horse trailer. It was the perfect size for an eleven year old girl.

Even Peter was impressed at how quickly his sister learned to ride the quick footed pony. Cathy awaited the natural request for a horse of his own, but Peter was content to watch Caroline ride, even to the point of helping her groom the little animal, as well as cleaning out the stall and barn. Ellen was just happy to sit in the saddle while Caroline walked Rusty around the round pen.

October arrived, but with the house hooked up to natural gas, there was no longer any concern about cold. Cathy was just walking upstairs to make lunch when a cold wind blew through the house. Walking through the rooms, there were no open windows, so it was puzzling when Cathy felt an even stronger wind. Crossing to kitchen, Peter was not at his usual spot.

"Where's Peter?" Cathy asked Caroline, who was spreading butter on bread. She just shrugged.

"He was just here a minute ago. Maybe he's in the bathroom. Oh… maybe he went out to get something from the barn." Caroline offered, licking jam from the knife. There was no reason for concern, but Cathy went out to the horse barn. Rusty was in the corral, begging for a scratch behind the ear, but no Peter. Checking the main barn, there was now reason to worry. As she stood in the middle of the empty space, Alex appeared in the doorway. A chill went though Cathy.

"It is time to end this." Alex said, as he motioned to Cathy to follow. Leaving the barnyard and walking into the tall grass, Cathy reached out to stop Alex, but her hand passed right through the form. "Stop!. I can't go with you. I can't leave Caroline and Ellen alone in the house." Alex stopped and took Cathy's hand. It was like holding a blade of grass.

"Cathy will look after them." Alex said, causing a vision of her great Aunt sitting with Ellen and Caroline in the kitchen, enjoying sandwiches and milk. They seemed quite content to be with a woman they did not know. Not quite understandings how all this was possible, Cathy took Alex's hand, following him through the old cemetery to the site of the collapsed church. She hesitated, but fearing her son was being harmed, went through the doorway, into the bowels of the hated building. They were suddenly in a room lighted by lanterns. Four women stood along the back wall, with two more standing by the Tsar and Alexandra. An older man, and a small boy, dressed in white, with no shoes. The blood drained from Cathy's face. This was the room where the Czar's family and servants were murdered. She could feel Alex's hand tighten on hers as the voice of the leader of the Bolshevik assassins echoed in the closed room.

"Nikolai Alexandrovich, in view of the fact that your relatives are continuing their attack on Soviet Russia, the Ural Executive Committee has decided to execute you." The man was Yakov Yurovsky. Cathy was frozen in place. She wanted to rush into the middle of the room and stop this madness, but became aware that she was witnessing an event that took place almost one hundred years before. She could not stop the act, but was weak from seeing her own son, Peter, as one of the victims. Once the shooting began, the screams of the dying rose like a thunder clap. Cathy tried to shut out the sound, but could not stop watching the massacre. Shooting and bayoneting the defenseless victims

became an orgy of death. With acrid smoke filling the blackened room, Cathy could not breath. Alexei walked to the middle of the room, and instantly, everyone vanished. The room was empty, except for Yakov Yurovsky who faced a young Alexei Romanov. Yakov raised his Mauser and pulled the trigger. Nothing happened.

"It is time for you to die!" Alexei said, his voice resonating in the room. Yakov kept pulling the trigger, trying to kill this young boy who had been following him since 1918. Yakov threw down his gun and ran at Alexei, a large knife in his hand, It was as if a wall had been built around the young Tsarevich. Yakov screamed at Alexei. Although they spoke in Russian, Cathy could understand perfectly. She was witnessing the end of a century old battle between the Romanovs and Bolsheviks. She realized the bearded man who had been killing and tormenting her ancestors was being put to death by the Tsarevich. Alexei raised his hands, as if to strangle his attacker. Yakov tried to fight off the small hands that were now choking the breath from his body, but thrashing in vain, screaming profanities did nothing to stop the inevitable. With a final kick at his ethereal opponent, Yakov Yurovsky went limp, and a moment later, evaporated into thin air.

Alexei looked over at Cathy and put up his hand to his forehead as a final salute, then he too, vanished. It was over. The tormentor was gone. The Romanovs were finally free of the Bolshevik menace.

Stepping outside into the fresh air, Cathy Romanov immediately, threw up. Looking up, she found Peter standing beside her. Wrapping her arms around her son, she broke into tears.

"What's the matter mommy?" he asked, putting his hand on her shoulder.

"Peter. How did you get here?" Cathy asked, looking around for Alex. He was gone.

"Alex brought up here and told me to wait at the door. I didn't know you were here." Peter replied, not quite understanding the importance of the moment. Taking Peter by the hand, Cathy walked through the grass back to the house on the hill. Entering the kitchen, she looked around for her children. A sudden fear went through her, but laughter from the living room allayed her anxiety. Entering the room, Cathy could see the form of a woman walking down the driveway. Caroline and Ellen came and took her hands. Walking with her back into the kitchen.

"Auntie Cathy was really nice, mommy. She said she would come back to visit someday." and an even more excited Ellen added, " she even made us peanut butter and jam sandwiches." Resuming their positions around the table, Cathy was more than happy to refill their glasses with milk, as well as making peanut butter and jam sandwiches for her three healthy and alive Romanovs.

The ordeal at the old church convinced Cathy that the building had to be completely demolished and its parts ground up and burned. Contacting a disposal company, it was only a matter of days before the crew arrived on site. Creating a clearing for the debris, it wasn't long before moldy pieces of the walls and roof were broken up and piled, ready to be mulched. There was a great deal of satisfaction in listening to the sound of breaking wood and timbers. She was startled by a knock on the kitchen door. The Foreman was standing there, with hardhat in hand.

""Excuse me Ma'am, but there's something you have to see. We can't go any further until you make the decision." The worker was quite serious. She was hoping that no one would be injured on the evil place. Nodding her head, she grabbed a jacket and walked back up to the church site.

The contractor had accomplished quite a bit in a short span of time, but everyone was standing around awaiting Cathy's arrival. The Foreman directed her to the edge of a pit. Standing in the dirt, Cathy looked down and could see the excavator had uncovered, what looked like another room in behind the first. It was made of concrete. The church itself was built completely with wood, so seeing the concrete was a complete surprise. The Foreman invited Cathy down into the hole.

"You see that?" he asked, " that's a steel door. It's locked. What do you want to do?" he added. lighting a cigarette. Cathy walked up to the door and hit it with her fist. Who would have constructed this? It was time to rid the building of all of its secrets.

"Tear it down. It may be a furnace room, but the church was heated with a big wood stove upstairs. Whatever is in here, it's got to go!" so the decision was made. She stayed and watched as the excavator began rip at the corners of the mysterious room. Finally, after it resisted for ten minutes, the door was ripped free of the concrete wall. The smell of death arose from the pit. Jumping in, the Foreman took a flashlight and looked into the darkened interior. Moments later he fell back, holding his face, regurgitating his breakfast. Other workers put their heads in the doorway, all of them following the Foreman's revulsion. Cathy took the light from the foreman and looked into the room. She was shocked to see skeletons, some, their bones fastened to a wall by chains. Piles of bones littered the floor. Controlling her stomach contents, she climbed out of the pit, directing the Foreman and workers to take the rest of the week off, with pay. It was an offer none of the crew objected to. Walking directly back to the house, Cathy phoned the nearest RCMP Detachment. Within two days, a team of forensic Investigators had set up camp on the Romanov property. It was a gruesome task, assembling multiple sets of bones to form a human skeleton. Three of the prisoners had been chained and died of dehydration. They had simply been placed in the concrete bunker and left to die, probably all the while seeing others already dead. The fact that DNA identification was available, allowed investigators to pinpoint family connection. During her journey through time, she was made aware of children being abducted, like her brother, while other children just vanished without a trace. The bodies of both Abigail and Dorothy Romanov were identified. They had been chained to the wall. The third person was Tony

Mercedes. It was a surprise. Cathy tried not to let on she knew who he was, even though, on her trip back through time, she and Tony often spoke of getting married.

A total of nine bodies were pieced together. There were four young children, two of whom were identified as Danny Wagner and William Stevenson. The bones of a male baby, Alexander Romanov were found mixed with the skeleton of an unidentified female. The results were printed out and handed to Cathy. The Osteologist, working with the bits and pieces, was able to reconstruct all the bodies so that the RCMP could photograph and start a file. Cathy did not interfere with their investigation, although she knew it would lead nowhere. A pair of Geneticists were intrigued at the thought of finding Romanov bodies in the small town of Admiral. Jodi Wilson and her Lab partner, Jared Butryskaya, were convinced that there was a connection between the Romanovs in Saskatchewan and the Romanovs in Russia. Contacting friends in Moscow, they wanted to know more about Peter Romanov. After considerable digging, they discovered the notes from the Doctor who attended the birth of Nicholas Romanov in the birthing room of the Alexander Palace in Tsarskoye Selo outside of St. Petersburg. The notes, having been hidden from view for a hundred years, were smuggled out of the records department of the Kremlin. Sent to Regina by Courier, both Jodi and Jared were sworn to secrecy. Laying out the document, they studied it carefully.

With Jared's understanding of Russian, being born in Kazakhstan, it was not a complicated affair, but the second page proved shocking. May 6, 1868, Maria Feodorovna gave birth to twins. Identical twins. Mikhail was born first, then two minutes later, Nicholas arrived. Their father was ecstatic, until he discovered that Mikhail had a deformed left hand. His index finger had not completely developed. The Doctor tried to explain that it was not a problem, but Alexander was livid. He did not want his son, who would be the Tsarevich, to be laughed at because he was a cripple, so he forced the Doctor to change the order of birth. Nicholas was deemed to be Tsaverich and Mikhail was removed from the room and taken to a wet nurse in town. The Doctor did not specify who took the baby or what happened to him. There was no mention of the other brother as Alexander proudly brought forth Nicholas 11, claiming the continuation of the Romanov Monarchy was assured.

"Well, that's an interesting development. What we have to do is compare our Romanovs with the DNA from the bodies they found in Russia. I'll contact Dr. Rogaev, and get a copy of the results. It's doubtful that they would have all the hand bones, so we wouldn't be able to prove the deformity, but we can see if any of our Church bones are related to the Russian Romanovs." It was an exciting prospect. Within days, the results were emailed to the Lab. Placing the graphs side by side, it was immediately apparent that the bodies from the old church were related to Czar Nicholas 11 and his family.

"Now what? Does this mean that Peter Romanov was Mikhail Romanov?" Jodi asked, studying all the results carefully. Jared sat back and closed his eyes. "I wonder where Peter Romanov was buried?"

With the RCMP returning bones identified as Romanov, it was up to Cathy to have markers made to place in the Romanov gravesite for her ancestors. Her mother, along with Grampa Arvid, who drowned in Notukue Creek in a foot of water, were the last to be buried. It had been 17 years since she stood on this spot in the Admiral cemetery, and realized her children would someday be here looking at the long row of Romanov headstones. As she watched the machine expertly dig holes for the small caskets, she recalled the laughter, love and pain she experienced during her travel through time. The passion of Abigail, the joy of Dorothy and the sadness of her mother with the loss of Alexander. The strength of Arvid and her father, Leo, as well as the beauty of Tzeitel and Patricia.

They were all here now. Burying the three small caskets presented the opportunity to allow Jodi and Jared to study the body of the patriarch of the family, Peter Romanov.

Cathy asked the digger to carefully expose the nearly hundred year old coffin, as there was some forensic work that had to be done for the Police. It was a lie, but, the less questions asked, the better. It was time to learn the truth, and with Cathy's blessing, the still intact cedar and oak casket was uncovered and carefully raised to the surface. Asking the digger to leave, it was finally quiet in the Admiral cemetery. Cathy watched as Jodi and Jared carefully removed the lid. The remains of Peter Romanov were completely intact. Her great great grandfather died in 1911 on the same day Arvid was born, leaving a 21 year old Petrov to manage Romanov's growing influence. Cathy thought back to her dream time, and how real life seemed with her brother and sisters. She looked down at the man who started it all and felt a great wave of sadness. Jodi and Jared delicately inspected the clothes, removing only what was necessary to see the left hand. With a monitor set up on the edge of the casket, Jodi moved the small camera to a position where they could identify the bones of the left hand.

The proof was there for all to see. Peter Romanov was, indeed, first born, Mikhail Romanov. Jared stared at the screen and shook his head. "Bugger!" was all he said.

Cathy Romanov knew what Jared meant. Would Russia have dissolved into revolution if the true first born Mikhail, instead of his less aggressive brother, Nicholas, been chosen as Tsar? She would not exist, nor would any of the Romanov family in Admiral. Jodi looked up at Cathy and smiled. With a nod of her head, the casket was resealed and lowered back into the ground.

The ghosts of Admiral would remain locked away, revisited only in the dreams of the survivors.

END

Made in the USA
Monee, IL
02 November 2021

80911159R00128